I0715970

THE FREE AGENT

OLIVER TALMADGE

The Free Agent

By Oliver Talmadge

First Edition 2024

Copyright © 2024 Oliver Talmadge

Author Portrait by Michael Armand Altares
Cover design and image by Reprospace, LLC using OpenAI DALL-E
Editing by Reprospace,. LLC with the help of OpenAI ChatGPT

Paperback ISBN 13: 978-1-952685-87-3

This is a work of fiction. Names, characters, places, and incidents either are the product of the author's imagination or are used fictitiously. Any resemblance to actual persons, living or dead, events, or locales is entirely coincidental.

Kitsap Publishing
Poulsbo, WA • USA

"I've missed more than 9,000 shots in my career. I've lost almost 300 games. Twenty-six times, I've been trusted to take the game-winning shot and missed. I've failed over and over and over again in my life. And that is why I succeed."

—Michael Jordan

"The most important thing is to try and inspire people so that they can be great in whatever they want to do. —Everything negative, pressure, challenges, is all an opportunity for me to rise."

—Kobe Bryant

"I think the reason why I am who I am today is because I went through those tough times when I was younger. —You have to be able to accept failure to get better."

—LeBron James

FOREWORD

by the Author

My name is Oliver Talmadge. I'm sixteen years old, and I've been captivated by stories for as long as I can remember. Growing up in Renton, Washington, in a house bustling with five siblings and two amazing parents, I found my own little corner of peace through writing. It all began back in elementary school, when a simple classroom assignment turned into a gateway to a world where I could shape anything I imagined—where my thoughts and feelings could transform into characters, places, and adventures.

I've never been the type to dream small, but writing a full novel seemed far beyond my reach. Instead, I channeled my energy into crafting short stories—little windows into different worlds that I could complete and share. It wasn't just about the words, though. Writing gave me a sense of purpose and belonging, even in those moments when life felt overwhelming. It was a place where I didn't have to compete, prove myself, or fit in—I could just be.

Outside of writing, I'm on the basketball court, finding another kind of freedom. I play for my high school team at Lindbergh, and I push myself hard in every practice and every game, not just for the win but because basketball, like writing, demands heart and dedication. Many parts of my novel are glimpses of my life on the court—small victories, painful losses, and moments that shape who I am.

But it was during a parent-teacher conference that my path took an unexpected turn. My English teacher mentioned an after-school club that gave students the chance to write a novel in a month. I shrugged it off. I wasn't ready to take on something that big. But my mom, always believing in me more than I believed in myself, told my teacher that I had a knack for storytelling. Suddenly, what seemed impossible started to feel—maybe, just maybe—within reach.

So I took a leap of faith. With encouragement from my mom and unwavering support from my dad and siblings, I started writing. It was exhausting. It was exhilarating. And in a whirlwind month, I hit fifty thousand words—something I never imagined I'd achieve. When I finished, I realized that this wasn't just a story; it was a piece of me. And I wanted to share it.

Then came another surprise. Kitsap Publishing took a chance on my manuscript, and that's when I knew—this is what I'm meant to do. My dream is to continue honing my craft and one day become a full-time author, bringing stories to life that move, inspire, and maybe even heal others in the way writing has healed me.

For now, I'm still a high school student, a basketball player, and a Young Life student leader working to support youth in my community. But above all, I'm a writer—someone who sees the world not just as it is, but as it could be, and is unafraid to put pen to paper and bring that vision to life.

Oliver Talmadge

FOREWORD

by the Publisher

We, as publisher, are always on the lookout for stories that offer fresh perspectives and explore the complexities of the human experience. "The Free Agent" by Oliver Talmadge is one such work that captivated us from the very first page. This novel is more than just a story about basketball; it is a compelling exploration of ambition, identity, and resilience set against the backdrop of the high-stakes world of professional sports.

In Abel Richards, Talmadge has created a protagonist who is not only a gifted athlete but also a young man grappling with the weight of expectations, both his own and those of the people around him. Abel's journey through the tumultuous terrain of the draft process and his unexpected path into the league is a story that resonates with anyone who has ever faced adversity or dared to dream beyond their circumstances. It is a narrative that speaks to the power of determination and the importance of staying true to oneself, even when the world seems to be against you.

What makes "The Free Agent" particularly special is Talmadge's ability to weave a tale that is as emotionally gripping as it is inspiring. His attention to detail and deep understanding of the sports culture bring Abel's world to life in vivid detail. But beyond the basketball courts and locker rooms, this book delves into the personal and often difficult choices that define a person's character. It shows us that the real game is not just played on the court but also within the hearts and minds of those striving to make their mark.

We are proud to bring this remarkable story to readers and believe that it will leave a lasting impact. "The Free Agent" is not just a sports novel;

it is a story about finding one's place in the world, about family, love, and the strength to rise above the challenges life throws at us. Whether you are a basketball fan or simply a lover of well-crafted fiction, this book will offer you something to cheer for and reflect upon.

We invite you to turn the page and join Abel Richards on his journey. May his story inspire you as much as it has inspired us.

Sincerely,

Ingemar Anderson, Kitsap Publishing, Poulsbo, WA

Chapter 1

A Cigarette and a Voicemail

The television casts a cold blue light that flickers through the room, its low whispers of voices echoing off the walls. The small screen hosts a lively debate between two sportscasters.

"And what exciting news at that! It'll surely be a very tight race between the two, Randy. I mean, we've seen amazing things from each player consistently throughout their time at TSU and Washington. Would you say one has an advantage over the other? Is there some gap that separates the two?"

"Now, don't look at me funny, Michael," Randy replies, his hands gesturing animatedly, "but I just have to say there is a slight gap in athleticism between the two, not to mention the sheer drive and defensive capabilities of Khalil Henderson. Let's look back at his collegiate career. He dominated all four years in basketball, averaging four rebounds over his first two seasons as a Tiger. Then, we saw an improvement—eight rebounds in his next season, eleven the following. There is a constant trend of improvement in Khalil's game that I have a lot of respect for. I expect him to go far."

"If you're going to talk about improvement, you have to mention Abel's performance this last season," Michael counters, straightening his suit as he turns back to the camera. "He led the league in points and nearly every other offensive category. Khalil sold out arenas, but Abel? He sold out cities. The kid is only twenty."

"Who won the finals last year, Michael?" Randy interrupts, making a grand display with his hands.

"Tha—" Michael's excitement is cut short as Randy continues.

"-No!" Randy chuckles, scoffing at his co-worker's opinion. "Khalil Henderson is the real deal. He averaged thirty-five points per game in the tournament throughout all four of his seasons. Instead of winning just one championship, he built a dynasty over three years, securing three straight national titles." He straightens out his papers, his eyes shifting dramatically to the camera. "I'm sorry, but there is no discussion to be had—"

CLICK.

The TV switches off, and the room returns to its dimly lit, ordinary state.

Abel sighs. "I can't believe—no, it doesn't even matter."

He moves sluggishly around the hotel room, his legs stiff like two wooden boards. He squeezes himself into the small crevice between the countertop and the barstool. The smooth granite is a nice material—a perfect surface to scatter the various empty and full plastic containers of food sent by family, friends, and neighbors. These gifts were all filtered by his mother, who made sure to label them because she knows how picky he is about certain foods, especially those lacking a homemade touch. One of the dishes is labeled: "spaghetti and meatballs with no meatballs." This makes Abel chuckle, and on a whim, he pops off the lid and throws it into the microwave on top of the dresser. The peculiar placement of the microwave never fails to amaze him.

The digital clock beside the microwave reads: 9:50.

9:50.

9:50.

BEEP!

The steaming pasta comes out of the microwave looking like it came straight from an Italian restaurant. All that's missing is a thousand-dollar bottle of champagne to celebrate. In his own way, he celebrates by walking over to the phone, trying his best to press the voicemail button without hitting every other one.

One message.

"I just know you have time for your mother. You didn't think to call tonight? What? Are you too good for me? Too famous, maybe? Damn, you got me stressing out," the voicemail pauses, and Abel can almost see his mother reach up and rub her forehead.

His way of coping, however, involves pulling out a single cigarette from a pack of Marlboros and grabbing the lighter already in his left pocket. As if she were watching him at that very moment, she continues, "You better not be smoking while listening to this message, either. You're not grown; you're only twenty! And you know that stuff is bad for you. You're a basketball player; you need to take your health seriously, especially with tomorrow being a big day for you. I need you to get rid of all those things, all of them, and I mean it, God, so help me... Anyway," another regretful sigh fills the pause, "just know that we are praying for you, and we'll see you in the morning. The flight was pretty rough. Listen, don't worry about what's to come. That's not your job; just focus on what you can control, okay? Okay. Goodbye, son."

The message ends, and Abel drops the cigarette and lighter onto the counter, muttering something unintelligible.

Cars streak across the view of the skyline, making the roads seem invisible under the packed traffic of the nocturnal city of Las Vegas. All ears and eyes are on who will be called forth the next day. Across the country, couches will be filled, and their occupants will be shoulder to shoulder, watching the TV and placing their bets. Hundreds of thousands more will pray that their team doesn't mess up their one chance to improve their fortunes and mental well-being with a draft pick that could set them up for success in the coming years.

The asylum of the hotel room rests just above the beautiful chaos of Las Vegas—the stark contrast between the dark and the vibrant overcropping of the city's hypnotic strip. The lights are unlike anything Abel's ever seen, not even comparable to the dim orange street light that watched over him as he grew up shooting hoops outside. "Jesus and a streetlamp is all the help you need," some might say.

Contrary to that, the city truly never sleeps, and the illumination is endless. The lights guide tourists down the strip, all waiting in line for the "adult Disney rides." Unfortunately, there isn't any fast pass to save them from the dragging, horrifying experience of using their virtue of patience.

Abel recalls a conversation with a friend before he left for Sin City. He was a basketball player too, older than Abel, and had been to Las Vegas more times than Dennis Rodman. "Man... all they got there is women, money, money, and women. Don't get into all that; trust me, it ain't all that." His friend's tone was light, almost joking, but Abel knew deep down he was serious.

He bets that if he wanted to, he could sneak out to a club and have a few drinks, with the only problem being how to escape his room. If he did get out, he was sure he could control himself enough not to overdo it.

It's just part of the game, especially during tournaments: leave the hotel around ten, stay out until three, come back at four, sleep until ten, then game at twelve. Coaches never know; no one says anything, and everyone has a good time.

A "good" time.

10:30.

Abel sits on the couch, resting his chin on his hands. He's realized that everyone's already offered their support, he's read nearly every ESPN article written about him, and he still can't look at his bed. He feels like a six-year-old on Christmas Eve—wanting to go to sleep but knowing it would only make him feel worse.

Instead, a tense, rapid feeling takes over his body as he uncontrollably taps his foot against the floor. The sensation taunts him, closing in like a Venus flytrap deciding it will escape starvation for another day. His lungs feel crushed under the weight of expectation, his stomach churning with nerves. His mind races, doubts and fears circulating through his bloodstream like a virus.

Scrolling through Instagram reels, reading random text messages, and listening to music only increase the tempo of each toe tap, wearing down his socks to the point where a small hole forms.

"Didn't I—" Abel finds himself on the other side of the room, reorganizing his clothes scattered around his suitcase, casually flipping each piece systematically. He comes across a crumpled piece of paper sandwiched between the only comfortable clothes he has: a pair of cotton shorts and a branded hoodie.

He tosses a packet of papers aside, letting it float down gracefully to the questionably designed carpet. Instead, its contents plummet like a penny dropped from a skyscraper.

BEEP BEEP. BEEP BEEP. BEEP BEEP.

Groans follow the assault on Abel's eardrums as he scrambles to silence the alarm. "Why? Why?" He rushes to his bed and slams the snooze button out of muscle memory and frustration. A few seconds later, he clicks a button on the back to reset the alarm. That's not happening again.

Abel has always been fine with getting up in the morning. If he's anything, he isn't lazy. The mere thought of missing a morning practice still haunts him.

A particular memory sticks out—a frosty December weekend. Winter break is a sacred time for basketball players—a time to relax but also to play games and interact with the sport. His coach started the season with a blunt message: if you ever couldn't make a practice for any reason, you needed to give an hour's notice. That December morning, Abel woke up, quickly slipped on his slides and shoes, and dashed out the door, shouting, "Love you, Momma!" as he ran to his school gym. He had been there for twenty minutes before the coach showed up, saw the low attendance, and said, "What is this to you guys? I'll see you tomorrow." The eight players who were there shoved their hands back into their pockets and called their parents for rides home. Abel, furious, trudged back home. The next day, the entire team showed up... and they ran.

So, Abel has no trouble waking up on time. The most overlooked part about waking up early is that moment when you swing your legs out and just sit there, getting a feel for your body like it's the first time you're inside your own skin. Abel goes through his routine, which is quite mundane, and heads to the room with the Marlboro cigarettes still sitting on the counter.

He glances over at the balcony next to him, where a bald man in a robe leans forward, his chest puffed out with sparse chest hair sticking out, blowing a massive cloud of nicotine into the air.

Abel can almost feel the devil on one shoulder pulling him toward temptation, while the angel on his other shoulder barely gives a nudge before giving up.

"Just one," he whispers.

With that, he leaves his room and heads toward the lobby, carefully putting in his wired headphones and lifting his chin as he walks down the hall. The elevator arrives quickly after Abel presses the button. Nobody else is inside, given he's on the top floor, but strangely, it feels crowded. He feels watched, as if someone somewhere is observing him with a pen and notepad, taking notes. This strange feeling travels with him to the lobby floor. He turns up his music in small increments, drowning out his thoughts until not even his own mind can be heard. Perfect, he thinks.

His mind drifts back to the pack of cigarettes left in his room and his mom's phone call last night. Even though smoking had never been a habit, his mother treated him like he was addicted to everything to ensure he never mixed with anything. Deep down, however, he knows she's right. It's only going to be today; I'll throw them away tomorrow.

Sooner or later, the inevitable future dawns upon Abel, perhaps reminded by the wave of cameras with flashes as he struts through the delicate glass doors and into a taxi. The reporters' questions fly faster than any human could comprehend:

"So what are you expecting from the association tonight?"

"What have you been doing to stay healthy?"

"Abel, would landing in Houston hurt your chances at a championship this year?"

"Would you consider yourself part of the Rookie of the Year conversation already?"

"How has your confidence shifted since the recent interview with Khalil Henderson?"

Abel's gears start turning with the last question, and he stops like a poorly oiled machine.

"What has he been saying now?" he blurts out suddenly, halting the crowd in its place.

The reporter who asked the question steps forward, the only one unfazed by his words. "Henderson said you're no different from the last time a fake player messed with him. He claimed you're still the same kid he messed up in college. What does that mean?"

Abel looks away, breathing deeply. "He doesn't know what he's talking about. Next time he wants to talk trash, I suggest he say it to me on the court. I dare him to; he knows what happens." Abel points up to a billboard, making a phone gesture with his thumb and pinky finger. "When you get one of those, come call me, bitch!"

The one thing he had on Khalil was a sponsorship. A broken one, but a sponsorship nonetheless.

Outrage ripples through the crowd, and everyone realizes that what they just heard has changed the course of the next twelve hours. The entire reporter community seems to fight for a piece of the action, straight from the mouth of a rookie. The chaos of the moment eats at Abel, making him feel prickly in his skin, his sweat flooding past his hair like a tsunami. His casual wear begins to weigh down on him, pulling him closer to the taxi door until he falls inside.

The taxi is immediately bombarded by reporters, their cameras becoming weapons and a message. A message that will be replayed many times by the association and interested teams, a few times by his little brother, once by Khalil, a hundred times by his mom, and a million times by Abel.

The image replays in his mind as the taxi speeds off.

Cough. Cough.

"You good back there?" the taxi driver asks.

Coughing some more, Abel fights to nod.

"Yeah. I'm good, don't worry about it."

"I've been following your career for quite some time. I got interested with that one game against Highline. You are quite the specimen, son. I never got the chance to finish my sophomore college season—I developed a heart condition, and I haven't played since. It's just nice to see someone with that passion and drive again. You can tell you truly love the game, and love what you do. I've been trying to teach my son to stay level-headed on the court, just plain and simple hoops. Let your game speak for itself. It's hard to find players like you, but that's why I show him a lot of the stuff you do."

"I—I—" Abel stammers, biting his lip, hoping the driver would just focus on the road.

A cloudy memory of a man and his son comes rushing at him. "Just like that, son, yep, dribble, dribble, shoot!" The man laughs, his grin wide as he demonstrates a move with a basketball. "I think you're getting the hang of it, shoot! Shoot!" He's developed a good sweat around his head from running around with his kid, still smiling and laughing. "You've got it. I think that wraps up today's hooping session, wouldn't you say?" The kid doesn't respond verbally, but his smile is even wider than the adult's.

Chapter 2

Don't Leave on a Miss

Six Years Earlier

In the world of basketball, certain unwritten rules transcend the game. One of them, as every young player knows, is that you never wear your basketball shoes outside the court. The sacred soles are meant for the polished, gleaming hardwood, not for the gritty concrete or dusty streets. But Abel Richards was never one to follow the rules blindly.

He grabbed his bag, mumbled a quick goodbye to his mother, and raced out the door toward school. It was only a few blocks away, a short sprint for someone as agile and eager as Abel. Today, he wasn't wearing his usual slides or trainers. Instead, he wore a pair of brand-new Kevin Durants. The shoes gleamed under the morning sun, the most beautiful thing that had ever touched the gym floor. They were fresh out of the box, a gift from his mother, though he had no idea how she managed to afford them. But he knew one thing for sure—he was going to ball out in them.

"What made you decide to put those on?" one of his teammates asked as Abel stepped onto the court.

Abel looked at him dead in the eyes, face serious. "What do you mean?"

"I mean, why are you wearing your hoop shoes already? You didn't wear them outside, did you? Look at the bottom."

Suddenly, the kids gathered around him, poking and prodding, searching for any flaw in the pristine sneakers. "You gotta get yourself a pair of slides, man. You're going to ruin those shoes. Look, they already got scuff marks all over 'em!"

Abel felt a flush of embarrassment rise to his cheeks. He had no comeback, no smart-aleck response that usually came so easily when talking back to his mother.

He knew all the rules, or so he thought. The unspoken ones, like the one about shoes, must have slipped through the cracks. His older friend in elementary school had drilled the rules into him like they were the words of the Bible. "Don't leave the gym on a missed shot," his friend had said. "It's the most important rule, trust me."

Abel remembered one day before a tournament when his team met at a local Boys and Girls Club to warm up. The hour flew by, and Abel was drenched in sweat, sinking shot after shot. As the coach called time, signaling the end of practice, the other players rushed to throw up a layup. Abel, however, launched a corner three as he dashed toward the exit. It air-balled.

If there was any lesson to be learned, it was that leaving the gym on a missed shot is a curse. That game, Abel went 0-for-12, his shots clanging off the rim. From that day forward, he made it a point to always leave on a make.

But today, all he could think about were his shoes. They bothered him so much that he could almost feel the microscopic dirt grinding against the seemingly clean floor—a sensation like nails on a chalkboard.

Abel might have been the only white boy over five foot seven in the entire school, but his height was the least of the team's worries. Luckily, some of the eighth graders were pushing six feet, and with a squad like that, the team would have no problem winning games. Abel's role on the court was simple and widely understood within the basketball community: his job was to shoot. Any shot was a good shot, especially that corner three he loved so much.

Not much about Abel made him the target of ridicule, except maybe his race, especially in contrast to his mother's. Brianna Richards was a proud African American woman from Seattle, a close family friend of Abel's biological mother, who had struggled with addiction and eventually succumbed to an overdose. With Abel's father long out of the picture and his extended family deemed unsafe, Brianna took him in and raised him as her own. Abel never knew any different.

Occasional comments about his background didn't bother him much. He always felt loved and supported by his mother. She was the loudest in the stands at his games, always pushing for his education, always fetching him from the principal's office. It wasn't that Abel was a bad kid; he just struggled to focus on one thing at a time. Teachers often labeled him a "disruption" due to his energy and inability to sit still. But on the basketball court, that same energy was an asset. His body moved faster than his thoughts, especially on defense. This set him apart from many of his peers in the late stages of middle school, making him one of the most athletic kids in the state—one who could both hit and be hit.

Abel's determination was unmatched. One year, he decided to ask his mom for a gym membership so he could access the weight room and basketball court. He spent weeks preparing his pitch, carefully crafting his argument. When the day finally came, his mother listened patiently to his entire plea, only to respond with a simple, "No." No explanation. No follow-up. Just a single word, delivered without hesitation.

The next morning, Abel found himself sitting at the breakfast table with eggs and toast. His mom, coffee in hand, walked over and handed him a flyer. It was an advertisement for a basketball trainer—someone Abel recognized immediately. This man was a local legend, known for coaching several great high school players. Abel wanted to be the next one. He was speechless. He looked up at his mother, who was smiling.

"Bring your things to school," she said. "I can pick you up, and we can go straight to his gym."

"Mom, are you serious?" He could hardly believe his ears. She nodded, and they both burst into laughter. "You can do great things, Abel. And I know you want it, so let's go get it!"

Abel didn't know then about the problems his mother faced—the late-night texts that kept her awake, the times she took him to stay with relatives so she could handle things without him around. He thought those were just fun sleepovers. He had no idea anyone was after her.

He also didn't know how tight things were financially. His mother always made sure he felt secure, that he had what he needed. For some reason, God had blessed Bri with a child who didn't need much materially, but instead, he wanted things he could achieve himself—things Bri could help him achieve. That's why, when an extra shift came in late one night, she went to Abel's room, kissed him on the forehead, said goodbye, and went to work. She understood the indescribable need to play the game, the feeling of being a puppet with no control over your body. She had played basketball in college, but that didn't last long. She was kicked off the team when she found out she was pregnant. The pregnancy was a shock to her, too. Despite having the privilege of playing basketball stripped from her, she decided to turn the page and prepare to start a family.

Not only were her basketball dreams short-lived, but so was the pregnancy—something she never spoke about.

Abel never asked about the miscarriage. Never.

After those hard times, the opportunity arose to take care of Abel temporarily before she assumed full custody of him. For the first time in her life, Brianna was content.

A few days after the incident with the basketball shoes, Abel walked out of the gym, expecting the day to end differently. His mother was already standing outside the doorway, her eyes fixed on his.

"Now, don't say anything other than—you know what," she began, marching toward the coach who was just leaving. "Is my son running today? Is he trying?"

"Mom, what are you talking about?" Abel asked, bewildered.

"You know exactly what I'm talking about, Abel James Richards! I found a pack of cigarettes in your dresser this morning! I can't believe you would do such a thing!" Her voice was rising, the heat of her anger radiating toward him.

"No! I wasn't—"

"-To answer your question, Ms. Richards," the coach interjected, "he's been a bit unmotivated during practice."

"I can't believe you would use those death sticks," she said, her voice cracking.

"I wasn't, Mom! I really wasn't! I was just upset by what someone said."

"Then why the hell did I find them in your dresser?"

"I was holding them for a friend. He said I should try them, but I never did! I haven't even touched them!" Abel continued to plead, feeling like he was on trial.

"That doesn't excuse your behavior. You still had them in your possession."

The rest of the night dragged on like an eternity. Abel swung his legs back and forth, occasionally banging his heels against the bed frame. He couldn't say anything, couldn't do anything, couldn't go anywhere. Every attempt to open his door failed.

Much later into the night, his mother slowly opened the door, holding something in her hand. "Look, I know you may not have smoked them, but I want you to understand that harmful things in your body can change you, turn you into someone you're not. We need to put good things in our bodies. That's why we eat decently, and that's why we're going to start feeding ourselves spiritually. You have to read this book. I don't care how long it takes; we can go over what you read every night. If you want to become a great basketball player, you have to treat your body with respect and care. Understand?"

Abel nodded, taking the book and lying back down on his bed. She left the room without another word. After she was gone, he debated with himself for a moment. The debate didn't last long; he opened the book.

"In the beginning…"

CHAPTER 3

The Rain

Mornings at the diner had a special magic to them, the kind that Abel Richards had always found comforting. There was something about the hustle and bustle, the clatter of dishes, the sizzling sounds from the kitchen, and the soft hum of conversations that drew him in. It was a place where time seemed to stand still, where the weight of the world felt just a little bit lighter.

Today was no different. As Abel looked over the menu, he found himself wrestling with a decision that felt far more significant than it probably was—Belgian waffles or biscuits and gravy. For Abel, it was always a toss-up, a fifty-fifty shot, much like his choices on the court. Usually, he would pick something his mom wanted, so they could share their meals, each getting a taste of the other's. It made these rare breakfast outings feel like a small adventure, a way to try something new without the full commitment. But today, Abel had a craving.

"I'll have the omelet with green onions and red pepper, please," Abel said, glancing up at the waiter. He half-expected to be recognized, but he was praying they wouldn't make a fuss. His voice sounded deeper than usual, still heavy with sleep, warranting a few awkward throat clears.

"Aren't you—" the waiter started, pausing mid-sentence. "Never mind. You said an omelet with green onions and red pepper. What would you like on the side? We have sausage links, eggs, and hashbrowns."

"The hashbrowns will be good, thanks," Abel replied.

"No problem, we'll get that started right away," the waiter nodded and walked back to the kitchen, greeted by the heavenly steam pouring out like a rolling fog. Even the sizzling sounds seemed to carry over to their table. But probably not to Mikey, who had his headphones in, lost in his own world.

"Hey, little bro," Abel said, pointing to his lips.

"Oh, my bad," Mikey responded. He reached past his outdated phone on the table, grabbed a napkin, and wiped it around his mouth. Across from them, their mother watched them intently, her silence eventually breaking into a warm smile.

"So, Abel. How were things holding up here in Vegas, all by yourself?" she asked.

"They're fine. Not a lot of people to talk to. Mostly just staying in the hotel," Abel said, his words coming out tight, his eyes avoiding his mother's, drifting instead to a spot just over her shoulder.

"You didn't seem to have any problem talking to those reporters," she said with a raised eyebrow. "You just said what was on your mind, didn't you?"

"Well, yeah," he muttered, glancing away.

"You realize everything you say is going to come back around, right? From now on, you have to be cautious about what you say. I know how you feel about Khalil after what happened—"

"No, Mom. Just—don't worry about it."

"Don't worry about it? I'm your mother!"

"I can't—"

"You're right. You can't keep acting like this. You just can't."

Mikey looked down at the table, careful not to get caught in the crossfire. He knew better than to step in when things got tense.

After a long pause, Abel finally spoke, his voice softer this time. "You're right, Mom. I'm sorry. It's just been tough. I've had too much time to think, and now I'm self-projecting."

"I accept your apology," she replied matter-of-factly.

The waiter returned with their food and a foldable table, quickly setting it up to lay down the fresh breakfast. "Here we are, enjoy!" he said, passing out the meals before collapsing the table and leaving them to eat.

Like a wolf, Mikey dug into his meal, creating a shockwave of crumbs and ketchup stains in his wake. Their mother rolled her eyes. She knew exactly what was going to happen—it was a pretty usual sight.

They ate in silence for a while, each lost in their thoughts. But Abel could tell something was on his mother's mind. The growing silence seemed to make her twitch in her seat, as if she were searching for the right words to fill the empty space. "So, Mikey, why don't you tell your brother what we have planned for later this week?" she finally said.

Mikey pushed his plate away, leaving no evidence of food except for the ketchup stains on a napkin to the side. "Yeah, um, we're going to go with you to whatever team you go to, like, the city, I mean," Mikey sputtered.

"You guys are?" Abel asked, his interest piqued.

"Yeah."

"How are you getting there?"

"I still have some time left on my timeshare from your uncle. And airfare isn't too bad right now. We're going to support you, Abel."

"That sounds great, actually," Abel said, taking the win.

"Can I use the restroom real quick, Mom?" Mikey asked, jumping up.

"Yes, be quick, please. I think we're going to leave soon."

As Mikey slipped out of the booth, Abel noticed something that caught his eye. Mikey's shoes were completely worn through. In one spot, a hole had formed, revealing his brother's sock. Abel inhaled sharply, balling his hands into tight fists.

Ever since he was young, Abel had felt more like a father figure to Mikey than just a big brother. During some tough times in high school, the family had lived off Abel's minimum wage job at Burger King. The rent got paid, but luxuries like new shoes were out of reach. Abel had assumed things had gotten better, especially now that he was getting some money through social media deals. But now, looking at his little brother's shoes, he felt like he'd let him down, like he'd let everyone down. The weight of responsibility was something he was only just beginning to understand.

"Abel," his mom whispered.

"What?" he asked, not expecting her to speak so softly, a rarity for someone who spent a lot of time shouting support at his games.

"I need to talk to you about something, not in front of Mikey."

"Okay." His heartbeat started to rise. He could sense where this conversation was heading, and he didn't want to hear it.

"Things... well, things aren't going so well."

"What do you mean? Are you talking about finances?"

She nodded slowly. "That's not entirely it, though. Mikey's father came back the other day—"

Abel groaned, rubbing his face, trying to wipe away what his mother had just said, as if it were a smudge in his eye that he couldn't get out.

"At your house, Mom?"

Again, she nodded, pursing her lips. There was a beat. "Mikey's father came back and took a lot of what we had left."

Abel's blood began to boil. The very mention of that man forced a blade down his throat, making every word that followed a painful struggle to get out. "All of it?"

"All of it," she repeated in a lower tone.

"Mom, I—"

Regaining her composure, she said, "I know! I know! But look, he didn't do anything else this time. He just took the money."

"How'd you get him to leave?"

She turned her head away and rested it on her hand, avoiding the question. Maybe she was dodging it for his sake, or perhaps for her own, trying to avoid spiraling into a confrontation. "Just know that he left, Abel."

Abel didn't pry this time. Instead, he let out a sigh and accepted the situation. "I don't get another check for a few weeks. I might have enough for you guys to stay with me for a while, but I still have to talk to Dell."

"I'm just saying we need something short-term. A short-term fix is all we need."

"You have that remote job, though, right? That should hold you over until I get the money from my socials, and then my first big check. Once we cross that checkpoint, we'll be fine." He reached out and took her hand, holding her fingers tightly.

A tear slid down her cheek, and though she tried to hold them back, they obeyed gravity and landed in her lap. "I'm sorry, Abel. I'm so sorry."

"It's okay, Mom. I'm here. We're going to get through this. And I need you to tell me the moment you see that man again, okay? Nothing will happen to you guys while I'm on this planet. I don't care if I have to fight with my bare hands; I've got you."

"I love you, Abel," she said, looking into his eyes, the same baby blue eyes that had always remained a beacon of light, no matter how dark things got. "And listen to me, failure is something you're so scared of. So scared of." She spotted Mikey walking back over to the table and pulled him under her arm. "You have no choice if you want to succeed. You can't let fear control you. Failure is just an abyss if you let it be, but you have to use it, let it fuel you to become who you're meant to be."

"I know, Mom. I know."

In that moment, Abel wanted to believe he was capable of great things. The sensation washed over him like déjà vu, but instead of memories of the past, it was visions of the future. Hoop dreams, a family, a legacy—these were the things that filled his thoughts, pouring into every corner of his mind like a high tide. For once, his focus was on what lay ahead, not what had dragged him down before. He could see his true potential, usually clouded by self-doubt. But just like clouds, these thoughts didn't stick around for long; they drifted away.

And then the rain set in. Unlike clouds, you can't always see it coming. The rain is like a constant reminder that, even when there are signs, it doesn't mean it'll strike. Sometimes it shows mercy, sometimes it doesn't. But everyone is at its mercy. Abel's mind shifted to darker thoughts—pain, poverty, loss, hate. These weren't specific visions of the future, just an onslaught of worries, flooding his mind with every possible thought he'd ever had, and some he'd never even considered.

With what little power he had, Abel lifted his head and looked at his family. He looked into their eyes, and saw the "memories" playing out within them, their eyes a perfect canvas for his own doubts and fears.

A single tear fell down his cheek, his body slowly releasing the grip that fear had on him.

"Are you okay, Abel?" Mikey asked, his voice soft and worried.

A noise could be heard inside the diner.

Pitter-patter. Pitter-patter.

Abel turned around, biting his lip. How could he have been so dumb?

CHAPTER 4

The Thousand Dollar Jacket

"It's no big deal, big fella. I can assure you of that. One slip-up won't change a thing. The attitude is for the coaches to deal with later. Trust me, I've been talking to people." The words echoed in Abel's mind like a distant drumbeat, a mantra he repeated to himself repeatedly, but he still had no idea what he had done wrong.

The stage was just finishing its setup. Hundreds of people lined up at every corner outside. Some were patient, while others couldn't rid themselves of the feeling of impending doom. For the fans, it was like a gamble. They felt a rush of excitement when they put their money in the pot, but the moment it left their hands, they dreaded the idea of losing it, despite the initial thrill. For Abel, standing with his family felt much the same. His hands trembled so much that you could register it on a seismograph. He could see the commissioner standing behind a large curtain wall, reviewing papers and being bombarded with folders. Abel knew that man would tell him his future—a scary thought, that one man could have so much power over someone's life.

The rest of the room buzzed with activity—agents leaning over tables, whispering with team representatives, each hoping to secure their player's spot in the league. Abel's agent, Dell, was in another section of the arena, surrounding himself with team reps interested in Abel's talent. It made sense; only a select few teams could consider adding him to their roster. Despite what any reporter or newscaster said, very few players in the league could match the top-tier talent coming from a quick two-year stint in college.

Spectators and fans poured through the doors, bringing with them the warm fuzz of anticipation. It started like the crackle of a record player but soon erupted into a loud roar, the sound bouncing off the ceiling and walls. The vibrations hit Abel's chest, making his heart race faster than Usain Bolt in the hundred-meter dash.

He glanced down at his watch. Thirty more minutes of self-inflicted torture and anticipation until he could be relieved of this madness.

"Abel."

The voice snapped him back to reality, his eyes widening as he focused on the source. "Yeah, uh, what?"

"Huge day, huh?"

"Yeah..." his voice trailed off as he tried to place the face. The man was someone he'd never seen before, yet there was something oddly familiar about him. He was dressed head-to-toe in designer clothes, from his cap to his socks, every piece perfectly fitted. "Nice fit, man," Abel added, trying not to fumble his words.

"Oh, thanks," the man replied with a grin, his perfectly straight, pearly white teeth on full display.

"You see, I need something like that," Abel continued. "How much did you get that for?" He pointed to the man's coat, an oversized piece with patches of famous basketball moments sewn into the lining.

"I don't know, something light," the man said slowly.

"Two hundred?"

"Something like that." The man began to walk away, then pivoted back on his heels. "What's your name, young buck?"

"Abel. Abel Richards." Abel raised his eyebrows. This guy had to be joking, right? Walking up to arguably the most talked-about player in the league and asking who he was?

"Stay safe out there, Richards. Keep it tight, brother." With that, the man turned and walked away.

For reasons he couldn't quite explain, Abel pulled out his phone and quickly Googled the jacket. Within minutes, he found it. His eyes widened at the price tag. The webpage read two thousand four hundred dollars. A puffer jacket worth two grand. This guy wasn't just another Joe from Vegas, a city built on temporary money and fleeting happiness. Intrigued, Abel dug deeper. A few more searches, and he found a special guest at the draft this year—Meek Fant, a current basketball player with a hidden net worth. No estimates were listed. Just a big, fat question mark.

"Weird..." Abel muttered to himself.

The room seemed to tighten up as the majority of the fans poured in. The giant jumbotron blinded anyone within view, displaying the faces of all the year's draft prospects in mock draft order. Abel, Khalil, Brandon, Terrell, and so on. Each name got a few claps, but the crowd was restless, hungry for the season to begin.

"What's going on, Vegas?" boomed a voice from the podium. It was the commissioner of the USBA, Patrick Ostrander, his hair tied up in a neat man bun, complemented by a suit worth more than Abel had ever made.

The crowd roared in response, the noise rising to a fever pitch. Tonight, aside from the draft, fans wouldn't suffer from their hands hurting from clapping but from the frustration of those whose expectations wouldn't be met. Some would stay, some would leave, and many would beg for their money back, but in the game of life, nothing is guaranteed.

"We want to personally thank the city of Vegas for hosting this year's draft. We also want to give a shoutout to all the fans who came out today to support these young men as they enter the world's highest level of basketball competition. Tonight, things will proceed as follows: each team, in their designated order, will have five minutes to decide on their draft pick. The next minute, it will be processed and announced. The player will come forward, hold up their jersey and hat, and exit the stage. And it continues in that fashion. So without further ado, the Detroit Titans are on the clock."

The giant clock appeared on the jumbotron and the stage. Five minutes.

"Don't sweat it," his mother whispered, gripping his hand tightly. "They already know who they want to pick."

Abel nodded, but his eyes were fixed on the clock as well. The minutes dragged on, each one feeling like an eternity. Whoever was in charge of time seemed to be punishing him for something he couldn't even remember.

Four minutes.

"Remember, Abel," his mother continued, her voice steady and calm, "what order you get chosen doesn't matter. It's about what you do with that opportunity. You have to make something of your situation, regardless of what the league thinks of you at this early stage."

"I know," Abel replied, his voice lacking conviction. Of course, your position mattered. How you were perceived by the league was one of the most important things. Your landing spot could determine the trajectory of your entire career. But somewhere in his heart, he understood where she was coming from. She had often mentioned players who were drafted first overall but ended up doing nothing with their careers. Right now, he wasn't thinking about legacy; he was thinking about survival, about getting that first paycheck.

"The pick is in. The first overall pick, going to the Detroit Titans, is..."

Abel held his breath too early. For the sake of the audience and the viewers at home, they liked to draw these things out, just enough to get a reaction before they pulled the trigger.

"…Khalil Henderson!"

The entire arena seemed to gasp in unison. Everyone's jaws dropped. The shock and disbelief were palpable. Whispers filled the room like a thousand bees buzzing.

Khalil's highlights played on the jumbotron, showcasing his greatest moments, the ones that made him look like a superstar. Conveniently, they left out his game against Abel in college. They wouldn't dare show that.

Abel's body felt like it was shutting down. His hand tingled as if it were falling asleep. He couldn't move, couldn't react. Most of the fans weren't even looking at the jumbotron or listening to the commissioner's background dialogue. They were all watching him, watching his shocked expression. Waiting.

"The Miami Rovers are on the clock," the commissioner's voice boomed, snapping Abel out of his daze.

Abel thought of the commissioner as the Grim Reaper. A mysterious man who said very little, all tied to his job, with the responsibility of taking things away. Regardless of whether it was his decision or not, the association with pain was hard to shake.

Somehow, Abel kept his thoughts forward. "It's okay to be picked second. It's okay."

"Abel," his mother said softly.

"Yeah?"

"Look at me."

Abel turned his head, staring at the brand-new shoes he had bought just a month ago, preparing for this moment.

"No, look at me!" she insisted, raising her voice.

He complied slowly. His mother's gaze was stern, almost angry.

"Tell me a time, other than winning the NCAA finals, when you were placed first."

He hesitated. "I-I don't—."

"Exactly. So why are we sitting here moping? You know exactly what you're going to do once you get into the league. You're going to earn your spot. I know you don't like Khalil, and believe me, I sure as hell don't either, but he's sitting comfortably on that little throne they've made for him. You, like always, are going to have to fight for your spot." She crossed her arms, waiting for his response.

"You're right, but I can't let you guys down. Like you said, right now, I need a short answer to our problems."

"It's fine. We can take care of that. Don't even think of it as a problem. I have several interviews lined up for the next couple of weeks. Even if those don't pan out, the pay will still be good on another team. That isn't the issue right now."

"That's good, mo—." He paused, unsure what to say next. "—That's good."

Snap!

Everything shifted back to the stage. "The pick is in. Wait, what?" A man wearing a Miami Rovers logo on his shirt, complete with an earpiece, whispered something to the commissioner and then quickly stepped offstage. "Oh, okay, wow... And with the second overall pick, the Miami Rovers select Adam Trellmac!" Another shocker.

Eight more picks went by, each player smiling broadly, their families beaming with pride, overwhelmed by their accomplishments. Another eight picks followed with the same results. And then another eight. Soon, the first round ended, and the grueling night continued. The basketball community was in disarray, all eyes still on Abel, standing still, still waiting for his name to be called.

He took a deep breath in and out, holding it as he spoke. "I'm leaving, Mom. Let's go."

Instead of arguing, she nodded, took Mikey's hand, and headed for the exit. The eyes glaring into the back of their heads didn't make things any easier, but they managed. Not a word was spoken between them on the way home. They just watched the traffic fly by, each lost in their thoughts.

Abel Richards's name was sure to be a hot topic tonight. He already knew articles were being written, stories were being developed, and interviews were being prepared for this historic night. Not once in basketball history had a projected number one overall pick not been chosen in the first round, much less not even in the second.

Sixty names were called before Abel that night. Sixty players now had a team, a paycheck, a reputation.

Abel Richards, however, had none of those things.

CHAPTER 5

The Agent

Abel sat slumped in a metal chair, his hands folded, his head hanging low. He felt like a kid being sent to the principal's office, waiting for the punishment he couldn't avoid. Beside him, his mother and brother sat quietly, offering little comfort in their silence. Across the table sat Dell Washington, his agent, a bald man in a suit that was almost too sharp for the occasion. Dell's fancy glasses glinted under the fluorescent lights, but there was nothing fancy about the situation.

"We've got a few options here," Dell said, his voice trailing off, his eyes scanning the room. He could sense the weight of disappointment hanging in the air, heavier than the contracts stacked on the table between them. "Look, it's not over yet. There are plenty of undrafted players who make it in the league. Sometimes it's not about talent. I'll work the phones, find a team that'll pick you up as a free agent—"

"But. What's the catch?" Abel's voice was flat, his enthusiasm long gone. He sat like a deflated balloon, the energy drained from his body. He had the look of a moody teenager, the kind who thought the world was conspiring against him.

Dell sighed, the kind of sigh that said there's more bad news coming. "The catch is, the starting contract is low. Very low. For the league's standards, anyway."

Abel raised his eyebrows, daring him to say it. "Just tell me the numbers, Dell. It can't be that bad."

Dell hesitated, knowing how those numbers would land. "You'll be paid once a month if I find you a team. But it's not going to be much more than a nine-to-five paycheck. We're talking maybe a couple thousand a month."

Abel let out a sharp laugh, rubbing his chin as if to calculate the futility of it all. "A couple thousand?" he repeated, the reality of his fall from grace sinking in. "That's it?"

Dell nodded, the guilt in his eyes barely concealed. Abel figured it wasn't easy delivering such news to a young man with dreams of grandeur, a kid who'd been told for years he was destined for the big stage.

"Alright, just get me somewhere, Dell. Anywhere," Abel said, resigning himself to the new reality.

His agent looked uncertain, as though he had more to say but was biting his tongue. It was the look of a man who knew the game but hated playing this particular hand.

"That's all I can do for now, Abel," Dell said, leaning back in his chair. "Don't stress too much. This happens. You just have to stay level-headed and keep your mind open. We'll find something."

Abel stood up slowly, arching his back, sore from all the sitting. Funny, coming from an athlete. His back pain was usually reserved for old men, but today he felt every bit of it. "Alright, I appreciate it, Dell," he said, extending his hand.

For a second, Dell didn't move. Abel didn't even notice the delay. His mother, sitting next to him, was also distant, lost in thought as she gripped Mikey's hand, not out of formality but necessity.

The two finally shook hands. Abel's mother gave a small wave, and they started to leave. Dell's eyes lingered on Abel, his face tensed in a way that made Abel pause.

"Abel," Dell said, his voice sharp, almost frantic.

Abel turned, his eyes narrowing. "What the hell, Dell?" His voice cracked with frustration.

Dell lunged forward, grabbing Abel's shirt, his fingers twisted into the fabric like a claw. "Just wait," Dell hissed, his breath quick, panicked.

Abel jerked back, trying to free himself from Dell's grip. He looked down, confused, his gaze locking onto something on Dell's arm—a scar. It ran down Dell's wrist, deep and jagged, stitched together poorly, as though someone had tried to sew up a wound with little care. A burn mark, dark and misshapen, bagged his skin like crumpled paper.

"The money—it's almost all gone," Dell said, his voice low, shaking. "We need this. You and I both need this. I don't want you going out in public for a while. Just stay low. You and I worked too hard for this... don't let it fall apart."

"Dell, don't talk to me like that," Abel snapped, pushing Dell off him. "Remember who hired you. I didn't lose anything! I made one little mistake, and now the world's acting like I blew up the damn World Trade Center! I'm not some kid!"

Before Abel could even process what was happening, Dell lunged at him, his hands wrapping around Abel's neck, completing a full chokehold. The room shrank, the air thick with rage. Dell's sleeves rolled up as they wrestled, revealing more of the horrors etched into his skin. His veins bulged, roots of a tree curling up his arms, angry and swollen. Abel, quicker than Dell's strength, slipped free and landed a hard punch to Dell's face, then another to his torso.

"Don't EVER touch me again, Dell!" Abel shouted, standing over him, his fists clenched, his knuckles white with fury.

Dell stumbled backward, blood trickling down his chin, his eyes wide and unhinged. "And who are you gonna go to, huh? Where are you gonna go, Abel? You've got nowhere. No options. No education. Nothing!"

He began laughing, a crazed sound, the kind you'd hear in an asylum. His smile stretched, blood lining his teeth. "Nowhere."

Abel stood frozen, his hands still balled into fists, two knuckles raw and stripped of skin. His flesh was a sickly white-yellow color, exposed and vulnerable.

"Don't ever mess with me again, Dell," Abel growled, his voice low, simmering with anger.

Dell's laughter filled the room again, echoing against the walls. "Just stay inside for a few days. Let me do my job. We'll talk again soon." He grabbed his coat, straightened his tie, and disappeared through the door.

Abel collapsed onto his knees, staring blankly at the floor. His body was drenched in sweat, his chest heaving as adrenaline coursed through him. His hands trembled, the blood on his knuckles seeping slowly. His throat ached, a dull throb from Dell's grip.

He raised his hands to his face, inspecting them in the cold light of the office. His fingers flexed involuntarily as he looked at the raw skin on his knuckles.

"What am I?" he whispered to no one in particular.

The streets of Las Vegas had never seemed so foreign. Dell Washington walked through the shadows, his silhouette blending into the night. The neon lights of the Vegas strip buzzed in the distance, casting a strange glow over the darkened streets. Dell's hand fiddled with something in his pocket, occasionally reaching up to adjust the white tape on his nose, scratching at the dried blood beneath it.

He turned sharply into an alley, slipping into a building as quietly as he had arrived. The interior was no better than the outside. Torn-up sofas, ruined desks, and papers strewn across the floor like confetti from a parade long forgotten.

"Hello," a voice greeted him from the darkness.

"Evening, Dell. What brings you here this late?" The figure was nearly hidden in shadows, the only visible part of him his eyes and mouth, illuminated by the dim light.

"It's about Richards," Dell muttered.

"Again? You still don't have a grip on him?" The figure's voice was steady, dispassionate. "Just control your asset."

"There's a problem—"

"I know. I know. We can fix that. But we have to stick to the agreement."

"The agreement?" Dell's voice faltered, a lump forming in his throat.

"The agreement," the figure repeated, stepping closer. His hand emerged from the shadows, ready for a handshake.

Dell hesitated, his hand barely lifting. "We need more than the agreement. You already made a mistake by not selecting him first overall. Not even undrafted?"

"There was no mistake."

"He's a generational talent! You can sit around playing games, or we can make business decisions—decisions that make us money."

"He will lose us money," the figure said calmly.

Dell's head jerked back in disbelief. "What?"

The figure remained still. "He will lose us money, Dell."

"At least increase his salary. We both know how good he's going to be."

"The contract will start low, and he'll come off the bench."

"Just increase it!" Dell's face turned red with frustration.

"The contract will start low, and he'll come off the bench." The figure's voice grew sharper, more insistent. Dell cringed, the sound like nails scraping across his ears.

Out of the corner of his eye, Dell saw a glint of metal.

A gun.

Dell went pale, stumbling back against the wall. "What are you doing?" he stammered.

"We accept your offer, Dell Washington. The paperwork will be sent to you by the end of the week. If it's a day late, we'll find you. We look forward to having Abel as an extension of our team."

Dell didn't waste a second. He bolted out of the building, disappearing into the cool night air.

CHAPTER 6

Good Luck

The call comes late one night when the familiar voice of Dell drools onto the phone, and he breaks the news to Abel. He keeps it brief and professional, "You're in, you start this Saturday, pack your bags, and head to New York. You'll play for the Breakers. We'll talk soon, bye." The quick snippet of a conversation sends butterflies into his stomach, although these weren't butterflies, but more like moths, making him feel extremely sick.

The New York Breakers quickly blew up into the conversation, mostly regarding the unreal events of no one drafting a talent like Abel. His name would blow up within seconds, bursts of popularity on social media surrounded the topic, and because of the quick nature of large cities like Las Vegas, New York, and Los Angeles, several hundreds of articles and other pieces on current events pile up.

Fans were speculating an amazing season regardless of what pick he came in, or even what backwater team he managed to find. Fans were fans and Abel let them be fans, it is the reporters that he hated, like spiders they spun webs of lies and misinformation for an audience reaction, just like a class clown craving the attention they never had. Cameras and those who wielded such weapons were a hard pass for Abel.

Shortly after Abel contracts the news he passes the information on to his mother. "YES! YOU DID IT! I KNEW IT I KNEW IT I KNEW IT!" Abel lets her bask in his light for a moment, holding back his tongue until she finishes venting, with nothing else to say but, "There is hardly anything there."

"There will always be something somewhere, you'll get paid for what you put into it. I'm excited for you, I don't care what you think, we both know that this is a good step."

"Mom-"

"What?" She says still looking at her task at hand, which is busy with the task of folding laundry.

"Where did I go wrong? Was it the interview on the day of the draft?" His voice dives off into a very concerned sigh. "I just can't stop thinking about it. Do you think any of it had to do with-"

"Possibly." The answer comes quicker than Abel's little brother, who lunges for the toast in the toaster as soon as the obnoxious ancient piece of technology springs up the darkened bread.

The conversation ends with that.

The next morning they head out to the airport, Abel's mother and brother get sent on a complimentary flight with Abel to The Big Apple itself. Not one person in the airport isn't fighting to breathe as every bit of oxygen is stolen by each other's shoulders and arms. Every type of person is represented in the lines leading to the gates, not to mention the security line going slower than a minute plank. By the time they get to the front of the line, they exceed the time they were supposed to board the plane by several minutes. The team manager and coaching staff expect Abel tonight. He peeks down at his watch.

"Damn. Late."

The lady behind the desk asks for information and all of the formalities that send all of them sprawling through their bags for things they weren't prepared for, "I see that you are flying with Delta."

His mother takes the lead on the dull comment, "Yes. It would appear so.

"Good luck then!"

"With what?" Abel chimes in.

"Oh. It shows here that The New York Breakers are flying you in. Good luck as in, good luck in the season!" Her chippy attitude draws a side eye from the family, nobody they've ever talked to spoke like a damn robot, not unless you wanted to get hit upside your head for talking such nonsense, it is just simply rude, and very unnecessary.

"Yeah…"

Abel's mom starts to back up when she chimes back in, "But I guess I could say good luck for the flight too, so good luck!" Multiple pairs of eyes follow the family as they continue down the line toward security, with a glance over the shoulder Abel finds himself looking right back into the dead eyes of the curly-haired blonde who worked out their tickets. Mikey grips his toy harder in his hand and looks forward at the ground, he puts one foot in front of the other in the same manner a drunk driver would have failed to do. Like a sharp jaunt, Abel feels the watch transferring from him to his little brother. He looks back again. She is just looking at Mikey. No facial expression, no other words, just pure silence mixed with a crooked smile splitting apart her face and forcing a whimper out of the toughest little kid Abel knew.

He thinks about confronting her, it isn't like the line is going anywhere, and she just won't stop staring. At first, it feels insensitive, but now, it becomes excessive. They weren't close enough to exchange a dialogue but close enough to shout something to her. Something bites Abel's tongue for him, however, like he can't get out what he wants to say. Instead, he faces forward, attempting to participate in small talk with his companions to lessen the awkwardness of the mood.

This all happens before his mother finally gets a glimpse of the insane blonde. "Um, No! No! You can look somewhere else, miss, you're scaring my little boy, there's no reason for you to stare!" The tone she conveys is a perfect combination of stern, and polite. She can't forget manners, no matter how mad she gets, she never forgets the words please and thank you… Unless of course, she was upset with Abel.

In a much softer tone, she responds, chopping her words up, enunciating every word clearly but swaying, "I am not staring at you. Or staring at all."

"Um, yes you were?" The situation causes her to pace forward a couple of inches, blinking faster. If anyone knew Abel's mom, it was Abel. Wasted time is always the bane of her existence, so it became his too.

"I wasn't though." Her face contorts. "Good luck!" When it rolled off her tongue it nearly sounded sincere, but something about it just feels off.

And then he caught it. A Florida Gators bracelet. The Gators were rivals when in the past of the league, things had turned violent at games. Things were thrown, and fights broke out. She isn't a fan at all.

Maybe she is just being kind.

A small voice creeps into his mind, telling him that she knows exactly who he is and knows exactly what she is doing.

She is in his head.

Pitter Patter. Pitter Patter.

"Next." The security customs officer proclaims, pointing towards the security gate. They all put their phones and other small objects into the tray which slides through to the other side. One by one, they step through the gate. Abel first, no beeps. His mother, no beeps. Abel's brother, no b-

BEEP! BEEP! BEEP!

The sensor started screaming, engulfing the rest of the airport in a horrible wail that echoed violently.

Mikey stops short. Standing in the middle of the walkway. Every movement is reduced to little to none whatsoever. The security manager walks onto the scene, finding the source of the noise. For a split second, he responds with nothing and then breaks the silence by barking, "Just get through it! Go!"

Abel's hands travel to his pocket, grabbing Mikey's hand, and tugging along his mother's coat, he can hear her start to say something but with the swift movement taking her away, her lungs stop and the brief sound is cut short.

The rest of the time spent waiting didn't happen to be anything more dramatic. The seats were relatively empty, the stretch of empty spots expanding back several rows. One other man sits towards the back of the rows, crunched over his phone with his glasses, attempting to figure out the foreign technology. The lady at the gate stands contained to herself, jotting things down on a row of papers unrelated to her job.

"Excuse me?" Abel reaches out to the Gate Agent.

She perks up like a rabbit in the grass. "Yes?"

"I am wondering when the next flight embarks."

She turns one-hundred-eighty degrees, looking at the clock. "Oh! This gate is closing in five minutes. You should probably board now."

"Ok, will do."

Abel grabs the bags and stuffs himself through the gate and finally into the plane. Hours and hours of lines and interesting interactions for this Moment. The flight attendant grabs their stuff and leads them to the back of the plane: first class. Abel had never experienced anything like first class, quickly learning that it wields any remedy to any discomfort at the press of a button or quick holler down the walkway. Luckily, the flight couldn't be more than five hours, yet the anxiety for the family is very visible from the expressions engraved into their faces. It takes several bodily adjustments for them to get into their seat and comfortable, even Abel pesters a passenger trying to get by in the aisle.

The mundaneness eventually gets to Abel and forces his bladder to contract every drop of liquid in his body, with this sudden urge he floats out of his seat and makes his way down the aisle to the bathroom, passing economy seating first.

Every head turns to him in synchrony, and then he sees their screens, on every single one, despite their age, is his face in a New York Breakers jersey.

"Good luck." A hoarse voice bubbles in front of him.

Abel turns towards the source of the sound; it's a larger man, slumped in his seat with a Coke and a bag of Lays. "-Thank you." He didn't know what else to say really, he already had handed out responses to those words many times that day.

He tries to decide if he's annoyed or just confused, there must be a lot of New York Breaker fans in this area. The thought that they all just want to support him never crosses his mind, he had his fair share of haters, but also a scary amount of people who would lay their hand on a blade for him. He concludes that he is in Vegas and so are the league fans because of the draft. Maybe 'Good Luck' became a social media tag that erupted with the announcement, but again, he has no idea the intent behind it and if it's supposed to be sarcastic and off-putting.

Abel nods, giving no other attention to him as the man returns to the screen in front of him, adjusting to his original seating arrangement.

The remainder of the trip to the restroom he feels the heads turning like a creaking door on the thirty-first of October. The cramped restroom holds little in terms of space which sends shivers down Abel's spine, but he has enough reluctance to get on with it. After completing his business, Abel gazes into the mirror. The bottom left corner catches his eye, it splits almost directly from the corner, striking the whole mirror. The interesting part, however, is the lack of visibility these cracks have, Abel has just enough attention to detail to make it out. This skill is developed early on, he had to think about things no one else did, or cared about. During the time of his obsession with self-improvement, he found himself plagued with an external vision of things that only he could see.

The damage in the mirror tempts Abel, leading him to trace his finger over the damage, finally ending, and changing directions sharply. He looks to the other side, seeing that there's another beginning to a line opposite to the first. He drags his finger over this new line, finding himself in the same ending the other one did. He takes two steps back, looking at the mirror in its entirety, there are five beginnings to the lines, all leading to the same spot about a foot from the center of the glass. Just like life, everything led to something important, a catalyst of sorts. These broken segments trail up and split the glass right where the most valuable part of his body is.

"Basketball is ten percent physical and ninety percent mental.

At the intersection of the cracks, the glass leaves a gaping hole right where his face should be.

CHAPTER 7

A Treadmill

Goodbyes were short given the time in the morning, four-fifteen is not agreeable for everyone, Mikey is dead asleep when the buzzing from Abel's phone shakes him awake, vibrating into his bloodstream and creating an odd sensation in his heart, feeling like the sound juggles it.

The cold night's crispness is multiplied by the city's reputation for its weather. Despite the time, however, there is no shortage of cars on the road and honking like their life depended on it. The walk to the gym is supposed to take around forty minutes, according to a next-door neighbor who happened to be an oncoming rookie for the Breakers, and they decided to leave the house around five, giving them a perfect amount of time to get there if they walked at an 'athletes pace' he called it. The difference is the athlete's pace is right in between a jog and a walk, some might have called it speed-walking, and Abel became very educated on the sparse topic during the venture with his partner.

"You got to check out my place, I moved in a couple of days ago. I'm telling you, nothing worked! I grew up in one of the most broken places in Florida and my stove still worked!" Abel's walking partner declares. It didn't take long before Abel figured out that his name is Warren as vibrantly expressed by a yellow plastic bracelet that suffocates his wrist.

"I know what you're saying…" Abel responds.

"I just wish our agents found some way to get that check lined up for us beforehand, I mean look at that one guy-" Warren snaps his fingers, trying to fill in his blank. "-Oh! Matt Brown! Yeah, that's the guy."

"I know what you're saying…" Abel repeats dryly. He isn't trying to avoid conversation, he's just not used to someone being so comfortable with him so suddenly. They had only met the day that Abel moved into the apartment. Abel came out into the hallway, headed downstairs to take a call when out popped Warren, dressed in cargo pants and a very oversized shirt that read some exotic designer company. One could say his fashion did not match his living situation, but Abel understood the weighing pressure of looking nice for the attention they were going to receive so soon. You had to look good, that is the bottom line, for some this came at the expense of a working faucet.

The meeting at the bank had happened a couple of nights after moving into his apartment, he went over the rent for the apartment and was informed that his choices were to live there for a month or stay with somebody and have the money to get new clothes. Unlike Warren, the apartment had come first, he had to sleep two more people besides himself.

Warren grabs something from his backpack, stuffs it into his pocket, and returns his bag to its resting spot on his shoulders. He carefully sneaks small pinches of something into his mouth, sneaky enough for it to be concealed by the hand closest to Abel. Abel doesn't think much of it and continues following the burden of a pace that is supposed to be walking. More than anyone he understood that being fifteen minutes early is on time and being on time is late, but he feels dragged down by some invisible weight that makes his body feel useless. The last stretch of busy roads ends after jaywalking past a street with businesses scattered along it. It's pretty entertaining watching all of these places that were so alien to Abel. An introduction of sorts to an entirely different lifestyle than he is used to, the atmosphere is so wrong but it feels right. Aside from waking up and feeling like hell froze over, his body buzzes with anticipation, and a realization that he's going to play for a professional basketball team.

"It's a little bit ahead from what I remember," Warren says, twirling his hand around in the air.

Abel feels blessed that with all he had to say, and many many inappropriate remarks on the walk that he couldn't remember, he didn't speak anything about his failed start of a basketball career. Unfortunately, it isn't even as if he could have slid by without the information, it's everywhere. There were even signs and billboards on the way to the gym with his face on them, welcoming the rookies with photoshopped profiles of them in the white and black jerseys.

Abel musters up the courage to find conversation, "What college did you go to?"

Warren throws his hand, "Ahh, you wouldn't even know them. I was nobody in college, no one knew who I was. Rode the bench to the point where I wanted to nearly end my career, I got lucky 'cause I got a once-in-a-lifetime opportunity to play for this one team in Germany. My confidence skyrocketed, and here I am."

"Oh shit. Good for you man." Abel braces himself for the follow-up, expecting something in the mess that he is in. Instead, for the first time on the walk, his lips remain sealed, and no sound escapes. "Are you nervous?"

"Nah." He doesn't look back into Abel's eyes, not reciprocating the same level of attention to the conversation. "They're all a bunch of bums, they could very possibly be hand-picked off the streets. Half the players were found in a soup kitchen."

"Damn, I-"

"I don't mean any disrespect by that. The program from my understanding is a wreck, nothing good has come from that team. The insane fans are the only ones who keep the team alive every year, but they just have false hope if you ask me."

The couple turns around the corner and spots the gym, it's around the size of a high school with glass ceilings and a very well-lit interior. Futuristic beams support the glass roof and curve down towards the entrance, the entire look of it is unreal.

"New, huh?" Abel stands in awe. Here's where it all begins.

"Must be. That's another thing that they didn't say on the call. This is good though, I thought the broke-ass program wasn't going to be able to pay us at all!" He laughs. "Look at it though." A Gatorade symbol hangs over a section of the practice facility, through the windows they could see a couple of figures stretching and working out with bare chests.

"We're here!" Warren shouts with enthusiasm, jogging over to the entrance. His entire aura is illuminated by his growing realization. The entire block is centered around this enormous structure, it's very similar to a college campus with green patches like Central Park and the occasional cluster of trees for the aesthetic.

Inside is even more marvelous, the lobby wears granite floors with furniture that you could sink in and take hours just to get back out. A woman and man stand by the front door, letting them in as both players flash a keychain with a paper card on it, signifying their clearance. The pair look around like children experiencing a theme park for the first time, deciding which ride they want to go on first. Abel leads the way through a set of automatic double doors that magically open for them, revealing the best part of all: the court. It's like peeking through a window and seeing the future, neither Abel nor Warren had ever seen anything like the majestic hardwood and screens surrounding parts of the gym. On these large screens, there's a name and a top-down view of halfcourt, there were x's and o's from spots all over the perimeter and inside. Each person's name has three separate categories: three-point, midrange, and interior; under these categories it shows a fraction and a percentage, tracking the player's accuracy.

Every player has a trainer with them on their section on the hardwood, with a couple of people to grab the rebound for them. From Abel's view, he can see about half of them hanging their head and cursing profusely, pulling their hair out, and absorbing a verbal onslaught from the coaches. Typical, Abel thought, every team usually had its fair share of strictness, and the line at where they drew it depended on the program. So far, it hasn't exceeded, but he figured that it's different getting yelled at when they were handing out millions of dollars for them to perform, for everyone there is a lot on the line, especially me, Abel thinks.

A trainer catches sight of them and starts walking over, drying his face with a towel, and extending his hand. "Welcome, my name is Chris, I work individually with players, mostly in development and weight room. You'll have to meet the coach later, he's out today, you guys are all mine for the next four hours, get your stuff ready."

After shaking hands they follow Chris towards the locker room, which to no surprise at this point, is also top of its class and has every resource imaginable. And to think I thought this team was going to have nothing, Abel internalizes, feeling a tad bit optimistic for the first time since the draft.

The start to his career starts easy, mostly stretching and flexibility work, the number one most dangerous thing for a rookie is if their bodies aren't in good enough condition to perform with athletes twice their size. The wear and tear on bodies is a huge risk for such fragile bodies, such risk had to be fought with hours of stretching a day, keeping their body in peak condition. All this preparation is expected though, the only surprising thing is the weight room session. Warren had expected them to be lifting long and heavy, but instead, they did more flexibility work and then eventually worked up a sweat with footwork and very light weightlifting.

"Good, good." The trainer says to the group of rookies, recently having grown from two to four. He doubted many of them would play many minutes this season, the teams usually grabbed extra players to make them decent and then sent them off to teams for better players, that would be the business side of the sport. Abel grabs his toes and holds them there, the good pain seeping through his leg up into the rest of his body, after a minute, his leg feels as good as new.

Several groans escape the mouths of the newcomers, not used to putting their body in a better position, many people see stretching as painful and unnecessary, not immediately feeling the effects. Abel thought they were in for a rude awakening when they would inevitably end the day with an ice bath. It's his mother who started suggesting self-care when he took basketball seriously in high school, she didn't want to see her son jump and come down with a broken leg, or immediately sprain his ankle because his muscles were too tight. She had become just as educated as a personal trainer in the medical respect, the knowledge passed down to Mikey at a young age. However, he's more interested in what's right around him, a science nerd would accurately describe him, and basketball isn't it. Abel never made fun of him though, he had once been laughed at for saying what he wanted to do, and he decided he didn't want Mikey to feel the same way he did, even though he made it. The unfortunate truth is that some people never reached their goals, as many people tore them down from their full potential.

Chris guides them back to the courts, putting each of them with their spot and their rebounders. They are instructed to put up as many shots as they can in forty-five minutes, a test of endurance, but also accuracy. Abel's arms become incredibly sore around halfway through, the repetitive motion slowing him down, everyone else appears to be suffering from muscle fatigue as well. Some of them put their hands behind their head for a couple of seconds, and Abel watches Chris shaking his head and writing something down, offended. This pushes Abel for the last stretch of the time, he couldn't fall behind and fail to make an impression, he is there to make money and play in the highest level competition for basketball in the world. The rookie group wraps up by completing laps in the indoor track which is suspended above the courts in a ring.

Another hour flies by and Chris dismisses them to go back to the locker room.

"Screw that!" A player named Jay yells. "Four hours? That shit took us all day! Look at the time." Abel can't tell who he is talking to, he takes a quick peek behind him and realizes that it's a general statement, aimed at everyone. That's bold, Abel chatters to himself, what a brave thing for someone to say on the first day.

"What is that?" Chris comes right back around the corner, turning Jay's face into a melted cake, his facial expressions distorting.

"I-I was just messing around."

"Well in this program we don't fuck around. Do you want to stay on this team? Go run a five-minute mile." He points to the treadmill. Jay complies and sets it up, hammering the speed button with his index finger.

He gets to the run. At his pace, he runs a near sprint. He's pretty fast and they all watch as he endures the next four minutes gritting his teeth and moving his legs as fast as he possibly can. In the last thirty seconds, he lags a bit behind, taking only a couple of seconds for him to become conscious of this and speed up even more. One foot in front of the other he is flying. Everyone in the room's heart pounds at the sound of the lunges, wondering about the outcome of his future. Ten seconds left and he is already past a mile, the spectators are relieved that he made it.

Out of breath, Jay wobbles off of the treadmill to face Chris who has his hands plastered onto his back to keep him up. "I did it." A large grin grows on his face.

"Yes, you did," Chris smirks, drawing a long dramatic pause. "Now get the fuck out of my gym, take off all of your stuff right here, and leave."

Everyone's eyes go completely wide as if they witnessed a murder right in front of them, they encircle him as each of the players tries to comprehend what happened.

"If any of you want to play basketball with this team I suggest you all get your big boy pants on, we got another five hours in this hellhole."

CHAPTER 8

One Unwelcome Introduction

The hellhole statement only solidifies Chris's outburst towards what the team thinks is the end of practice. Nobody could have predicted the curveball that was thrown, the team expected there to be some level of discipline, but no one thought that players would just be thrown out like loud-mouthed kids in middle school. The only other times that Abel had ever seen someone kicked off a team was when a middle schooler started yelling at his teammate over choosing a jersey number, the other player got caught at practice higher than Snoop Dogg if he was given ten minutes with several blunts. The buzz dies down immediately after the exclusion of Jay, no one dares to say anything despite having the ears of a bat. Abel's mind wanders to the unsettledness that Chris isn't even the coach, he's a trainer, who mostly worked one-on-one with athletes on the team, but instead, he is acting in the head coach's favor.

Warren and Abel decide to walk home, figuring public transit wouldn't be the best idea. Unfortunately, they arrive at their places in double the time it took them to get there, the soreness already like a tidal wave rushing through their joints. The duo say their farewells and diverge into their respective apartments, Abel being apartment two-sixteen, and Warren being apartment two-fifteen. "See you tomorrow," is the best that Abel can do with how exhausted he has become. As he shuts the door he starts to feel bad for his lack of effort to talk to Warren and start a friendship, he had made some effort to say something, but it had little substance. He realizes that he has only really given one or two-word answers most of the time while Warren is spilling every minute detail from his inception into the world. He decides to do better the next day, and to reciprocate the respect that he got before he completely enters his hom- living arrangement.

"Hey, Mom-" Abel spills before he catches that she's asleep on part of the bed aside from Mikey, who also is already catching his z's. He pulls a couple of blankets from a corner and sets them on the small sofa that sits dead center in the living room part of the space. He drapes them over the sides and folds himself underneath them fitting like a glove. The night passes lazily, and every couple hours waking up in a cold sweat and a painful sensation in his chest that could be compared to the chestburster scene in Alien. He wishes that he could return to normal when things were more simple when his family had an option of whether or not they needed to follow him across the country in the hope that he is good enough at a game to put them in a decent living space.

Abel wanted to speak to his mother about Mikey and school, school in New York is set for a couple of weeks from now. Instead of bringing it up to her, he figures he'd rather not. Even if he did mention something a bit out of his place, things need to be clear about Abel's promise to himself that he wouldn't drag his little brother around the country. He would not be responsible for ruining Mikey's childhood.

After a quick trip to the sink for lukewarm water, he returns to the sofa sipping on it, the glass satisfies him after the first drink even though it's nearly warm. Abel sets down the cup on the dusty hardwood, the type of hardwood that many moons ago he would hoop on, slipping on it so much that he developed ankles that stayed inflated.

Another trip much later in the night leads him to the bathroom. Upon his return to his sleeping arrangement his foot slips as he reaches his hand down to maneuver himself into his makeshift bed. The costly movement knocks over the empty cup aggressively, which is sent straight into the through, splitting down the middle in a sharp noise that pops through the air like oil and corn seeds.

The light from the other lamp turns on, and Abel's mother approaches him with her eyes draped with heavy bags. "What's that noise?"

"Oh, don't worry about it, it's just a cup, you can go back to sleep." His disorientedness grabs the attention of his mother quickly and before he knows it she is already responding.

"Why haven't you been sleeping? Something's been keeping you up?"

"Um. No, it's nothing."

"Nothing?"

"Nothing."

"Uh-huh." She sighs and places a hand on her hip, the other rubbing her sleepy eyes. "Don't worry Abel, trust me when I say that everything will work out."

"You don't know that-"

"-but I do." She says matter of factly, leaving it at that.

And Abel does leave it at that, pulling his blanket back over his body and returning to a place of peace, or so he wished.

The night seems to resume its normal schedule, plugging along as most of the time.

Finally, he thinks.

BEEP! BEEP! BEEP! BEEP-

The alarm shocks Abel's system, forcing him to nearly gasp for air due to the stress put upon his body.

After a few grunts, he manages to get ahold of his alertness and throw himself out of any form of comfort that now he didn't possess. The walk to the gym is much faster than it was the first day, part of this is because Warren doesn't have anything to say for half the time, which he later attributes to being sleep-deprived. Abel follows up on his promise from the previous night, "What do you like to do outside basketball, Warren?"

There is something about him that he likes, he was someone he simply wanted to have around. Someone real, genuine even. Through his digging, he discovers that Warren is in a similar boat to Abel, his grandmother had to live with him because there was no one else to take care of her, and he had given her the bed too. Helping his family due to drug problems, he had pleaded with his Mom to try to go to rehab, mostly because his little s take care of her, not someone who couldn't take care of themselves. A life that could have been Abel's.

"Welcome back," Chris says bluntly upon their arrival, dismissing his attention elsewhere, distracted by something else more interesting. "Get ready quick, coach is back."

Warren looks sideways at Abel. "Yup," Abel replies, that keeping things short and sweet with staff on the basketball team is a very useful skill, most of the time you couldn't show emotion, you had to be a blank slate, like a poker player. The poker face had to be always on. The locker room is a bit more empty because of the previous day's events. On the contrary, the rest of the players are either stretching aggressively with their heads down, or they struggle to tie their shoes with their heads down. Only one player is confident enough in their spot to talk out loud, and for some reason, profusely. He tosses out words that make Jay's words sound elementary, and the worst part is "I can't believe you'll be scared of the assistant coach, his homeless ass can return to the soup kitchens where he's from." This brings everyone's attention back as he doesn't flinch or stutter one more word, "None of y'all know, this year we're going to be even worse, our record is going to be the number of bodies this guy got." He points to another teammate.

"Man, what's your problem?" His voice raises, trying to conceal the echo of snickers that follow the punchline. "Let's not talk crazy, we all know that I grabbed you by your bootstraps and dragged you all on my back."

"Yeah." The confident one scoffs. "To a losing record."

"And that says a lot about you, I'll play without those fancy-ass shoes on your feet, I don't need to pose for any camera or have anyone blow smoke so that I can feel better about my failed career."

"Failed career! We play for the New York Breakers!" He starts to laugh hysterically, like a patient in an insane asylum calling for Clarice. "Talk about a failed career, look around the room! Especially this one, projected first overall to then go undrafted! Even this bum got drafted in the second round!" He points to Warren.

"Don't talk about me like that, or him. You don't own this team, and you sure as hell haven't done anything with this team." Abel says with a grin, showing off his pearly whites. He feels like he put a mask over his face, concealing the anger the best way he figures he can.

"You won't either."

"Watch me." Abel moves away from the harmful setting, becoming quickly joined by Warren as they reach the gym and start putting up shots. Something inside Abel is triggered, that is the first time that he is confronted about the draft and how he is robbed of an opportunity, a huge opportunity, all for one small complication regarding something he said. His teammates had said much more than he did, especially 'Zero' or 'Poser' he had decided to call him in his mind, poser for his confidence without skill, and zero for the amount of times he had been with a female.

The rain of shots doesn't cease to stop, the attempts turn into makes as he thinks about nothing except the next shot, he feels fulfilled in himself, a feeling he hasn't felt in a good time.

"Baseline!" A voice shouts out, sharp and strict. None other than the head coach of the New York Breakers, Brent Baird, makes his appearance in front of the team. To some, an asshole, to some just a coach, but to

Abel; a mythical figure. One that won several rings during his time coaching back in the heyday of his career, which was way back when the team had a dynasty instead of a bunch of failed prospects. He's a very slow walker, almost as if his feet were calibrated with his mind, making each step very intentional and thought out. "Welcome everyone. This is your first official day of practice and as a team, we want to establish some ground rules."

The Poser has a hard time containing a laugh, an awkward bubbling sound seeping through his mouth instead. Luckily, the motion is completely ignored by the coach. Abel crosses his eyebrows, the guy is acting like he has plot armor and certainly didn't care about Chris's outburst the day before. "First. You might've thought that basketball was your life before, but you'll soon learn that it literally-" He pauses to make his point. "-is your life now. You will have nothing else to do, nothing else to think about, nothing else to eat, yes, you will eat, sleep, and breathe basketball. Do you remember when you thought that sleeping at school was cute? Well, that's what's happening now, you will sleep in the bunks that we have in this very building, and before you say anything, yes, you have enough privacy to do personal things. If you don't follow anything I just said, then you can make a U-turn out of this gym and return your uneducated ass to your city of origin."

Luckily, no one takes off everyone is very stone-faced. Well, everyone except for Poser. The more that Abel observes Poser, he begins to pick up on his erratic movements and random things, including the irregular quips that he continues to spur.

Shit, Abel thinks. He's drunk. And Coach Baird has no clue, or so Abel believes.

Coach Baird quickly surveys the line of people with their hands behind their backs, or gripping their practice jerseys with the other hand. "Each of you will give everything you got in your tank twenty-four seven, and absolutely no excuses will be made." He pauses to regain his composure.

"Last thing, we have a system here in this organization. You each will have individual goals set by coaches and other staff members, these goals are not something you need to keep in mind to get better, they are an expectation, and around here if you don't meet your expectations then you don't play, you don't play then who will care about you? I sure won't. You'll get your goals as soon as you get dismissed. Keep in mind that these goals will only change once you complete them, and we can give as many goals as we want. You're just going to have to suck it up and do it because we said so." Another break for air. "Well fellas... that's it."

The group disperses, as one staff member matches with one player, a total of fifteen players. "Richards." Coach Baird says with a sharp whistle. "You'll be talking with me."

His heart skips a beat, and just like a ghost, he follows after him to his office. The workspace is very cluttered, pictures from the wall are distant memories of championships, boxes of clipboards and old jerseys sit in a corner, and even a decrepit shelf of books making their late debut. The rest of the junk are papers that he never got to, and news articles that were either never read, or violently tossed out due to some reason.

"Sit down." The order flies out.

Abel sits.

"I'm going to be straightforward and brief. We need you on this team."

"I know." This one wasn't so hard to respond to, it's more than clear that the team is desperate.

"And unlike the rest of the team, you need to do what I say more than anyone." Odd, but Abel still listens in, pulling down his sweaty shirt.

"What do I need to do?"

"You will average twenty-five points, five rebounds, and five assists per game."

"Okay... that's what I knew I was going to do anyway."

"Sorry, you're missing my point, I meant that you have to achieve those stats. It's what I call an Incentive. You either do or you will not play for this organization ever again, or any organization in this league, or overseas, hell, I will make sure that you don't play basketball for the rest of your life, you hear me?"

"Yeah- I-"

Coaches face winces, as his hands become involved in expressing his disturbance. "And you will not get one cent from this game until we win ten games in a row, right off the bat to start the season."

"Are you serious?" Abel looks baffled, now throwing his hands in front of him.

"Damn straight I'm serious. If you want to touch a basketball ever again, you better get in that gym. You're with us now Abel, a whole new world. Welcome to the New York Breakers, son. Welcome."

CHAPTER 9

Opening Night

The words from the day before still sting like frostbite on cold fingers. The beads of sweat drip off of him to the beat of some fast trap song, his heart feeling the drumming of the bass. Who does he think he is? Abel never heard of a system like Coach Baird had in place, one that demanded results that were incredibly difficult even for veterans to the game.

But then again, nobody wanted it more than himself, he at least tries to convince himself. Twenty-five points though, Abel thinks, and on top of that there hadn't been plenty of time to prepare for the new environment he is about to be thrown into. He could be compared to a baby zebra being tossed into the wide-open savannah, where everything wants to rip you apart. It isn't much different in the league, some people wanted to see the blood trickle down your chin as they stripped you of your dignity in front of a crowd worth hundreds of thousands of people. The big question is is this something that he is ready for, his mother told him over the phone that he had nothing to worry about and, that he would do just fine, but Abel neglected to tell her about the incentive for playing, the threats from the coach. Something held back his tongue from spilling all the reasons he's ever wanted to quit or all the reasons he's unsure about his talent and the future. Lucky for him, that magical guardian had continued to hold back his anxiety.

Confidence is something that slowly builds over time in Abel. The beginning of his freshman season would be rough. As he leaves the facility once more, he ponders the thought of riding the bench and watching his teammates fail and prevail. Sure he could benefit some from this, as a result, he would get to know the moving pieces better than anyone, he just didn't put anything into action. The possible scenarios just felt wrong to continue to stress over, but Abel's walk around the faculty can only be filled by the constant chattering of his brain. Later in the season if he could get a chance, nothing crazy, just a few minutes in the game more than what he could be given, he would worry less because he would most likely achieve his Incentive quickly and easily. He would have to make sure that he didn't care when he missed the shot, he couldn't care if he made a small mistake. Instead, if he missed a shot he would just have to take it again, or if he turned over the ball he would have no other option but to chase them down and get it right back. In this case, the coaches would have to start to admire his mindset and the rest would be history.

Abel's little thought bubble pops during his approach to another set of doors, relinquishing his attention from his thoughts to something more materialistic. A water fountain nearby quickly takes Abel away from the hallway. The taste of the water is horrible for a water fountain that resided in a state-of-the-art building, which is relatively new. Oddly the water reminds him of the hollowing nights where he would grab a cup and crank the faucet to fill it up. The night brings strong urges that were hard to explain, they were never spoken about to another soul. They never left the space inside of his head, it was like he couldn't comprehend the shadows that were descending around him, the overwhelming dread he felt.

A sports documentary clicks onto the screen nearest to Abel, almost completing his sentence in his head, "As much as basketball is tied to money, women, and fun, it remains a completely separate minefield for those that pursue it, the game kills relationships, and turns players into people they're not. It happens often, unfortunately, too many people are uncomfortable in their skin and get held back from achieving great things." Power off. This time from Abel's two hands, snatching the plug from the screen.

Abel grabs his possessions from his locker yet again. The bus is rumored to leave around ten o'clock in the morning for the first home game of the season, information found via literally any of the chatterboxes that made the program. This time just unfortunately is a hot one minute from now.

"How are you feeling?" The more peppy Warren says as he approaches him with his duffel bag full of stuff. Warren grabs his headphones which are the older model that have a wire running down them, and connects them to some device inside of his duffel bag. The music could be heard, but just barely seeping through the headphones, the older style mode of audio enjoyment was still a valid choice. Abel on the other hand is empty-handed, empty-handed in terms of music, not the water bottles that were arranged in his hands unwillingly. He hated listening to music before games, he indeed gets in his head a majority of the time, but there is something that he felt is even more unsettling for him than listening to music that would turn off the exact moment the game started, there is no calm environment on the court, so why should he adapt to one?

"I'm fine I guess." He looks back down at his feet, inspecting the same outfit that he's worn since his senior year of high school. No shame in his game, what worked, worked.

"Hey, what did Coach say about your goals, Incentives, or whatever? Is anything… weird?" Abel tries to put it in the least intrusive way possible, but still, it doesn't roll out of the mouth right.

Instead of a verbal exchange, Warren shakes his head on a dime, swiping his hand to his neck and signaling for him to cut it out.

"So you know what I'm talking about?"

He nods his head this time, "Just forget about it." With that, he leaves.

They leave the building, where two luxury-style buses rest, occupied by the handful of players that made up the team, the other bus is for the staff. Upon entrance into the vehicle, Abel realizes that the other players must've had a pretty difficult conversation regarding their future performances as well. He's sure that most if not all of them were at least reasonable, otherwise they just wouldn't have a team. He guaranteed that no one had even close to the expectation laying on him, the stakes were high, and he couldn't afford to mess it up. He had to do something that was done once every couple of decades by a rookie, scoring twenty-five, five rebounds, and five assists. The last time that was done… well… Abel wasn't even born.

He reads the room for now and decides he isn't going to interact, there's just not anything to say to these people, he isn't particularly close with them, except for Warren in a way. He hadn't even spoken to anyone about how Coach Baird had put Abel in his private court to practice, which is dark, dusty, and has a huge chunk of the backboard missing as well. He had drilled hard in there for hours, mostly accompanied by his thoughts on why the hell he was getting that treatment in the first place. When he first walked into that room, he was dead confused. He was in the nicest building that he'd ever seen, let alone go inside and explore the interior. And it had a basketball court inside of it that is worse than the conditions he played at home as a child. It is almost frightening, the ways of Coach Baird, along with every single one of his other spontaneous decisions to sit in a chair and watch him practice in the phantom court.

The bus ride is a short excursion to the heart of New York, and luckily enough, its minor length keeps interactions short, and minimal. Abel decides he would never try to accompany himself with the area, there are just too many things, and they are everywhere. Also, if he were to ever be traded, the whole process would require him to pack up his things in a matter of days, not weeks. Not that he had much, but it still made a difference to him. So everything is everywhere, and everything moves everywhere, a good summary of the city of New York.

Some things cross his stream of thought on his walk into the building, and none of them are the cameras or lights, not even the fans that will soon appear like a flashbang when he inevitably walks out of the gate and gets warmed up. Instead, he thinks about his family crammed inside a one-bedroom apartment with an empty fridge, one pillow to go between the three of them and food that they rationed out for the month. The only things that were getting spent weren't things that they deserved, they were things that were necessities only, and they were very sparse.

Abel remembers the job that his Mom had lined up for herself, she had seemed very proud of herself over the phone which brought a wide smile to his face. He missed when his Mom didn't worry as much.

Flash. Flash.

The cameras were much less blinding with the pair of sunglasses he borrowed from a friend in high school and never returned. It's a pity they were so expensive too, but that kid lived in a three-story duplex anyway, it's not like it mattered that much.

The locker room in the arena is much more compact than the expansive, innovative space that was assigned to the Breakers team. The cubbies for jerseys become snatched so quickly that Warren and Abel end up on opposite sides of the room; it doesn't feel like too much of a gap, largely due to Warren's size. Warren plays the power forward position, so his job is to be a defensive bully and big scorer, and he played the part well at six foot eight.

A side door opens with a creak that can be heard for miles, Coach Baird. He sports a clipboard with a handful of papers on it, one hand holding them down and the other one helping him talk to the team about the game plan. Abel gets a quick glimpse of one of the papers, and they are none other than a tally system for keeping track of each player's Incentive. He spots Warren's, his paper requires him to set a total of twenty screens in the single game, below the box that looks like it would hold the tallies, there is another one that tracks how many feet he needs to push the other teams players while going for a rebound. The goals are so diverse to each player, nobody has the same goal, and no one wants to be the one to find out what would happen if you were one small mark from him filling in your boxes.

"Are we going to win today?" Coach Baird says in a monotone voice.

"YES!" They yell in unison.

He flattens his tone even more, "Good, 'cause we all know what needs to happen." He smirks, looking at Abel.

And that's it from him, the blank slate stays blank.

With that the team jogs out to the floor, dressed in warm-up outfits, which consist of athletic sweatpants and a loose sweatshirt. This is it, Abel thinks, hearing his breath as loud as the bass on the court. It takes a few seconds for the numbness of the mix of excitement and utter terror to wear off, and he realizes that he's been shooting around. The basketball finds the rim with every shot, but it doesn't roll in like it usually does, it's a rare occurrence that it even touches the rim in the first place. Usually, it's either swish or no bucket for him. Shot after shot, shot after shot. The same motion that he had been through millions of times before begins to feel like it isn't him shooting like he has no feeling in his arm and he's using someone else's. He keeps a level head for as long as he can, but he feels the disappointment of being shot at by his coaches, teammates, and opponents. After that Abel doesn't stop cursing himself out, adding a little extra force to the end of each shot, as if by pure aggression the shot would magically go in.

"Aaaaaaand welcome! To opening night with the NEW YORK BREAKERS!" The announcer booms, covering the arena with more anticipation for the Moment they had been waiting for four months.

"Hey. You good?" Abel's teammate Ray nudges him, placing another basketball in his hand to shoot. "You can't worry about the other team." He must have caught Abel returning glances with the opposing team, The Storm Titans, the best defensive team in the league, based out of Texas.

"Yeah. Yeah, I'm good." Abel bounces his focus back to the motion. Swish. Finally, the basket drops, giving him some source of relief.

"There you go, get the misses out," Ray says, throwing his leg behind his back and grabbing his foot with his hands, putting himself into a deadly-looking stretch. Abel figures he must have been comfortable in his skin to be as flexible as he is.

Ray had been chill since they met, he showed Abel a picture of him two years ago and from the picture in perspective, Ray looked like an entirely different person, it would be very safe to say that he lost some belly fat. He put himself through tough conditions and suffered through it to make gains for himself, respectable.

The shot goes up again and misses. The cold streak continues up until the buzzer, which sends his stomach on a roller coaster ride to the depths of the underworld, straight drop.

His brain turns off for the announcement of the other team, when it finally gets to his turn to walk out to the starting five, he sleepwalks his way to center court. In retrospect, he doesn't even know how he remembered to fistbump the referees with the dizzyness that his nerves brought him.

The basketball court is indeed a stage, for Abel, it is a stage of sounds just as much as a stage of entertainment for the fans, every aspect of the court translates into a sound that fed a growing symphony that hypnotized the ten players on the court. The whistles, the squeaks of the shoes on hardwood, the clapping, and cheering, the flicks of the camera, the basketball bouncing, one, two, three-

"Jump ball!" The ref throws the ball into the air and Shawn Wilson snatches the ball, possession Titans.

The game moves fast, buckets are made quickly, and buckets are made often. For the first five minutes, Abel damn near looks clueless on the court. He manages to get one lucky rebound after a horrendous shot attempt from one of the bigger players on the Titans, but his focus gets brought back to the checklist. It is do or die. Twenty-five points, five rebounds, five assists, or no basketball.

The first quarter wraps up with Abel contributing a couple of fast break layups after a quick steal or rebound, it could be worse, so he doesn't feel too bad. The timeout huddle is not for the faint of heart, things start to get thrown around, spit apparently could be used as a projectile that flies out of the coach's mouth.

And for some odd reason, he completely ignores Abel the entire time. Not one word.

Luckily, in the second quarter, he is given a short break to catch his breath. He has his eyes on number fifteen, Isiah Yen, the multi-faceted two-way player, equally as talented on defense as his scoring ability. The things coming out of mouth also aren't short of a travesty, he doesn't stop his onslaught of insults towards Abel one second.

"First overall huh? Must've been nice." He chuckles. Abel isn't going to give a response, he refused to give in to something so little in the hindsight of his past mistakes, just for lashing out over words that carried little weight. Abel had expected these exact things to be said, so for now, no comment. "What? Pretty boy doesn't have anything to say now?"

Still, no comment. After the trash-talking, Abel finds himself less focused on the people around him, and more in tune with his movements. This is second nature, he knows exactly what he has to do and what he is going to get out of it as a result, this is the give-and-take nature of basketball.

Every time the ball leaves his hands, something magical happens, it either went directly through the hoop or made its way to the hands of one of his teammates who got it done just the same. Sure, they weren't consistent, but they were enough to get him all his assists for the night which left him one-third of the way there. By the time the buzzer rang to signify the end of the first half, Abel had scored twenty, rebounded six shots, and assisted on five possessions. He jogs off the court smiling on the inside, not on the out, deciding that he is going to keep the same blank slate that his coach did. Primarily because he is going to obliterate the Incentive and he could forget about the agreement on winning ten games straight. Just for the night. One thing at a time.

Abel had never heard of such things as Incentives happening in a structured basketball league that was a national organization. They are globally spectated and have millions and millions of dollars lying around as chump change, if he worked for them, the contract said that they had to pay them.

Or had it? Did he read the fine print? Was there a fine print?

Halftime is a space for the flood of thoughts that carry with him, the team is pretty hyped to be up by five going into the half. The turnaround in the second quarter greatly shifted the momentum and mood of the game, now they were all feeling it.

Tweet! "Ball in!"

The slow start of the first half fuels Abel for the next fifteen minutes, he is a defensive menace for the first time in his entire basketball career, he isn't the best defender, but he wanted it, and he wanted it badly.

The clock eventually reads two minutes left in the final quarter, tie game.

Warren passes the ball to Jauque Torres, the starting point guard and they advance to half-court, meeting their predecessors head-on. The opposing team picks up their feet and swings them outwards to block the path of Torres faster than the speed of light, The Breakers have control over the play, any bucket is needed as the clock dwindles. The ball gets tossed down to Ray who nearly immediately departs the ground to shoot a layup, but is heavily contested by the largest human that Abel has ever seen, Yen. Ray luckily recognizes this too and makes the split-second decision to kick it out to Abel who is wide open for the three-pointer. It is wide open. Largely due to a failed scrambling of the Titans, who run around like they are chickens with their heads cut off, fighting for their chance to deny Abel any chance to put points onto the board.

The shot goes up!

But so does Isiah Yen, the freak human. His entire seven foot five inches, two hundred sixty-two pounds crash straight into Abel's chest, sending him hurtling towards the ground like a meteor.

Is it over? Abel gets to let out of his system. All before the most beautiful, and brightest lights that he has ever seen dim until there is nothing left except Abel's twenty-four points light up the scoreboard, all as a flurry of medics rush onto the scene.

CHAPTER 10

Eight Hundred and Two Missed Calls

The ambulance takes the most direct route to the hospital, which is around fifteen minutes, still a long time for an emergency. The arena remains in total shock and disarray, the majority of people holding their hands over their heads with a large gap in their mouths. Both Breaker fans and Titan fans have their eyes wide, even those viewing from around the country and globe keep their hands covering their mouths, holding their remotes in a static state. Abel Richards is taken out of the game with twenty-six points, seven rebounds, and. An amazing first-game performance for someone who desperately needs to essentially break records just for a paycheck.

He remains unconscious for the entire ride to the hospital, and then hours and hours in a bed, being administered frequently. In that gap of time, Abel feels awake, but unable to control any part of his body, even his eyelids that keep him shut away from the light. He gets to thinking about many things, but for the first time, basketball isn't one of them. His mind acts like someone on anesthesia or laughing gas, he isn't himself in his head, and he can't control the intrusive thoughts that form into a vision. The vision takes place in the real world, but instead of New York, he's in Seattle, the jewel of the northwest, home. The urban area of Seattle is plagued with hills that dress the salad that is the landscape. His mind places himself on the crest of a hill that is surrounded by a cul de sac of two-story houses, each with a default mailbox and a newspaper in the perfectly paved driveway. The houses are laid out with a large window that has a view of the living room, the second largest window is right above the door. As for the garages, they are either a level below the rest of the house, or they are the fancy double garage doors. The neighborhood isn't familiar to Abel, but he pleases himself with the thought that the place that he had created is amusing. Weirdly he is the builder of something by complete accident, and instead of tearing it back down, he decides to let out whatever story he had inside of him surface and reveal itself to him.

It doesn't take Abel long to figure out that the event of the environment around him was by his design and not, real, possibly only taking around five seconds to look around his world to find out that he is, , seeing things. Because of this special type of environment in his head, he can regain the power to move his feet and arms. He indulges himself in strolling through the neighborhood, passing by the empty streets with no signs of human life, not even vehicles. After a good amount of time, he gets bored of the mundanity of the setting, seeing the same houses over and over again, the houses are addicting to him though, they tickle something inside of Abel that makes him feel bittersweet about his existence in this plane.

After too much of the radical feeling, he decides to switch things up. With that, a path appears to his left, covered in gravel and dirt, with patches of grass fighting to grow up into the lane. He takes the detour with no second thought, approaching a wired gate with the sign: Trespassers are prohibited, the City of Seattle. He grips the top of the gate with both hands and leverages himself over, feeling a sharp pain in his head with his first attempt at jumping halfway up the gate. The pain causes him to stumble a little, but he recovers well and throws himself over. The path led down to an open expanse with a view of the city skyline from afar, in one corner of his vision he could see the buildings reaching high into the sky, and in the other corner he saw the mysterious sea, which dove further in depths, each were their accomplishments. Abel found it funny that as humans reached higher into the atmosphere towards God, God was going in the opposite direction that nobody else wanted to explore, a feat of nature, and a feat of humanity.

This wide area is a stretch of power lines, which are sprinkled pretty abundantly across the Puget Sound area. These large structures run for miles over the rolling hills, ever so often down the powerline, there are little sheds. They aren't supposed to be used by anyone except for kids who want to mess around during the summer or act plain stupid. The sheds are locked on the outside, and the only way in is to place a foot on top of a wood piece extending up and outwards to reach the wired part of the fence. The wooden slab that is attached to the fence is fascinating to Abel, it's littered with graffiti art, taking a more jagged and rough look. The words are scrambled out of any order, so no sentence could be constructed with the odd grouping of words. Gone. Far. Behind you. You're here. The words would've been unsettling to Abel if he hadn't known that his brain had come up with the words on his own, not some mystical force threatening his existence. To his benefit, he isn't afraid of his creation.

Was God ever afraid of his creation?

Should I?

He starts to climb. This time, he avoids going too fast at risk of his head splitting brutally down the middle, that would suck. Taking his time, he gets to the other side of the fence, ending up in a relatively tight space, he can just barely grab the other side of the fence by reaching his arm out. The fence isn't for nothing however, all it takes is for Abel to peer his head down to see the hole in the ground.

An entire staircase runs down this hole, molded with compact dirt, bending the laws of science a tiny bit. Abel's intelligence regarding science didn't go very far, unlike the tunnel that he is now immersed in. He grabs the sides of the walls as he makes his way further into an abyss, the light slowly fading away from him, until he relies purely on his other senses to navigate the labyrinth.

Enough exploring goes by for him to find several different passageways that don't seem to end. He knows there is a purpose that he placed into this dream, he has to go deep and find the heart of it.

BaBUM!

The sounds start to erupt out of the ground, causing tiny little pebbles to pop off of the ground with every beat.

BaBUM!

Abel turns his head in the direction of the echoing noise, is it his own heart? The one in his chest? He feels his chest, waiting, waiting, waiting. Nothing. No pulse or return of any signs of life in him. He is dead. He checks his pulse by placing two fingers up to his neck, still, nothing.

He starts to run, crashing his body into walls, but bouncing off of them just as quick as his impact against them, not caring where he ends up. "HEY!" He screams. "WHAT'S GOING ON!" The crisp air is the only thing that accompanies him throughout his break through the maze, breathing it in hard, and lashing it back out of the same passageway.

His intake of oxygen is synchronous to the tunnel, every time he breathes out, he makes a sharp turn in the tunnel. The same process goes by in what seems like hours on top of hours.

And then it stops.

The labyrinth ends abruptly. He enters the last room which is surrounded by dirt and roots. The room couldn't be any bigger than a classroom, and in the far corner, he sees himself in a perfectly intact mirror, one that isn't a reflection. In the glass Abel sees his doppelganger lying down in a hospital, eyes closed, lifeless. A nurse stands over him, with a clipboard and a pen, shaking her head, completely unaware of Abel's presence and observation. She shakes her head more, frustrated with her failure. He is intrigued by the scene, not cognizant of whatever is going on in front of him. At the very least, he knows that he is the one in the bed, but why? He watches as long as it takes for the nurse to make a one-hundred-eighty-degree pivot and catch sight of him, initiating a staring contest. The nurse looks like a deer in headlights, remaining calm and beginning to advance slowly. She can see me? Abel thinks.

"Come." The nurse waves him over, and he feels pulled deeper and deeper into his vision, tied to the end of a rope. As he draws closer, he starts to want to resist the force dragging him to the hospital bed.

He tries screaming, but nothing comes out.

His brain explodes to the new pain that pulls him back to the surface. He looks up to see a nurse, she looks familiar to Abel somehow. He starts gaining the feeling of deja vu, the room looking familiar. He is unfazed as he is rushed and surrounded by the supporting hospital staff, poking and prodding and shining blinding lights into his eyes. Abel tries hard to comprehend what happened, trying to recall the not-so-real steps he took while his soul was on vacation from his body.

"Can you hear us, Mr. Richards?" is the first thing he allows himself to focus on, the rest of the people look like fools the way they mouth the words to him.

Abel tries to talk again, but when nothing comes out, he settles by giving a quick nod. As soon as he regains strength in his muscles, he puts his hands to his mouth in a drinking motion, signaling for water.

"Oh." One of the doctors runs off at his request.

"You've been in a coma, Mr. Richards, you..." she trails off. "You flatlined. We thought you were dead."

"My family," Abel mutters, sounding like a drug addict asking for his next fix. His mouth's as dry as the Sahara so he gives himself a little grace because he can't talk at the same leisure as a normal person.

"What about them?" The nurse gives a quick response.

"Where are they?"

"We don't need them."

"Yes, yes I do."

"No, you don't." With that, she turns around and exits the room.

A vibration comes from a device next to his table. It is his mobile phone. How the hell did it get here? He thinks, managing to reach it, and looks down at the blue light that radiates out of its small surface area.

Eight hundred and two missed voicemails.

"What is this?" Abel says, gripping the phone tighter as he scrolls down on the times of the calls, they go back a week ago and have been called damn near every minute since then. He's been gone for a week.

His fingers turn into lightning that strikes the keyboard on his phone, typing into the gray search bar: 'Breakers vs. Titans'. The score was one hundred-ten to one hundred-eight, the Titans winning. Under the tab that has the score, there are recent articles, with red highlighted words that say 'breaking'. He scrolls furiously through the articles, each of them garnering his name on the headline, 'basketball star deemed dead at last night's game'. He reads and reads and reads, trying to make sense of the predicament he blindly fell into because of his waking up. It feels like a whole new world that he had stepped into, subject to others' preservation of his memory.

The nurse turns back, having the hearing of a bat, and turning right back around, "Oops! You weren't supposed to see that." She put a couple of fingers up to her mouth to express her surprise.

"Why wasn't I supposed to see my phone?"

"That isn't your phone."

"It has all of my things on it, it has the same password too." Abel scoffs, it doesn't help that he wakes up from a coma and everyone plays dumb.

"You can't take that with you."

"Take it with me? It's mine." He says the sarcasm is starting to wear off.

"You are being released from the hospital tonight, and no, it's not yours."

"Aren't you- what's wrong with me? Why hasn't anyone told me what's happened?"

"You were in a coma because of direct contact and pressure to your brain, we thought you died, but somehow you came back. Now, our readings say you are good, you are free to go, your coach says to immediately report to the training facility, no going home."

"I can't believe you- I." He pauses, suspending his jaw in the air. "You're acting like everyone else-"

"Goodbye now." The nurse completely dismisses him, ushering him out of his bed. His brain sharply spikes with pain, forcing him back down to the bed. This doesn't stop the nurse from continuing her motion by pulling Abel out of the room, and nearly throwing him down the hall, pointing to the closest exit with her gloved hands.

The frigid air welcomes Abel into its painful environment, adding more severity to the parasite squirming violently in his head. He walks towards the bus stop, hands in his pockets, realizing that he left the phone on the bed.

The voicemails would have to remain unanswered for now.

CHAPTER 11

Media Day

The abrupt re-entry of Abel Richards remains a very talked-about subject amongst the athletes, the coaches however, could give a rat's ass that he came back the moment he woke up from a coma.

The first thing he does is eat something, his stomach starving from food that isn't in liquid form or forced down his throat. After that, he tends to the missed calls that were frantically left by his protective, not necessarily overprotective, mother. His brain is slow to process the proceeding amount of stress that he puts his mother through, and when he realizes that he is injured and in a coma, he snatches his phone from his pocket at superhuman speed and dials the number.

Every dial leads to something strange, the ring immediately stops and hangs up. Every time he calls anyone actually, he tries his friend, his Mom, hell, even his ex to see if anything is going to go through. All it takes is a quick trip to his contacts to find it completely blank, with no alphabetical organization, no search bar, nothing. The contacts app is stripped bare bone down to an unusable platform.

He groans, frustrated with the constant failure at things being clear, especially surrounding his very decision to continue doing what he loved, every moment he feels like his future in basketball is at extreme risk.

Abel's next plan of attack is to bring this information to one of the coaches, knowing that they probably had something to do with it, it isn't hard to tell that the nurses and doctors at that hospital had been conveniently influenced to do certain things for them, which is why they delivered a message to Abel while he was leaving the hospital. He is no detective, but he does have half a brain. This decision to say something to the staff is quickly shut down with the threats echoing in his mind, swirling around like it got thrown in the washing machine.

Abel walks up to the coach, who is sitting down on a chair at center court, staring around at the basketball hoops. He is turned in the opposite direction from the point in which Abel is moving towards him, so doesn't have direct sight of him as he makes his approach.

Before he makes it into too close of proximity he says, "You're back."

"Yes, Coach. I'm back, it isn't too serious of an injury I can play on-"

"I don't like you telling me how to do my job," he grinds through his teeth, throwing away a piece of lint on his blazer, quickly sweeping his pants with his legs, and standing up. He adjusts his tie very formally, pivots without stepping forward, and looks him directly in the eyes. "When you mean serious injury, can you explain?"

"No, I can't really."

"Oh, so you can't, that's it?"

"Yes."

"In all the things I've ever doubted in my life, I haven't doubted your capabilities, I'm not just talking about basketball, things go deeper than basketball. The game is just a tree, and I am watering the roots, these points of interest are what will boost you up into the sky, just like said tree. Now imagine if you were sent somewhere else, let's say they pay you often, and it's forty million on a two-year contract. This imaginary organization will deprive you of the energy needed to grow, they will fatten you up like a cat, and turn you into a gluttonous pig. You don't want that believe me, but when I say I believe in your capabilities, I also believe you are intelligent, and all I wanted is a response that told me what happened, I don't care for anything else, just, what happened?"

"My head hit the ground." He pauses to salivate his Saharan Desert of a mouth. "I went to the hospital because I went into a coma at the game."

"Ok. That's it. Not hard? Just wanted to know what happened."

"You were there- I mean, so what's the problem, can I not play?"

"Well did you meet your Incentive?"

"You tell me!" Abel's frustration builds up to a peak of explosion, similar to if one is simply talking with their parents and they raise their tone on accident, knowing what pain across your backside is going to happen roughly three seconds after the last syllable. Abel immediately regretted talking to the man who had his career resting in his fragile, cracked hands.

"I will tell you. The shot was short. But lucky for you, you fell into a coma, and the coma landed you right to today, media day."

"Media day?"

"You and the rest of the team are going to take pictures for our profit, and you still have some goals to complete so the money will have to stay with us for the time being."

"How is it that you can just withhold money from us, I could call somebody right now, and get you gone, and myself with at least enough money to pay for a home."

"You can't call anyone."

"What do you mean?"

"I mean, your phone will not be able to call someone."

"How?!" The temper is starting to build, Abel becoming steaming because Coach Baird could be so level-headed with something so criminal, it had to be, there couldn't be any way that anyone else would be accepting of his methods.

"I am watering the roots. And calling won't do anything, I have connections everywhere who have very similar ways of coaching, how do you think I've won seven championships?"

"You're a bastard, you know that?"

"A damn good one too, Richards. There will be no more talking with your family, they are a distraction made for being the wind that blows you off course into a place where you had success, but you never used any of it. You are special, and so, you are going to use your success and become one of the brightest stars in the league. It's a partnership." The extension of his hand adds mystique to the conversation, he is like a bipolar Tasmanian Devil, whirling around the dialogue making little to no sense, and saying things just to say them, struggling to convey concrete things that were digestible for Abel.

"What are we agreeing to? You don't understand, I need to have some form of pay."

The hand drops. "I hate repeating myself, Richards. If you're going to make one cent from the team, you are going to do it my way, if not, you can leave. I have no problem with you taking yourself off of my hands. But if I can't have you as a talent, you can count on no one else either, you have no idea what I can do. Now, you are going to tap your head a couple of times, make sure it's good, and then complete the expected stat line."

Abel's mental stability relies on him not saying another word, worried that if that were the case, his head might explode.

"Go get ready for media day, it's at our home court. Outfits are in the locker room with your teammates."

Abel stands in place for a couple more seconds and exits the gaze of the dark abyss of Coach Baird's eyes, he is a snake, and Abel is a rat. The snake is extremely fast, out-maneuvering the rat whose stubby legs and lack of defense leave him six feet under before he is even touched. The strangling is what is happening now, the life being drained out of him, his close encounter with death didn't even register as a real event that happened to him, rather taking likeness to a nightmare that he couldn't wake up from. Coach Baird's demeanor is stone cold, emotionless, and internally driven beyond anyone's comprehension for something that hardly any people ever touched, providing a feat in the books alongside climbing Mount Everest. Everyone is driven towards that trophy one way or another, but some athletes had completely different captains and boats than the sinking catastrophe of a season that most of them were attempting to endure.

The loss is still engraved into Abel's mind, along with his cryptic time while he was in a coma with some undiagnosed brain damage which the cause was suspiciously withheld by the nurse. Not only that, but even tampered with his phone, rendering it useless.

The atmosphere that Abel joins as he reunites with the gym is very atypical of the team, primarily a group of younger adults who all flaunt their recent adventures to the doctor's office, "-Got my physical shape like three months ago." One of his teammates tries to explain.

"-Went to take myself to a health screening like two weeks ago." Buts in Devonte.

"Damn, everybody's been going to the hospital for something- Abel! Abel!" Most people surround him instantly, even the people who might not have liked him the best. They all seem genuinely blessed to have Abel back to play after the traumatic experience a couple of weeks before. Abel quickly learns that their record is one win, eleven losses. Most of them secretly agree that one of their Incentives was to get ten straight wins. Some of his teammates had just received their first paychecks in the mail for completing their basic chores on the court during their very limited time running in the games. They did their part, and Abel hasn't done his.

The team quickly loads onto the bus as per usual, Abel still feels a bit rusty in the process of loading onto the bus and getting through. The rest of his teammates are already much more comfortable with each other and the way they act around each other seems almost friendly. He'd missed out on two weeks of getting more familiarized with his environment, and his supporting cast of teammates. Abel fumbles the bags pretty severely on his trip up the stairs leading to the bus seats, "My bad." The bus driver, who is a sweet old lady, bends her head down a tad, placing her hand up, showing that it's no big deal.

Abel continues towards the very back of the bus this time, the three seats per side turning into just two because of the bathroom that extends out into the walking lane. He sits down, throwing his bag on the inside seat, taking the window spot, and propping his head on his hands. He grabs his headphones and scrolls through his phone until he finds the right song, he taps the button, returning to gazing out the window. He waits a few seconds for the song to come on, assuming that his internet just needed to figure itself out, but when it didn't start playing he reopens the app and presses play again, this time with more pressure. As a result, the music starts playing, causing Abel to start to turn off his phone when he decides to check his contacts again, still empty.

Luckily, the bus isn't too loud for the moment so he quickly dials his mother's phone number into the phone, holding it up to his mouth to talk. The phone doesn't even ring. Abel looks back down at the mobile device, seeing that the numbers he dialed in are gone. He types them in again, with the same outcome, the numbers immediately vanish. He continues to try to call, but the phone simply does not let him put in the phone number.

The rest of the team in front of him didn't have their phones out either, In the first game, the majority had been watching videos, or listening to music, but this time he was the only one. The ride to the arena is much quieter as well, the lack of atmosphere dragging down the mood, seconds before they had seemed social, and now they were dodging. It would be understandable if it was a game day, everyone has their methods to lock in and mentally prepare for the task at hand, but they were all taking a ride to get their picture taken for media support.

The New York Breakers Arena is in full business, the fans run around rampantly trying to find their favorite players in hopes of some horrible marker scratching across a valuable piece of clothing. The fans find it valuable and cherish these items.

Today, Abel feels like an asshole, an asshole who didn't want to sign hundreds of jerseys, hats, and places on the body that shouldn't be mentioned.

As expected, the media has a huge presence, not only the media that organized the photos and other questions there, but plenty of third-party companies try to film content for whatever fake news they plan on stirring up. Abel thinks of the Pixar movie Finding Nemo, making the responsible choice to just keep swimming, remembering the consequences that diseased him the last time he had a small interaction with a member of the paparazzi. The tunnel of cameras starts to form around the players as they enter the back doors to the arena, quickly taking shelter in the one place where they legally couldn't harass the players.

The players group up in a large room to the side of the hallway, getting greeted by more and more camera lenses. Coach Baird appears out of a large metal door by himself, surprisingly he is alone.

"Alright," he says, snapping his fingers and aiming them at a couple of lockers, "get dressed."

Most of Abel's teammates have outfits similar to his, they were basic and looked like hand-me-downs from their father. The reality is that most of them have drained pockets like his, the outfits are most likely from the time when they stopped growing, when a lot of them had stopped growing in the seventh grade at six foot six. They each opened their lockers, finding something that widened their eyes, Abel saw the contents and diverted his attention to his dirty outfit. Inside were designer outfits, each for the most part matching in general style, color, and brand. Abel's outfit is a set of Dior clothing, in all black. He rubs the material, getting a feel for the lack of money. He hadn't gained one penny in months, living on his last check. He had to get himself to a point where the Dior clothing was his. He grabs the clothing and quickly dresses along with the rest of the Breakers, taking their place in a room surrounded by white panels and lights, getting the right setup for the perfect photo, the photo that would bring in money for everyone else except him, Not for long, he thinks.

"Can we get the starting five to stand right here," the camera woman walks over to the more diluted group of players, gently putting her hands on them and adjusting their stance in front of the camera. They stand on a blank white box that holds them above ground level, they inch their feet to be angled towards the camera, then are instructed to shift their faces to reflect the damage they are going to inflict upon the Seattle Orcas coming tomorrow. Several flashes indicate that more than one photo has been taken, the managers of the photoshoot have them pose in multiple different positions and arrangements, eventually doing individual photos and a whole team photo with the coaches and staff included.

"Mr. Richards? Could we have a photo of you with Coach Baird?" A man says, just like the rest of his crew, they are wearing all black, and this particular person wears a black hat and a pretty thin headset over his ears.

Abel looks over to Coach Baird who is conversing with a small group of people, bringing his phone up every once in a while to show something, they seem to be in a general agreement, and he is pulled aside from the man who asked for their picture.

"Picture?" Coach Baird inquires, dropping his things and preparing himself on top of the subject area of the photos.

"Yes please, we are going to send this one into Drip, they are having you two as the next cover and main story."

Abel chuckles a little bit, they wanted him as the cover athlete and he's played a total of one game. He knows that the game was pretty incredible for a rookie given that it broke records, but usually, it's about veterans already tearing up the league, or consistent and promising rookies, one game is not enough to judge someone's game. The only real reason that he made the cover and main story is because of the recent past with his becoming a free agent and barely scraping by onto a team that won't pay him, and then with his injury that no one has second-guessed, not even Abel.

"Oh, okay." He bites his lip, continuing to try to remain emotionless, not Kobe-type emotionless, but to keep himself hidden.

The two are again instructed to bring different props in and pose with them, getting several different types of photos. The media day coordinator puts her thumbs up after looking at the screen that fed the display of the photos. "We got what we needed, thank you!"

Coach remains still as Abel attempts to leave the stage area, getting pulled back by Baird, he slowly gets dragged back to his starting place, careful not to make a scene by flying backward. His rough hands feel like sandpaper as they scrape across Abel's body until he finds Abel's hands, dropping a small piece of paper into his open fist, and then he snaps back into character and puts back on his smile, returning to the staff members.

Abel pockets the paper, sighs, and returns to the locker room, undressing out of the fake clothes and putting on the more comfy clothes that he rocked. As per the directions of the team, he is to report individually to the press room where he has to undergo an official USBA interview. Abel remembers this as the last part of media day if he recalled correctly, hopefully, it wouldn't take too long.

The press room is surprisingly full with even more reporters and cameras than outside, everyone is trying to get a piece of what Abel Richards had to say. He manages to sit down quickly, being the type of person to get things over with rather than endure past events.

"Hello everybody," He musters up the best opening he could think of, not exactly going the route that he had planned, but at this point, he couldn't care less as long as he didn't repeat previous interactions that damaged his career.

The room doesn't waste any time filling itself with the frantic voices of the reporters, but when it finally calms itself down, a reporter stands up, "What can we expect from you after your injury? And can you explain what happened?" There are plenty of nods of agreement with him, most of them having the same couple of opening questions.

"Well the latter part of your question will remain disclosed, and you can expect the same from me as the first game, I'm here to bring it, and I'm not here to mess around. Next question."

The next reporter stood up. This person, however, looks very familiar, it's someone who he has talked to for sure. The name floats around somewhere in his brain, but he can't figure it out, focusing on the person who is on the tip of his tongue.

"What is your mother's reaction to your injury and game?"

"I-I-"

The man with the thousand-dollar jacket, that's who it is, and he is standing right in this room pretending to be a member of the press.

"Is she supportive?"

"I don't know, I haven't spoken since the beginning of the season."

"How come?"

"I- don't know. But I do have something to say: Mom, if you and Mikey are watching this right now, I can't call you, but I'm doing fine and hope to see you soon."

The flashes all turn off immediately, security running in and snatching the man that had the thousand dollar jacket, Meek Fant, the previous USBA basketball player. They carry him out of the room very quickly, and the rest of the press clear themselves out of the room quicker than if someone had said that everything at Best Buy was one hundred percent off.

Abel stands up, fighting the urge to follow the same people that he wanted to run from, but he is quickly joined by Coach Baird, who looks as if he has seen a ghost.

With little hesitation, Coach Baird slams Abel into the table in front of him, grabbing him by his neck, "This is strike two!"

As soon as it starts, it ends even quicker with the release of his neck, leaving him gasping for air.

Abel reaches into his pocket for the piece of paper that had been placed into his without context. He unfolds the bent edges and reads.

The next few hours are dependent on one choice and one choice only, we will extend your contract to four years, or you can be removed from the USBA entirely. The extension on your contract is pending two things: you delete your family's info completely, with no contact, and you follow the goals we have in place. You can follow those simple things or your little brother, Mikey Richards's terminal cancer will go untreated and unpaid for. Your final decision will be dependent on if you return to the practice facility tonight.

Signed Coach Baird.

CHAPTER 12

A Nokia and the Medical Bill

Terminally ill? Cancer? The world seems to spin faster than usual, tipping Abel over in a sickening fashion. He has no other choice than to continue with the USBA and the Breakers as long as Baird is telling the truth. Knowing him for a few weeks caused him to wonder if it was a ploy to get him to sign something that he would regret minutes later. In some cases, he would have no way out of the contract if he wanted to live.

Mikey is just eight, he hasn't made it out of elementary school, and has been healthy his entire life, it felt impossible for him to have cancer, he just couldn't. Abel's racing heart is pulling in the direction of the double doors with a bright green sign that says exit above it. He feels the tears starting to build up as his heart speeds up in a way that it feels like it is slowing down but still is going to explode out of his chest.

And he runs, he sprints past security and the twisty hallways finally leading to the last door to make it outside, the handle is a bar that has to be pushed. Abel stops and tries to regain control over his body, remembering to think about his actions and the effect that his actions could have. If he left he wouldn't come back, he would rejoin his family, but if Coach Baird is telling the truth, then his brother would die, and the blood would be on his hands. It is that or he can sign the contract, given the opportunity to make money and pay for whatever medical bills need to be paid. There's no option, Abel has no extended family, nobody to borrow money from or ask for help, he hasn't talked to his friends since senior year summer either, there is no option, none. He releases the bar to the door, slowly letting the pressure recede as it clicks back into place.

He turns back around, walking with his head down, sorting through the thoughts that attack him. The return to public transportation leaves him unbothered. Fortunately, he draws his hood, trying to mask as much of his face as possible. The last thing he needed right now was a fan to confront him and say something that upset him, especially with the stains of tears that scar his face.

The route as shown by his phone prompts that the bus is going to take thirty minutes to bring him back to the practice facility, too long.

The sky outside turns dark enough for unlit buildings to disappear completely. Everything is closing in. The claustrophobia that the world inflicts sends him to curl up in a ball, taking up two of the seats.

The only thing that feels right to him is reaching for his backpack and finding the Good Book. The backpack has bent up the stack of thin pages, it isn't in its prime days, but it would still work as long as the words were still there. He can't remember the last time that he had opened it up, but it's marked with small bookmarks on certain pages with brief notes in pen on each of the slips of paper. The Bible had many words that were universally important to indulge in, and Abel understood this internally but hadn't put it to work. His mom is the strongest person he knows, and if she read the bible as much as she said, then it had to be beneficial to her drive and ability to climb obstacles.

Right now, he needs some stability, something that is constant, which he finds in John. He reads and reads, scanning the page in the amount of time it takes a sports car to reach sixty miles per hour, and then reading the same words again, and again, and again. This repetitiveness helps sink in what he is reading, forcing the words into his brain, and engraving them in his eyes as if someone stared at a light too long and then blinked.

His heart rate starts to recess back to his normal resting heart rate, and the bus also decelerates to a complete stop a couple blocks from the training facility, which isn't on the busiest street due to the preferred privacy of the building. The crosswalks are all in the crossing mode due to the lack of vehicular travel through the particular area, making the couple blocks that Abel travels even quicker. Abel already knows exactly where Coach Baird is going to be when he stomps in, he would most likely be planning someone else's demise over a small notebook on his desk.

Abel rushes right into the facility, giving a quick look to the person who works the front desk, giving a slight nod. For him it becomes hard looking at other people and not releasing tears, it was the thought that his little brother is dying and he had to carry that with him and nobody else would ever know unless he were to explain.

He walks into the office put together, refusing to sit down and have to look up at the monster that is Coach Baird. Baird sits down, but quickly recognizes the power that Abel is threatening and dramatically exits his lower half out of the luxurious white leather chair.

"I'm glad you chose the easy way. There is no need for the blood to be on more than one person's hands, wouldn't you say?"

It takes every ounce of energy in Abel's body not to lunge across at the devil himself and strangle him to death just as Baird had attempted. Instead, he grits through his teeth, "You have no idea how much I want to beat your face in. You're a lucky man."

"And you are unlucky. You've never hurt another soul in your life."

Abel reflects solemnly, wishing that he was wrong, instead, he tries bluffing, "You're wrong."

"The only person that you've ever hurt is yourself, Abel Richards."

"I–" Abel sputters, "no, you're still wrong, you're manipulative, conniving. You're sick!"

Baird doesn't take the comment smoothly, also putting some restraint on his conscience, grabbing a packet of papers bound by a paper clip, sliding it across with gentle fingers, and keeping the page as crisp as possible. "Sign." His hands follow the action by folding themselves in front of his dainty, fragile body.

"What about the money?"

"What about it?" He slides the papers closer.

"I need the money, and a guarantee, none of this Incentive shit."

"It's a system that works. I'm not going to fix what's not broken, as they say."

"You're going to have to, but I'll strike a better deal. I'll choose the Incentive."

"What is it?"

"You pay my brother's medical bills until we lose, if we lose up until the end of the month, then you can continue to manipulate me for your profit on a four-year contract."

"You seriously are gambling four years' worth of pay on the last, what? Six games?"

"Yes."

"Well I'm not going to think too much into it, we have a deal. You're going to remain unpaid for the next four years guaranteed Richards, you probably didn't look at the schedule. We play the Titans. The rest of this month is going to put you through hell and around the corner, the top teams in the league! You messed up Richards!" He brings back his maniacal laugh, obsessing over the idea that he could gain millions of dollars from the lack of payment towards a player. The stupidity for someone to gamble the money away on a whim, which in hindsight, is how gambling works.

Abel grips the ballpoint pen and reads through the contract completely, finally striking his initials into stone.

It is done.

"Good," Baird says, grabbing the paper and walking out of the room with no further comment. Abel is left in the crowded room, looking around. He pauses and realizes that he is by himself and Baird is gone. The opportunity would only come once, so Abel drags his feet outside the door, draws the blinds to the window in the door, and checks both ways down the hallway, making sure there is no foot traffic in the area, and then he starts searching. He doesn't know exactly what he will find, but whatever it is, it has to solve some of the mysteries surrounding his entrance to the league, this team couldn't be typical in the league, it just couldn't be normal.

A good five minutes go by to no avail for Abel, nothing is sticking out in the pigsty of an office, most of the stuff is old newspapers and plaques of his high school basketball career leading up to his coaching stint from high school, college, and then the USBA. There is nothing out of the ordinary for a well-off coach of a backwater basketball team.

The fact of the matter is that he had inevitably fallen off after the dynasty that he built up completely crashed.

Crash. The word grabs Abel's attention, lying down on a news article in the corner of the room, pinned by a bookshelf. He pulls the paper out of the crevice, tearing a small piece of the corner off in the process. The article is named after the man from that day, Meek Fant. He had been in a car crash the day after the Finals, the year that they had lost, the end of an era. There were many documentaries surrounding the topic that Abel had watched alongside millions of other people worldwide, everyone was captivated by the subject and the show went in depth. The show didn't say anything about Fant getting in a car crash the day after game seven. Abel scans the rest of the article, each word adding more strength to the grip he had on the paper, Meek Fant dies in a car accident following the loss in the USBA Finals.

Abel doesn't believe in ghosts, he never has. It didn't stop him from being intrigued about such a topic, he did believe that there could be something that isn't explained in the Bible, some unexplained event that somehow tied together the book, some coincidence perhaps. Meek Fant had appeared twice to him, the draft, and the interview, How is he not found? Some people know that he is alive. But maybe that isn't the point, maybe a small circle did know that he still breathed. If not, the people that took him were about to find out.

Abel exits the room, first folding up the old article and sliding it into his pocket, it will have to wait. He continues down a winding set of hallways and stairs, leading down, until he makes it to his bunk, his personal belongings are stuffed underneath the bed in a small compartment. He unzips a duffel bag and pulls out his wallet, quickly flipping through a couple of twenty twenty-dollar bills he has left. The drought of income is going to end soon, he is going to beat everyone that stood in his way.

After taking his wallet, he quickly leaves the facility and starts his journey to the nearest Target. Abel has no idea where he is going, but he figured if he headed in one direction for a long period, he would probably stumble across the white chick magnet. Sure enough, he only walked for forty minutes before the bright red bullseye stared back at him. This particular building is part of the city block, rather than a standalone building, and as it is in New York fashion, escalators are separating the three floors of shopping. Abel wastes no time by stepping on the escalator aiming for the third floor, instead of standing still on the moving stairs, he trudges upwards.

Making it to the electronic area, it takes a decent amount of time for him to find what he's looking for, he just needs one thing, and that one thing is going to have to be under forty dollars, there is no other option. He searches down the aisle, quickly growing more anger as he surveys the items. Luckily, God is dishing out blessings like Oprah does cars, and he is given the sight of a Nokia flip phone. On the other hand, God didn't listen through his entire prayer, and the label below the phone explained to Abel, that he couldn't afford such a high piece of technology in the year twenty-twenty-three, ironic. It's also locked behind glass, the only way to access would be to call over an employee.

Buzz. Abel presses the 'ask for help' button and is quickly greeted by a member of the staff.

"How can I help you?" The man with an overload of facial hair says unenthusiastically.

"I'm looking at that flip phone, would you mind if I could check it out at the front, I plan on doing a bit more shopping."

"Yeah." The blandness of his response makes Abel feel more confident in the actions soon to come.

"Thank you," Abel quips as the worker unlocks the case and hands him the item. As soon as he touches the item, he starts walking in the other direction, trying his best to hide it before completely stuffing it in his jacket pocket, which is just big enough to hold the box. It isn't big or stocky by any means, but it creates a slight crease in the jacket which warranted questioning if a person looked too close.

Abel keeps his eyes up, trying to remain as unsuspicious as possible. On the last floor, before he exits the doors, he makes sure to buy a couple of snacks with some of the money that he did have, this makes his pockets full, and hid the phone. He also is sure to grab the receipt and keep it in his hands as he walks out, just in case an employee looks his way and sees his full pockets, and with that, he walks out of the store.

He pulls around to the nearest alley he can find, ripping the phone out of his pockets and quickly dialing some numbers.

"Please, please, please." He begs.

The phone rings, and the line stops, Abel expecting it to end. "Hello?"

Abel nearly cries at the sound of his mother's voice, almost forgetting to talk. "Mom. It's me."

"Oh! Abel!" He can hear her start to tear up on her end, breathing heavily. "Abel, what's going on?"

"I haven't been able to call you, the team has removed all my contacts and blocked all of them."

"Look Abel, your brother-"

"-I know." The voice that he hears on the other end feels broken.

"You know? How?"

"My coach told me. I made a deal with him though, the medical bills will be paid."

"Abel. Nobody knows, there were no visitors and hardly any doctors."

"What do you mean?"

There is a long pause, and Abel hopes that the connection didn't break, he has no idea how he is going to tell his mother about his situation, but everything is going to be okay. The money is going to come, it has to, Abel thinks. It would trickle down at first, as most of it would go to the medical bills, but the cancer is going to be abolished after a certain amount of time.

"I mean, your brother..." There is a very long pause, giving Abel too much time to think about what is going on, and rightfully so. "...he's gone Abel, he's gone." The words barely escape her mouth, deforming them into words that are nearly impossible for someone to translate, but Abel knows, he knows.

And his entire world shatters.

CHAPTER 13

A Silhouette and the Little Tikes Hoop

The buzz of the stadium builds up static in Abel's chest, the rest of the night is going to be rough mentally, the insurmountable pressure bubbling to a climax that causes tremors in his body. His entire being feels weighed down by the dirty hardwood floor, covered in the faint outline of basketball shoes outlines.

"You ready?" Warren pats his back, unknowing of the emotional damage growing in his insides, squirming around and trying to wrench itself out of him.

"Yeah." The lack of emotion is brought by the lump that is formed in his throat. He has the same look as a killer, making the final decision of the horrible act to come. The Orcas are going to get an entirely different person to guard than Abel James Richards, the straight-A student from a decent high school. His ears filter through the music, extracting the bass and internalizing the feeling in his chest.

The rest of the team is warming up and preparing by putting more shots up. Abel already knew his attempts were going to go in, now isn't the time for that. It's the time to lock his brain in, fighting the urge to picture his little brother.

He figures the funeral will be small, and exclusive to the very sparse amount of friends and acquaintances, the majority of the attendees would be the church, coming to support.

Towards the end of the previous phone call with his mother, she had explained that she rarely visits the apartment anymore, instead, seeking shelter in the word of God and the congregation. She had acted as if she folded her hands enough and prayed the hardest that somehow, she would open the door and find little Mikey sitting down, trying to ignore her because of her embarrassing affection towards him.

The phone that he used is now stored away very tightly in his bag, his income and his life are held in the hands of no one finding the ancient Nokia in his possession. The worst feeling is knowing that his mother is suffering even more than he is, and he had to sparingly call her, unleashing comfort every once in a while instead of crying every step of the way through it with her. After telling her about the contract she agreed to his decision to stay with the organization, the money isn't going to walk into the bank and his checking accounts, and for the moment, his mother couldn't land a job just yet.

The lie that the coach told Abel sends him right back into his office that night when he screams, spits, and threatens his existence. At the end of the day nothing had even mattered, the coach had no verbal response, and his twisted soul only looked like a broken man in his eyes which stared back with the same intensity.

The first check is going to come minutes after the game upon a victory, it is a couple of million dollars. A couple of million dollars that should have been less if his brother had medical bills to pay for, instead of the money he plans to cover his funeral. With two million dollars, Abel has so much to pay for but so little purpose in doing so, he decides to be honest with himself and thinks that he doesn't have any plan for the massive income that is going to be a career. His thoughts initially had been about cars, houses, and personnel to work things for him, the exact opposite of the way he grew up, and the exact opposite of what his mom had told him was important growing up.

He's certain that he is going to hold up his end of the deal and win every game for the rest of the month. His eyes reflect his burning torment and adrenaline coursing through his veins. He deeply feels that he can annihilate every single person who stands in front of him on the court. Annihilate.

Years before…

The day is very cold. A lot of traumatizing things happen on cold nights, Abel just happened to be a part of the cliche. His father is a man of good stature, and well respected in his community, and also the home in which he lived. Now, this father of his isn't his birth father, who is never there for even the very earliest stages of human life, his father is his mother's husband, an Asian American man whose arms were twice the size of Abel's torso. He faintly remembers the interactions he had with Mark, he had gone out fishing with him, and exposed him to all sorts of activities at a young age, most not sticking to begin with. Basketball isn't something that is spread thin in the household, however, and the constant cheering and trampling around in the living room supporting his favorite team on the television.

The couple that raised Abel, had met in high school. They were young teenagers hoping for a summer fling in the offseason of both of their basketball seasons. The summer league had just started that year and it was a quad night, meaning that the girl's team watched the boy's game and the boy's game watched the girls. Mark had done horribly in that game and was beyond embarrassed to perform in such a way in front of his future wife. In a desperate attempt to woo Brianna, he told her to show up to the next game played it off as a mistake game, and then proceeded to ask for her number. For some reason, Brianna thought his behavior was cute and handed him a crumpled piece of paper with the digits.

Needless to say, Mark didn't perform the next night well either, Brianna is more of the baller, and Mark took up cheering in her stands. Things took off from there with several large details dropped out of the story by Abel's mother during her retelling of the story, for obvious reasons.

Abel is the first child, taken in by Brianna without any consent from Mark. He eventually warms up to the idea of taking care of a baby after a not-so-quick trip to the bar to reflect on his life. Once he sees Abel, his mistake comes from doubting Brianna at all. This warmth in their house only lasts another five winters before it is all stripped away.

Brianna knows he's a drinker, and yet never expected that it later in life would contribute to his sudden departure from their residence with no note whatsoever, just an empty car in an empty driveway. For the majority of Abel's childhood, both of them thought it was their fault for the actions of his father. The only thing that Abel remembers from that day is a quick look out the window on Christmas Eve, wondering if Santa's sleigh was flying across the sky towards his house, in anticipation. Instead, he saw a different mode of transportation leave the driveway slowly, avoiding the large bump that made a lot of sound. The neighbors had not been very appreciative of any cars leaving at night, but Mark made it so that no one could hear him leave. He did it successfully, there was no sound associated with Abel's memory, just the blinding red taillights that dimmed as they got further from the parking lot.

Brianna cries like she would when her second kid comes into the picture during the middle of the night, Mikey.

Now, it is a year before the exodus of Mark, he allows Abel to discover the most important thing that he had ever laid eyes on or participated in, and that is a red and yellow Little Tikes basketball hoop. The basketball hoop stands only four feet tall but he quickly adjusts to the height and frantically imitates famous basketball players' dunks, specifically throwing the ball off the backboard and using two hands to slam it in. Mark is the official rebounder for Abel, making sure that he throws as many basketballs as he so leased, and not only that but attempting to explain to a toddler how to correct his jump shot form, something that didn't make a lot of sense then, but would hopefully start to take shape later in grade school.

"Just like that, son, yep, dribble, dribble, shoot!" Mark laughs, grinning wide while demonstrating the move. "I think you're getting the hang of it, shoot! Shoot!" He's developed a good sweat around his head, running around after the kid. He won't stop smiling, laughing, "You've got it, I think that wraps up today's hooping session, would you say so?" There is no verbal response from the small child, but his smile is even wider than his parents'.

Who knew that a child could smile so much? Mark surely doesn't.

He is a very good husband to Abel's mom and made sure to teach him at a very young age to respect all of the women around him. He's also passionate, something that grips a human being and forces them to forge their path through the human experience. He was an ideal person who constantly appeared happy, fulfilled even.

Sometimes Abel wonders what would have happened if he stayed, and what life would be like if his mother didn't live a circus act with so much to juggle, including two kids that were an absolute handful.

The name Mark would not be spoken in fifteen years by his mother, aside from the occasional story, and she never led her children to hate him, not at all.

The hatred only blooms because of himself, not because of how he left Abel, but because of how he left his mother staring at her reflection with the glass broken, her eyes sore for the emotional beatdown, and the bathroom door just wide enough for Abel to peek in and see the strongest person he knew vulnerable.

She turns around, frightened at the scene she had displayed for him, "Hey baby." She says softly, wiping her tears and wearing a smile.

"Hey."

"HEY!" Coach Baird screams at Abel.

He snaps back into it immediately. Things weren't going to be good for him if continued dozing off much longer, no matter the conflicts that conspired between the two in recent happenings. Abel looks up from his downward-facing gaze, realizing that the entire presentation that introduced the starting five is going on right now, and he's up to go through the tunnel.

"ABEEEEEEEEEEEEEEEEEEL RICHAAARDSSSSSSSS!" The announcer booms over the intercom. The crowd cheers in excitement, ready to see what the young buck can bring on his second game with the team.

Abel looks back at Coach Baird, who returns the same look. Tonight is the night, and this is his time, nothing is going to stop that. If he didn't score twenty-five points, then neither would the entire enemy team. Today is the day for the small things, and the attention to detail that he has, it is the time to use that trait to dominate. With that, he jogs off, doing the team handshake with the teammate that had to memorize them instead of the plays, because his hands did more clapping and dapping up than actual playing. After the quick handshake with Joshua, he runs over to the check-in counter to deposit his number and fistbumps the refs, here he goes.

"Let's have a good game this time son." The older ref says with a similar look that Coach Baird wears often, it is one that Abel hated. Well, that isn't fair, he hated every look that that bastard gave.

"You'll remember today." Abel chips back, apparently not loud enough because there is no response from either of the three referees. It didn't matter if they heard it anyway, he understood that some referees don't like to talk back to any remarks and choose not to respond to them about really anything. The only thing they put up with for some reason, perhaps because it's comical, is when the athletes complain about a foul they didn't commit, but if they had looked up at the jumbotron milliseconds earlier they would see their entire elbow descending upon a frightened looking face, preparing to be woken up violently.

"I'm sure we will." Chuckles the shooting guard for the Seattle Orcas, and Tristan Johnson, the pretty boy who played for his hometown team. He had been in the league for a few years, and Abel appreciated his game. Before a couple of his college games, he watched a film on Tristan to see what he was doing right so that he could translate it into his game. Tonight, that is an advantage, the previous respect he had for him is gone, he is going to expose every single weakness that he saw in him from the late nights huddled around the bright light of the computer, watching his games.

TWEET!

"Jump ball!"

CHAPTER 14

Polaroid

The game ends one hundred-five to a whopping sixty points, the team was bats-off insane, and Abel just as he had said, dropped forty of those points. This ultimately led them to victory. He doesn't say anything to the opposing team either, heading straight for the locker room with a smirk on his face. The smirk is all he needed to shut up the crowd and the team, it wasn't expected, and it only solidified the fans' excitement to see what the young man could accomplish given more time. This promising game doesn't make him cocky, his sly and straightforward attitude toward the win is in stark contrast to his exuberant teammates who completely lose their marbles once they step a toe into the locker room.

The energy is unmatched, but Abel doesn't participate in the celebration. They act like they have won the USBA Finals, a torch that the program has been waiting to carry since the early days during the dynasty that the coach was a part of. Unfortunately, like all dynasties, they died out, and when the Breakers died out, their flame was completely snuffed. Snuffed until now.

Hopefully.

"Let's go!" Warren exclaims, patting Abel's shoulder with a bit too much spice. Since he is a bigger person, the hits have a bit more punch to them, not helping, but not bothering him either. The smell of salt and hard work permeates the air, creating a more humid environment than Florida at the peak of summer.

"Good game, Warren, we gotta keep it up," Abel says, rebounding his attention after he had moved on from his overflowing excitement.

"Yeah, Abel. You got us to where we needed to be, you're a special man, I hope you know that." Warren says, pointing into his chest with a couple of small jabs.

Abel nods his head in respect, Warren has been one of those people who always made sure to be the best teammate he could be. A lot of the culture surrounding basketball nowadays is the constant mentality that they were a one-man show, and had an emphasis on highlights and a good-looking stat sheet rather than a win. He didn't want to become one of the players that took over the team and made his teammates resent him, and then the game, and then inevitably the sport of basketball.

There isn't any arguing with his impact on the court, and for now, Abel planned on continuing that same thing that made them win.

The only person that has their head down the entire time is Aiden Foss. Abel hadn't known his deal except he rarely saw his face on the court, just by the look of him he didn't exactly make people turn their heads and recognize that he was a professional athlete. Anyone could tell that there was more going on inside his head, and no one decided to say anything to him. So much for the team being connected.

The locker room starts to clear out slowly, the players filtering to a separate room to watch the film on the game. The only people who stay are Abel because he is running behind on packing up his things, and Aiden. Abel grabs an empty water bottle from his previously inhabited seat, and stuffs his basketball shoes into his backpack, making sure they have plenty of room and aren't pressing up against anything that might stain them, cut them, wear down the traction, or even loosen the laces a little bit.

Many many athletes made sure that they had a weekly rotation of shoes for their games, choosing to focus on looks or functionality as one of their worries. Abel has one pair where he likes the colorway, so they have to be functional for him to wear them. He prays that the endorsements would start to come in soon, sending some extra digits into his bank accounts, and possibly some new kicks in the mail.

"Man- why-" Aiden murmurs from the opposite side of the room, causing Abel to cross his eyebrows in confusion. He decides to ignore it and walk straight by him and out of the locker room, becoming a steam train that couldn't be stopped.

Until it broke down. "WHAT THE FUCK, RICHARDS!" Aiden leaps out of his seat and straight into the direct vicinity of Abel, sending phlegm streaking across the short distance and onto his face.

"What are you talking about Aiden?" Abel tries to calm him down, putting his hand on his abdomen and pushing him away. There is nothing more unsettling than a grown man in your face and you were skinny and not seven foot tall. A problem that Abel has always had, and unfortunately, was out of his hands.

"I- YOU-" He stutters out, slouching his head again, bringing his hand up to his chest, in a tight fist, tense enough to pull on his skin causing red spots to appear where the pressure takes place.

"WHAT!" Abel starts to match his level of intensity, starting to become restless. His recent emotions cause him to run a very thin tightrope, where if he leaned a little in one direction, he would overcompensate by falling the other way. Now Abel starts to mutter to himself, trying to calm himself down, why am I so angry? He tries to figure it out as Aiden's temper tantrum ensues, but instead, he ends up tapping his hands rapidly on his leg.

"YOU RUINED EVERYTHING!"

"What are you even talking about, I have nothing to do with whatever you're talking about!" His voice cracks and even a little bit of yelling causes him to burn out, he guesses that the use it or lose it rule applies even now.

Aiden screams out in anguish, throwing himself against the lockers, creating a loud ruckus, crashing on his way down. The locks on each of the lockers clank and resist the gravity being put onto them, the few lockers that aren't open in the area of Aiden's crash become tilted open, revealing them to be empty. This comes except something that catches both of their eyes.

It is a photo, a Polaroid photo, not something that is typical of their period and generation. Aiden drops his act, both of them leaning in to look at the photo, Abel snatches the photo before Aiden can look at the photo, and then checks the locker to find any sign of the name of the locker or property.

This isn't a player's locker, it is Chris's locker, the trainer's. The trainers got lockers along with the rest of the team to carry around their backpacks containing things like athletic tape and different commodities to contribute to the athlete's health on and off the court. Chris had already grabbed his backpack on his way out of the door so nothing was hanging on the hook, but this one little photo had made it to the bottom of the metal coffin.

"What is that?" The now calm Aiden ponders, looking over Abel's shoulder, who shrugs off his hand that's reaching for the photo, stopping him from nosing his way into view of the picture.

"It's- oh."

The photo is of Coach Baird standing over a man, his fist clenched, and his other hand concealed by the darkness of the photo. The person on the floor looks mangled, maybe a bit hurt, but by the look in his eyes, he is scared. The poor lighting from the Polaroid camera suggests that it's night and there is a light source other than the natural light that fought to peek through whatever windows were nearby.

"Abel, let me see. I want to know what that is."

"You are crazy Aiden, absolutely crazy." He replies, grabbing his things and starting to leave back towards the bus. There isn't even a little bit of his body that isn't still writhing from the unsettling image of seeing a grown man freak out in front of him and lose their mind just to immediately chill back down at the sight of something out of place or missing.

By the time he mutters his last words, Aiden is already gone. Abel is oblivious to how the rest of his teammates spend their nights, forced to stay at the practice facility with only a certain amount of time allowed outside for small things like shopping for personal things.

The idea of becoming family with his teammates is not something foreign to Abel, his high school basketball team had found many opportunities to grow in friendships and become young men together. The big opportunity came when the team was offered to join a state tournament at the Seattle Orca's court as teenagers, the surreal experience strengthened the bond that they all had.

In this case, the current curfew that they had for certain things and the lack of access to family was way too far of a stretch, and Abel figures that it can't continue to be followed perfectly and to Baird's strict rules. If he can do something about it, the photograph might help in some way, anyway.

Abel decides to stick around the arena and put up shots instead of heading straight towards his 'living quarters', a slight act of rebellion but oh well, he thinks. It wasn't like the lights were going to go out as it isn't completely abnormal for some players to want to stay around the arena, so long as he made it back to stretch and then head to sleep. Rest became more important to Abel in his college years, while his teammates and peers were out partying and doing other things late at night, even if it was finishing a paper due the next day and they had just started it, Abel learned how to fight the procrastination and make better use of his time so he could maximize the time he spent playing basketball. Think smarter, not harder.

He doesn't decide to do anything overly strenuous to his body, starting with stretching. He bends over a few times to adjust a small strain on the inside of his thigh, if it doesn't work itself out now then it would just have to go through his stretching stages. The first stage is finding somewhere peaceful and stretching there, at this place he could put himself into awkward poses that if given enough time were extremely relieving and fought the pain very well. If the area of tightness isn't solved in this stage he would get out a foam roller, where he would try and see if he could force the tension out of his body by rolling himself on it, this is the second stage. The last two stages are using a massage gun targeting the tight area, and plunging himself into an ice bath if no one kicks him out of the building. This tension would have to be resolved by going through all four stages, another time-consuming feat that would take him later into the night, damaging his seven hours of sleep policy. The seven hours would have to be put in the evening, so that when he finished the first part of practice that day, he could nap until he needed to essentially repeat the process, ending the day by getting food delivered.

Luckily for him, stage one suffices, and he moves on.

Abel acts nonchalant as he drains his free throws one after another, continuing the flow that magically runs through his fingertips which flick the ball into the hoop. The team is lucky enough to own a singular automatic rebounder, which after the basketball is shot, is filtered down into a machine, and the ball is kicked back out to you. This allowed Abel to put up plenty of shots in a little amount of time.

When the lights start to dim again as the fatigue catches up to him all at once. The empty expanse in his stomach is also calling out for attention given that the last thing being consumed is a few Gatorades before the game and a small protein bar after.

Although the lights becoming less bright is a sign of Abel's last time in the arena, many custodians and members of the event staff for the building go up and down the aisles cleaning the seats and the absurd amount of garbage and food. No doubt were they blatantly placed there to make everyone's life a bit harder, but work is work.

As Abel leaves the court the rest of the staff closes in on cleaning the court floor and putting up the seats for the bench and the high-paying fans. They put the high-end seats on their special rack that they lock up with a long extended cord that holds in place a bar that blocks the chairs from being removed from the rack. Such chairs are a travesty, the cushions were like a cloud, at least that is Abel's understanding from the few arenas that he has been to. If anything, the chairs deserve to be locked away in some remote vault off the coast of an unknown island in a country that repels tourists due to being boring as fu-.

The picture.

Abel remembers the odd assortment of objects in the room of the polaroid, one of them being a chair like one from the courtside, the only similar styled furniture is in certain offices in the arena, not the practice facility, not in people's homes.

The picture. This is it.

Abel whips out the photo again, revealing nothing of meaning to him other than the fact that the picture most likely had to be taken in the arena, and someone's office, at night. This is odd in itself, no one is in offices late at night, they would be heading back to the team building because the only time it is dark is after a game. Unless it is a day where there is no game.

Could it be his agent? Dell. The man who vanished right off the planet is most likely the puppeteer behind a lot of young men suffering.

No, it can't.

Almost like a thumbtack, he slaps his hand straight into his forehead, gently turning over the hardstock photo making sure not to brush the film on the front to add his dirty fingerprints to it, tainting the image.

In red pen on the back, it reads a name etched out:

Meek Fant.

The victim.

CHAPTER 15

One Screenshot Later

For some reason Abel feels drawn to leave the arena immediately and search for him, but on second thought that doesn't seem very logical. No one knows where Fant went because no one knows that he's alive either. He could be anywhere on the planet, given that it had been at least a few days since media day and his mysterious reappearance in close vicinity to the coach. Additionally, with the things that he had to take care of, it didn't seem responsible to leave behind any chance at getting paid to go on a goose chase for a ghost. Especially given that the next game is in two days, the second to last game of the month.

This time, they were going to be met by resistance. Khalil would have to wait a few days after that game to get his first piece of Abel, who is yet to surpass him in points per game due to the gap that he left during his coma. For the games that he played, however, it's an entirely different story. Khalil is a roadblock that has the potential to strip away millions of dollars from him and his career, all he has to do is beat one of the worst teams in the USBA.

For now, at least, he finds it a good idea to remain where he is and he returns safely to the practice facility.

The building is very quiet upon his arrival, nothing out of the ordinary takes place, which is pretty uncommon given the circumstances, but still. Abel walks up a short stairwell, down a hallway passing a steam room, and finally up one more set of stairs to a door that stood by itself on the stretch of the hallway. The rooms are like small apartments, they have very typical beds, nothing special, and they have access to ice and other materials to soothe the owner's muscles and body after a long day of work. To Abel's understanding, the rooms are spread apart across the entire facility, it is rumored that it is so to avoid players mingling during their off time and focusing more on seclusion and self-gain. This makes sense except for the fact that they need to be a cohesive team, they are supposed to act as a unit, striking down their opposition on the hardwood battlefield as comrades.

Abel unlocks the door and steps inside, the bed is freshly made and the sheets are drawn out nice and tight to reveal no wrinkles that would make his eye twitch. It would all be disbanded a mere twenty minutes later when he decided to crawl himself under the sheets pulling the perfectly strained blankets up and over his chest up to his neck.

He's conscious of his busy mind, there are too many things to think about and worry about. He starts reminiscing on times when he wasn't where he is now when Abel Richards was the scrawny white kid that nobody knew played basketball.

He remembers thinking he had no chance growing up that he could even make it into a league, much less the league. He did however crave the attention once people did notice that he played, boosting up his ego, although he would never admit it. He told these people that he only wanted to go semi-pro, trying to set goals that were more realistic and weren't going to be near impossible for him to obtain. He's short in comparison to most and short isn't something highly valued on any basketball team. As much as certain trainers and coaches say height didn't matter, it had a huge role in the construction of some teams, so much so that Abel left those teams for somewhere he had a chance.

He is lower than low during these times because he knows he's ten times better than everyone who stepped on that court, he just isn't looked at the same by the people who made the decisions. Not only is his skill extremely important, but he pushed through every set of conditioning and running that the teams put them through, and he always made it first. It didn't matter to him that his body was screaming for a few more seconds for him to avoid slamming his legs back into the ground. The coaches looked at him succeed in his way, gaining confidence, and stripped it from him when he couldn't even start in the game. The starters that had similar positions to him, were far behind in everything skills-wise, and even speed which was surprising to him, but still the coaches chose the players with a couple extra inches on him.

College is a different story, not many people knew what had happened with the first college that Abel attended. Many people didn't even know that his first wasn't the one he left for the USBA, his first college put him on the same team as Khalil. He had entered the college's basketball program after receiving a brief letter during his senior year to join them for a mock tryout of sorts, a shorter league that exposed him to college basketball but is on the private side of things.

He had done extremely well and surprised the coaching staff, they had made it to the season, and by the time the opening tryout was over, Abel had been the clear choice for the next starting shooting guard and then came Khalil. Khalil was already committed to another college for basketball when he decided to transfer to Abel's. Khalil had four inches on Abel, and after a practice that he half-assed and just showed up for, he had put him in Abel's spot. The coach had seen more potential in Khalil and diverted all his attention to making him the better player instead of building up players that he had already committed to, he switched on his ways and made it about them. This changed the entire format of the team to revolve around Khalil in a way that isn't focused on winning, but rather the personal gain of Khalil.

It took that one practice and one more to finalize Abel's growing frustration over the incident, without much else to say to the college and the basketball program, he left completely, in search of a team that valued him and valued the team as well. His thoughts were that he didn't want to get in the way of his teammates' dreams just by being there, he wanted to be a positive influence that helped boost them up and make them better players.

The next college that he had in mind didn't seem to care about his short stint with another team, he was welcomed onto the team with open arms and is well respected by the entire community at the school, in addition to the staff of the team, and the players. His starting spot was secured and he started to develop a bond with these people. It was very interesting for him to be exposed to the different kinds of people that were on the team, the ones that had money didn't value it as much and tended not to do crazy things with it, and the ones that didn't did the exact opposite, often spending their money on things that were stupid and were pretty immature for people who support their families. He had learned a lot about the value of things in college, the value of friendships, the value of hard work, and the value of family, all through becoming part of someone else's.

Long story short, he is glad he didn't quit, because his path wouldn't have gotten him to play professional basketball, a thought that would've made his late middle school to early high school self laugh, and it surely would've made his coaches, teammates, and classmates slap their knees as well.

The thing is, they wouldn't be laughing now. The 'impossible' challenge that he overcame is something that he will hold on to and cherish forever, he had set himself up with an opportunity to be successful, something that he had a hard time with in other things, this is his chance.

His chance couldn't be wasted, he didn't travel to where he is now for nothing, yeah, he thinks, I didn't.

KNOCK! KNOCK! KNOCK!

The door receives three firm taps, each louder than the previous one, the person on the other side of the wooden plane pivoting to make sure that he or she is heard.

"Just a second," Abel replies quickly, trying his best to crawl out of his comfortable spot in his bed by leaving it easily accessible when he comes back.

KNOCK! KNOCK!

"Just a second!" Abel calls with more volume, he shakes his head, slightly frustrated by the urgency of this person when he is just trying to sleep. He slides on his funky-looking slippers, resembling basketball shoes but much more comfortable, and he makes his way around the clutter.

KNOCK-

"Damn! I'm coming!" Abel swings the door open with a force that could pull the infamous sword out of the stone, quickly reacting without fully comprehending who is behind the door, "Man, what do you want-Warren, hey."

Warren looks dazed. It looked as if he had seen a ghost, just as pale as one that's for sure. He turns around periodically looking for something. He tries his best to keep his breathing back down to a normal speed, for an athlete it would be relatively slow, so now he is in a range exponentially larger than what is average for him. His short hurried breaths into his lungs were followed by an attempt to drag out his carbon dioxide, distress hanging all over his face. "Abel."

Abel guides him inside, lunging towards his trash and clothes and kicking them under the bed, including a pack of cigarettes that he makes sure to kick harder out of the way. He pulls out a chair from a small closet in the corner and places it in front of where he assumed Warren would be if he had followed him while his back was turned, instead, he is still under his door frame.

"Are you going to come in?" Abel says, waving his hands over to the chair. "What's going on?"

Warren finally nods and complies, slipping his way into the chair after very slowly closing the door, giving a quick peek down the hallway before finally closing it with as little sound as possible. "Abel I'm not supposed to be here."

"I know- but it's not that big of a deal, the curfew is stupid anyway, I don't think they do shit about it, Aiden was out partying one night too-."

"-I'm not talking about that, Abel. I have something else to talk to you about."

"Yeah, no problem, I got you." Abel assumes it's something about his salary getting cut or his inability to communicate with his family. In their free time, they couldn't even see their families, at first, Abel had wondered why someone couldn't use their free time to see them, but that was before he saw himself being watched from a Toyota Camry very carefully. The tinted windows and dark shadows within did not cease to let up a fifty-foot or so distance from him. From then on out, he stayed his distance, instead using his phone on the subway where he couldn't be followed by a vehicle.

"It's about the league, Abel. It's not what we ever thought."

"I know. I haven't told anyone about the deals that the coach and I had to make just to get me paid, have you been paid?"

Warren nods his head, "Yeah I've been paid, been paid millions. I can't even use it on things that I want, instead, they gave me a flyer for real estate saying that if I am interested in my place in the area these were good places to start. I researched the real estate company because I was just curious about other listings they had because these places weren't very functional, they were just luxury."

"What do you mean not functional?"

"Dawg, these places didn't even have wifi, and they were over four million dollars."

"What the," Abel says, trying to keep up with Warren's path of conversation. "So what is the deal with that?"

"Well when I looked up the real estate company they didn't even show up, and I was just scrolling and scrolling and scrolling, trust me. They were trying to scam me again, that's all that this league is, it's one giant scam, they're controlling my income and what I do with it, can't you see? I gotta get out of here, Abel, I can't keep doing this anymore."

"What about getting paid?"

"It doesn't matter Abel, I value my life- and that's not it, Abel, I found something that could change everything."

"What is it Warren?" Abel braces for the worst.

"The league controls us with the money, it's not real Abel, none of it is real." The tears start coming out of his eyes. "None of it is real Abel! Real estate is just a way to recycle the fake money, they get bought from and because they're independent, no one knows. No one knows Abel! It's just me, you, and Fant."

"You know about Fant?"

"Yes, Coach- he is hiding something-"

"There were too many red flags, I messed up Abel!" He continues to panic, finally getting grabbed in his shoulder by Abel.

"You're fine Warren! You're fine! Pull it together!"

"Baird- he's not who you think he is-"

"Yes, I do! He's a murderer! He's got to be!"

"Abel!" A tear barely slips from his cheek, nearly falling in slow motion towards Abel's feet. "You're wrong about everything. You're crazy! You're crazy! Baird isn't the problem! It's-"

He is stopped short by the window cracking and a quick and mostly silent whizzing sound. Abel hears it for a split second before he catches a lightning-fast glance at the tiny object. His eyes widen.

"WARREN!"

But it's too late, the damage is already done and the bullet penetrates through Warren's forehead.

Warren is gone, and so is Baird's secret.

For what it's worth, the secret is safe with him.

CHAPTER 16

The Gutter

The paramedics arrive on the scene with very little to do to save Warren, his heart rate had flatlined the moment that Abel cried out his name. His room is taped off from the world and he's launched back into solitude again.

The Breakers staff have a spare room that he can stay in for the night, but it doesn't stop his mind from wandering to the moment that he will have engraved in his head forever, a picture that won't ever fade and constantly reminds him that he has a memory of such a thing. To be fair, Abel isn't the type to think about death often, with the rare exception that he had read the Bible saying certain things that didn't sound right at first. Death is something that he figures he is inevitably going to experience, and so will everyone else, but that's just the way that life is, there is no detour or long way around it, it just simply is. This doesn't take away from the horrifying direction that some people have died, and this is one of the ways.

Abel remains in isolation for a long time before he is brought before a cop, who decides that right then, in the few minutes after midnight, is a good opportunity to have him reenact the crime scene, "for a better understanding."

He feels forced to comply, and it takes several minutes for his head to digest every bit and piece of what happened. Thankfully the officer doesn't go into logistics and the topic of discussion of course, but instead focuses more so on the sequence of events before the shot, and everything from the predicted spots where the owner of the firearm could even be, to any reason that he may be killed. Abel very carefully thinks through his decision to not give any such information, partially because he believed that there was no reason for him to be killed.

There is no reason. There is no reason. He repeats his thoughts back to him, trying to prove the innocence of a man who had never done anything but try to endure with him and do what he could to win.

The detective pulls out a paper from behind his pocket, unfolding it and examining it closer. He grabs a pen and starts to jot things down. "So, Abel. We have some bad news for you."

Pfft. "I'm sure you do." At this point, there isn't very much that could faze him, and he still stays through all of it. Why? He thinks to himself. Why do I keep staying? He continues to try to conclude, I'm not a quitter, that's why. But he knows deep down that's not the reason, there is more going on that keeps him stagnant, that keeps him grounded.

"Unfortunately, this isn't the first time that something like this has happened to this particular organization, we assume that something is connected with these events. We don't know right now."

"So what does this mean?"

"It means that we have to investigate your entire organization, just in case something is going on internally, it's not very likely, but it's my job and I have my reasons."

"But what does this do to us?"

"You are all going to be monitored very closely for at least a week. We will put police and other members of law enforcement to investigate the scene, the entire Breakers organization is required to stay there, and by entire organization I mean the entire organization."

"I hear you out," Abel replies, taking his time to think about the options, maybe it is time for his exit while he has the chance unless that is what Warren was being prevented from completing. What he was attacked for was something that he tries to run through his head, Warren didn't do anything crazy and didn't speak out either.

Wait, he thinks, Warren was cut off right as he was going to say what Baird did, he was about to tell him something.

He takes a stroll out of the area, finally being released by the detective back to his spare room. Nothing makes sense, and his brain took an immense amount of processing for him to make it through the morning, nothing is going to be the same.

What if I took it in? Very early into the morning, he begins to venture, his mind trailing to a separate reality where he shows law enforcement the one thing that remained of Meek Fant, the polaroid. That could be evidence, and he hadn't taken his one possible opportunity to end Baird, the man that he hates the most.

The next morning isn't going well for Abel, he wakes up with large bags formed under his eyes, looking like he got punched in his face and inflated. Sleep is a hard commodity to come by for him due to the past night's events. He walks over to the window, peeking ever so slightly through the blinds, squinting his eyes to make out what is outside. The exterior of the facility is nearly surrounded by cop cars and bulky vehicles with some personnel coming in and out of the scene. He is quickly drawn to Coach Baird who is fully dressed in business attire. From top to bottom, he is completely dressed in a suit. Abel sees Baird roll up his sleeve, checking the time on his luxury watch, finding that the time is calling him to leave the area. Without wrapping up the rest of his conversation with a member of law enforcement, he checks both ways like a little kid is taught to. He silently dips behind some cars and crawls into another vehicle in a parking lot to the side of the building. The car blazes off faster than Abel has time to blink again.

He's gone.

They weren't supposed to leave, even the staff must uphold the same rules, and this meant under any circumstances.

But still, Baird is gone.

The city is way too large for Abel to attempt to find him or follow him, it would be especially difficult if the team were suspicious of him or caught him leaving. Abel recognizes the car, which is ironic because the vehicle is hardly ever in the parking lot. It's often on vacation, along with its owner.

He draws the blinds again, slides on his coat, and decides to go on his trip down the hallway to the gym. The gym is full with every single player on the team, trying to put up shots with their extremely broken jumper.

With a closer look, Abel notices that each one of their arms is shaking feverishly which forces the basketball in a wide arc to the side of the gym. Today the morale is so low that the team doesn't even get on each other for the horrible shots being taken, the only one who sinks their shots is Abel, each shot is controlled and calculated. Once they catch sight, the group starts to form around him, everyone looking at him like a travesty, he's the one who was in the room with the dead body. He saw the red sticky liquid exit Warren's body, not any of them did, and yet Abel was the only one to remain to appear unfazed.

Abel recognizes the group around him, giving him looks that are certainly judgmental, "What are you looking at me like that for?" He lashes out at the circle.

"Nothing..." They all say in unison, returning to dribbling the ball.

Luckily for them, Abel drops the conflict, instead focusing on his problems.

Swish! The ball sinks through the net without touching any rim at all, a flawless shot from Abel. As the ball falls back down to meet the ground, the ball is kicked by Chris into the corner. The ball bounces off the wall, hits the wall, and rolls down the stairwell to the locker room.

"What the hell Chris! What are you doing? Weird ass trainer." This time he lashes out at the coaches with the same resistance that Jay had.

Chris shrugs and takes a step towards him, looking like he attempts to say something, but nothing comes out. Abel keeps on running after the ball, flying across the court and down the stairs towards the locker room.

He spots a small part of the ball behind a locker, running back over to it.

THWACK!

A fist crumbles Abel's facial expression. He yells out profusely, cursing and trying to find the source of the impact. Left and right, there is no one there. "HEY! I KNOW YOU'RE HERE."

A deep voice emerges out of the shadows of the dim locker room, the bright white lights flickering as fast as his eyes blinked, trying to keep awake to defend himself. "I know, Abel." The person's voice is foreign to Abel, he hasn't ever heard anyone with the level of deepness and roughness that he said his sentence with, dragging it out long enough to add a level of drama and suspense. They remain hidden as they continue talking, "Now you're quiet? You are so used to talking and running your mouth, sound familiar? That is just to wake you up, I assure you." Abel hears the sound of knuckles cracking, making him twitch, it's like listening to nails across a chalkboard.

"What are you doing?"

Then his ears pick up on what he believes to be latex gloves slapping against the skin, he can't pinpoint the location in the locker room that the voice is coming from, it is like the voice is on the intercom and hits all sides of his brain.

CLICK-CLICK!

A gun.

There is a gun.

"Look Abel, we made this pretty simple for everyone, and yet this batch would just not cooperate, that's all that we asked."

"Baird?"

The voice chuckles, blending into a louder laugh, "No, no, no. No, I am not."

"HELP! SOMEONE!"

"No one can hear you, Abel, you are alone with me here. We will take care of this like grown men, won't we."

"Did you kill Warren? Because I swear to God I will kill you myself!"

"I don't think that that will happen, Richards."

"Who are you then? I want to know whose grave to visit."

More laughs follow his quick comment, "You have heart, I do have to say, but you are so easily controlled, Baird did a decent job."

Again, a flurry of punches lands on Abel, forcing him to the floor. There is nothing for him to do, he is completely prone on the ground, not having enough balance to raise any sort of defense against the oncoming attacker.

After the adrenaline-fueled conversation between the two, the other voice ceases to emerge again, choosing to remain silent behind the veil of his surroundings.

And then as he had before that one night, he blacks out.

"What do you think about this one?"

"It's beautiful."

"Just like you." A pause. "I think I want to give you this one."

"Are you sure baby? It seems like a bit much."

"No, I want to do this."

"Look, we should probably get home, I got to get something to eat."

"Let's just stay out then, we can make it a date."

"I would- but-"

"But what?"

"Well… Basketball."

"Basketball?"

"I need to get back in the gym, I thought we talked about this."

She puffs, "You know what, I just can't anymore, I really can't return the damn necklace, I need a break from you."

"But… Oh, come on! We've discussed this, you know how important basketball is to me!" The shout is not returned with any further dialogue, instead, he is left to himself.

Abel starts to walk out of the store, keeping his head down, and his chest bent over. By the time he gets to the parking lot every single spot is filled up, causing several more cars to roam around preparing for new spots. Abel doesn't have any vehicle so these automobiles just make his trip across the sea of traffic more difficult, leading to the one bus stop for miles.

HONK!

A man in a car presses down on his wheel, waving him in front of the car trying to get him to leave his stationary position while waiting for him to cross. He can see the man mouth something but he can't tell what is being said.

As he drives his leg into the ground he feels something rough coming from his pocket. "Oh shit."

It's the necklace. The necklace is in his pocket, and he somehow walked out of the mall with it in his jeans.

He thinks about turning right back around and giving it back, claiming that it is all a mistake or maybe that he found it outside, but something caused him to put it back into his pocket and keep walking, instead of the bus stop, he skipped over a street and heads down the sidewalk for another mile or so, here he reaches a near run-down sign that says: King's Pawn.

There was nothing he could do to justify his actions, he just had to do what he had to do. Money is important, even if it is for the sake of others, it has to be done. "Hey, I need to sell a necklace. It was an engagement gift, but it didn't work out." The lies fly out of his mouth effortlessly, not of the failed engagement, or the need for selling the necklace, so maybe he tells no lie at all.

"Here let me have a look." The bearded clerk grabs the necklace from Abel's outstretched palms, setting it back down on the glass counter in front of him.

He observes it closely, and for some reason, he never looks much more into it than his surface-level eyesight. "Yeah, I can do that one for a thousand or so."

"Deal." Abel began to become frightened of any further options, taking the first route out of that store and out of the view of the cameras as soon as he could. One thousand dollars? That could go a long way for Abel, so it would have to do, even if it is a bit lower than the retail price at the store in the mall.

He leaves the store with ten hundred dollar bills in his wallet, breaking into a slight jog once he gets around the corner of the store, finally choosing to make it to the bus stop.

The ride back makes him feel sick to his stomach. It has to be done. I need this. I need this. These thoughts surrounded his head like a current flowing through the Pacific Ocean serving as a highway for creatures as perfectly illustrated by Finding Nemo. Only Abel didn't have a father to dap up for his accomplishment, not that there is one. He didn't doubt that he had done something of this sort before, he wouldn't put anything behind that man.

A dollar is and still is a dollar, right?

CHAPTER 17

A Living Situation Somehow Worse Than the Last

The room stinks. Like, really stinks. Somehow this is worse than the last two places that Abel stayed in back at the practice facility, but this isn't the facility, this is something entirely different. A whole new beast.

Abel's consciousness is not regained while he is back lying in a cozy hospital bed like the last time, but instead, he is chained to the exposed brick wall, the paint coating torn off in streaks. Aside from his bondage by his ankles, his arms were free to hold his knees to his chest due to the incredible wave of chilling air being circulated into his immune system.

He is alone, again, not greeted by the devilish voice that brought him to the hotel-looking space. However, unlike a hotel, there are no windows or points of access like doors from his point of view.

He faces forward towards the only object set in the room, a television. The television ran a somewhat normal program, starting with popular sitcoms and later going into basketball games and pregame reports. The Breakers were on, he had been out for another two days, he should've been at that game at this very minute. The TV volume is very faint at first, eventually blending into a louder sound as he starts getting used to the silence and straining his ears for the noise.

"Abel Richards, is out another game due to injury, such a shame for a player showing so much promise. Coach Baird is joining us, what do you have to say?"

"The Breakers are praying for him and his family through this time, we had some issues with clearing him for the upcoming games after his episode and coma a couple of weeks ago."

"That's too bad, the whole basketball community will be excited about his return and, hopefully, ready to go in full motion without any thoughts about the injury."

"Yes, thank you." Coach Baird wraps up, stepping away from the camera and clapping on his way back to his team during their warmups.

"Thank you, Coach. Back to you Marrissa."

"Liar," Abel whispers, finding himself too weak to scream his lungs dry to the point where his head is driven to a point of extreme pain. For once he decides to attempt to be reasonable with his well-being, both physical and mental.

All of the previous stress forced upon his back has quickly caught up to him. He still has a hard time figuring out whether or not he is living a fantasy or not, things like this simply didn't happen in the real world, it was as if he had entered a new one since he joined the USBA.

All of what he was going through just to play basketball, something he loved. At least he thought he did.

He continues to spend time delving deeper into the reason that he wants to play basketball and accepts the fact that he is plain and simply being manipulated for the gain of the organization every day. With the multi-million dollar paychecks that were supposed to be in the mail, one could say that there is a high enough amount of damage done to him that he should get compensated for that and some. Perhaps the real reason the athletes get paid so much is because if they are still in the league, unlike players like Jay, then they would be blind to nothing else than pleasing their organizations, like puppets.

It has to be a ploy, a plot destined to attack the most vulnerable of people who were devoted to something so simple, yet so complex. A sport. One that required putting a circular-shaped ball into another circle suspended higher off the ground. It's just a game, and yet he has treated it as if it were his life.

It is my life. It's all I have.

Hours have gone by and he determines that he isn't going anywhere. The game that he plays is his life, he hasn't done anything without it, and he hasn't made much of his opportunity either.

The only driving force keeping him going and away from the exit to the fake world that surrounded him was his family. His family made him stay. They never said anything to him about it, but that's what gives him purpose, and comfort in his decision to carry out things that impact the health of his family, hopefully for the better. They never said they wanted him to continue to play basketball, but he continued.

But, but, but. Abel thinks of every possible scenario to make him feel better about his whole situation. To be frank, it doesn't work. It doesn't work because his mother never forced basketball on him, she only supported him down his path, she never mentioned that it was just a pastime he should commit to either, it's something he adopted as his own.

The overwhelming amount of time he spends craving the next step in his career is a blind one. Quite literally as well, as he can't see the railing that keeps him up.

One side of the railing feels straight and made of a strong material, but the other side of the railing is deceptive to him, he leans in a bit and puts weight on that side, but the structural integrity of it would probably send him back down the stairs, breaking the bones in his body and making the climb back up a more grueling process.

It still isn't clear to him what the invisible force shoving him was, it may never be. He has been punched an awful lot more in the past few months than he ever had.

He doesn't have time to walk the crosswalk of possibilities in his head because, for the first time in hours, he hears a noise coming from around a wall, sounding like a person is walking up the stairs, hollow ones at that. As the noise gets closer in its pursuit of Abel, he starts to pick up on another pair of feet not far behind the first, this one whispering something. The dialogue between the two makes Abel's back tingle due to the wall that he rests on, trembling from the waves of sound traveling through them.

"You think he's still asleep?" One of them says.

The other, not the voice that he had heard in the locker room events, speaks, "Nah, it all should've worn off by now, the effects weren't made for his death. That still isn't the plan."

Abel's heart races, he isn't supposed to die. Then why is he here? Why put him through all of this, the constant beatings? The repetitive pounding through his head starts to reach its way to a pulse in his head, the thumping sensation coming from the rush of blood.

"We need a bit more time to prepare him for the next stage."

"Next stage?"

"Why are you always so clueless?" He scoffs. "Every time." Abel can hear the eye roll despite sitting behind a wall that separates them.

"You can quit it now, damn. It isn't that serious."

"Sure. Sure." The first one says to reassure the other, still hiding a sarcastic tone behind each word.

An unearthly sound echoes throughout the hollow room, reverberating its way through his bones, sending back the vibration and finally releasing out of his body. The buildup of the noise is quickly filled with the void of silence, sending a ringing sensation through Abel's ears. He tries shaking out of the chains, obviously not having any gain on his attempt out of the prison made for him. There isn't even a keyhole to the chained cuffs on his ankles, at first glance, there isn't a way out.

Something is in the works for him, which is quickly answered by the slamming of a door in the same area, crashing against something wooden behind it, sending several books into his view, revealing a very small part of the floor in the doorway, it is metal.

"Hello?" A new voice emerges, Abel isn't as alone as he expected, these people were here for him. A sort of old familiarity pops from his next words, "Ah, Abel. You made it, now we can get started."

It is Dell. His bald head shines from the dark and dim lights in the room, only coming from overhead instead of any natural light or lamps.

"Dell? What are you doing? What is this?"

"Abel, you have been asking too many questions since I met you. You got the drive, but you are blind."

"I don't know what you're talking about." Abel feels drawn away from eye contact, feeling tired which in turn makes it impossible to look up at him.

"You have no idea how much we've done for you, and instead you just make our job harder."

"So you're punishing me for playing basketball, great."

"You got involved in something much deeper, you just don't understand. The Breakers organization asked simple things from you, and for a bit, you followed our guidelines and expectations. This is up until your little coma stint. We've been putting you through an experience, a multimillion-dollar-making experience, and we can't have you interrupt our processes by being aware of it."

"What experience? You're accusing me of things that I don't even know!"

"You have been put under a procedure with a small chip in your head until you fail your expectations, the chip shuts off your brain, for good. The price for the removal is one hundred million dollars." Each syllable of his death debt rings out. "Once you retire and you don't pay, or you can't, we discontinue the chip, and you are replaced."

"Replaced?"

"Replaced. An actor of sorts."

"I don't believe it- this can't be real. All of this isn't even real, you're not a league-"

"Exactly, we are a business, we exist to make money. And you should too, it's the only reason that you keep going isn't it?"

"You're wrong, I do what I do for"

"For my family, whatever. We already know. You're wrong, and you don't even know it. The only reason that you can have the chip in your head is because of your defining negative trait, greed. Money is the beginning and it will be the end of your problems. Your Incentive won't be met, there is a game tonight, and you won't be there to play."

"You're bluffing."

"Trust me, I can't make these things up."

"Then prove it."

"Rub your neck, you will feel a lump. That isn't a coincidence."

Abel follows his instructions and finds the cold lump that he is mentioning. It's there, clear as day given enough pressure.

The sensation it gives off is almost a buzzing or odd feeling in the back of his throat, making him feel like he is a bit under the weather and developing what would later make him sick. Abel rolls it around with the tip of his finger, fiddling with it impulsively because that is all that he can think of at the moment, it is like once you noticed an itch you just couldn't get rid of wanting to scratch that area, despite if it is constantly bugging him.

"Why am I here Dell? Why bring me through this whole elaborate plan, just to put me in a room, locked up."

"You can consider this a reverse orientation, it's kind of like maintenance for the rogue players of the league. We would've had to run your face through a scanner to get a perfect match for an actor, but because you have too many intricacies we are going to prepare you for a common situation that will end your life, and keep the feds out of our business."

Behind Dell, he begins to set up the television in front of Abel, bringing the TV closer to him and grabbing the remote. For some reason the television itself is ancient, having the technology of a few decades ago with the two antennas that stuck out of the top of the TV connected with wires that led to a nearby outlet, this is a bit counterintuitive to the fact that Dell uses a remote to navigate the menu screen on the old device. "Here we go," Dell says in satisfaction, gathering a few of his things off of the floor. "And by the way, you're welcome. I've been waiting to say that, it's been hard to rat you out and become a birdie to the city, I could have done that since it happened?"

"What happened?"

"You don't know?" His genuine confusion shines through. "Come on, don't play dumb."

"I'm not you sick man."

Dell chuckles, "Alright, that's enough." He turns around slowly, waltzing his way away from Abel.

Now, Abel isn't one to believe in a lot of the things that the media glamoured, such as what is considered 'lucky' for the main character, something that just so happened to work out but is extremely predictable in the first place.

But when Abel catches sight of a screwdriver exiting Dell's backpack and gaining velocity towards the ground, he reaches his feet out quickly to grab it, unfortunately for him, he cannot grab it with his hands, and he has to stop it from hitting the floor and gaining the attention of Dell. The screwdriver flips through the air at a decent speed, landing perfectly facing south as it impacts with Abel's bare feet. Abel's mouth bubbles up immediately, trying to catch himself from screaming the loudest insults, and agonizing in pain which would bring Dell right back to him. The screwdriver is at least an inch and a half inside of his foot, impaling the thickest part of his skin, striking anything but the bone. The warm and sticky solution begins to pour out of his extremities like a stream, just like his pain. It begins mildly for him, but it only grows as it continues to get exposed to the air. Slowly, he retrieves his foot with his hands, constantly looking up at an unsuspecting Dale, and then back to the screwdriver to time when he is going to brace himself to welcome the wound fully to the outside world.

One. Two. Three!

The screwdriver gets yanked out of his foot, causing him to whimper uncontrollably, seething his teeth and completely blocking off his oxygen supply to not make any more sound. He vies a slight toss to the metal tool behind his back, shielding it from the eye of sight of Dell, this is his way out. The lock is an odd size, and Abel tugs the lock, resting his hands underneath the chain to not let it clank against the floor. With the metal tool tucked tightly inside his fist. As soon as Dell turns the corner he lunges the screwdriver inside of the lock, plunging it deep into the interior and lifting it as hard as he could up to the point where it got stuck. He jabs again with force to no result. He jabs again and again to no avail. Frustrated, he quits exhausting himself, and hides the tool behind his back.

The television stops its usual program and makes an alien-sounding whirr! It is almost as if the gears are turning inside of the box and trying to think as hard as they can to conjure up an image.

Pop!

The television screen restarts, drawing out a quick horizontal bright line before entering the world that is visual communication. In this case, the screen displays a man, an old man sitting down in a leather armchair with elegant stitching that could be seen clearly from the camera angle. The old man sits in front of his mahogany desk with a cup of coffee resting on the top of a coaster.

"Hello." The old man gets out. "You are probably wondering what you are doing here, there is no speedy explanation, unfortunately, so your proctor has already filled you in on the basics. This is an official message from the New York Breakers announcing your severing from the team, we are sorry that you can't continue to be a part of our program but if you are seeing this message, you have already done enough damage. What is about to happen is custodial work to clean up your little mess, and swipe our hand over the entire thing, now no one has to worry about it!" He coughs after his rant, releasing some spit before promptly cleaning around his mouth. "Sorry about that." He gets re-acclimated to his environment and what he previously had said, "Oh yes! The USBA's little invention."

Abel rubs his neck again, fiddling with the pebble-sized lump, remaining unsatisfied.

He continues, "As the owner of the New York Breakers-"

Abel tunes out the rest, remembering the Polaroid that he had gotten a hold of. There are two people in the image, one is Baird, and the other is behind Baird and has the same flair as the jacket. He had only seen the silhouette, but it was enough due to the flame-like design at the end of it. It made sense now, The Owner and Baird were there, huddled over his body, but for some reason, Baird was the uneasy one.

"-and that's the end of our little… orientation if you must. Unfortunately, these next few steps will take some time before- you know." He waves his hand across his neck in a cutting motion. "We are to transfer your assets back to our accounts, which includes money made, money saved, or any properties gained in New York for the next batch of rookies. They will take the same apartment and undergo a very similar experience to you, except hopefully, they meet our expectations. We are in a winning sport you know." He draws in a tight breath. "Sit tight while we extract your assets, and again we would like to say thank you for the small amount of time you've had with the New York Breakers, the rest of the world will remember you for having drowned yourself in your bathtub. Trust me, it's not the best thing that I could come up with, but it made the most sense because of your rough patches with your family, especially your brother... and mother."

Abel's strength begins to fade again, trying his best to regurgitate whatever feeling is lying deep in his stomach, forcing him to take fast breaths that pierce his lungs. No amount of screaming would help, or do anything in this case, the tears have been cried, and his knuckles have already been destroyed.

The worst feeling in the world is being helpless, and he's completely useless to some things that are frightening to him. There are too many things that can't be changed for the better with everything that goes on in the world. Some call it fate, others call it bullshit, either way, Abel wishes that he could've changed certain things.

Thinking about his family, he makes a last-ditch effort to drive the screwdriver even deeper into the lock. With enough force, the lock goes flying into the ground, breaking open with the speed of a cobra strike.

The lock is free from the chains that bind him, Abel quickly slides the lock off of the chain and unwinds himself.

Nothing can stop him now as he reaches his hands and pushes himself off of the ground and onto his wobbling feet. He beelines towards any form of exit that he might be able to take, making sure not to cross Dell or anyone else in the area. Dell can be heard a couple of rooms over talking in a very monotone voice, trying his best to conceal his words from any eavesdroppers.

He is busy. Good. Abel thinks while he crouches down and moves across the wooden planks, avoiding absorbing impact with the balls of his feet. With precision he finds his way across the gap between walls, averting any way that Dell could be alerted.

The walls are very hollow to Abel's understanding. The other sides of the wall must be paper thin because of the clarity of the sounds coming through them, everything is crystal clear now.

"He should've just finished the video." Nothing can be heard from the other end of the phone, and he pauses for a second before continuing again, "Yeah, I got it. Stop worrying about it, it's already done, he's out, and we just got to get past the game, does it start soon?" Another pause. "Alright, we're good then, bye." He sighs and starts to stomp his feet down, causing the floorboards to creak and echo throughout the set of interconnected rooms.

In response to the growing noise, Abel dashes across another living room area to finally reach the first door he has seen in what has felt like days. He violently twists on the sticky door handle, but due to the sweat flowing out of his palms, it progressively becomes more difficult to twist it open. "Please. Please. Come on. Come on." He begs anyone who might be listening in the extremely large expanse of space to listen, just once for something to work out for him. With enough finesse, he manages to twist it halfway to a full turn, holding it there in fright that it might slip out of his hands again and escape his grip. In an unexpected turn of fate, it barely cracks open just wide enough for Abel to make the split-second reaction to pull the door as hard as he could to his chest, turning his neck slightly over his shoulder as he completes the motion.

Out of the corner of his eye, Dell stands silent, his mouth completely closed and his eyes hellbent on Abel. He's holding a metal baseball bat that has paint scraping off in flakes.

"Look, Dell. I've beat you to a pulp, I can do it again. Don't take another step, I swear to God." He says as he starts to back up away from the weapon.

Step. Another step. The consistency of his steps only increases. Like a robot, he follows his program and moves towards Abel.

"Dell. Dell." He tries to verbally nudge him away from him, unsure of any actions that will follow if he makes it within arms reach of Abel.

Abel's palms start to itch, shaking from the tension he is being put under, the itching feels like a need to fill the lack of holding something, without anything in his hands. he is vulnerable. His hands tremble their way to his back pocket, feeling for the cold steel dragging his fingers down until he feels rubber. He grips the screwdriver until the white in his knuckles can be visible from ships at sea in the night.

In the span of a millisecond, Dell lunges towards Abel for a repeat of weeks ago.

The grotesque sound sent shivers down Abel's spine.

What is done is done.

It is eat or get eaten.

It is do or die.

And now he didn't have to carry around the screwdriver.

CHAPTER 18

Likes, Shares, and Consequences

The elevator's large metal box interior greets Abel with the opposite of a warm and comfortable environment. There's a column of flashing buttons with layers of dirt around them, and below them resting on the floor is a sign that says Out of Service, also extremely worn out. Abel knocks on the metal walls softly, wincing after a third knock. At least it isn't hollow, a hollow elevator probably wouldn't even work, or it would likely be undergoing some sort of maintenance on the exterior. After deciding that he has no other option than to press one of the buttons, doing so emits a piss yellow color at a couple-second intervals. Now all he has to do to prepare is glue his feet to the floor.

Whirrr. The sound reminds him of the spaceship-like qualities of the new cars that some of his college teammates whipped around for fun. One of the nights he made the immature choice to hop in a car with one of them, it turned out that "good driver" didn't determine how safe they were, but rather how many laws they could destroy on one stretch of the road.

Clank! The elevator drops for a split second, dropping Abel's heart and sending a spiral of thoughts about the end through his head, and then it quickly accelerates back up regaining the distance lost in its travel upwards. The sounds are very uncomfortable to listen to for the rest of the ride, and a constant fear is transmitted to him, he wants to avoid freefalling as much as possible, he was told to spread his wings and fly as a child, but he doesn't think that this is what they meant.

Ding! He reaches the peak of his summit towards the surface of the world. Because the automatic doors aren't working, he has to repetitively slam his hand into the manual button, eventually opening it just a tad before shutting down. The little slit is all he needs thankfully, he had been hitting the weight room since a freshman in high school, so he makes light work of pulling apart the two doors from each other. The light shines brightly upon his exit from the metal death box. His first fresh breath of air and sight of natural light as a new man. A man whose shadow has encroached on more than half of his body and has continued to follow him around.

The shadow was always there.

Abel stumbles out of the twin doors of the unregistered, rotting building. The sun shines above him and for some reason, he is still covered in a shadow.

He makes a one-eighty-degree turn to get a full view of his point of exit. The building is an old laundromat with a sign half hanging by what looked like a thread, the rest of it etched out completely. The busy streets of New York don't stop for him and no one picks up the role of the good samaritan, they continue to go about their day despite the sticky red liquid covering various parts of his clothes and his skin.

Abel hardly has enough strength to call out, not that he would, he could help himself and that was final. So in turn the people further fulfill their part as faulty pedestrians not deserving of cars stopping for them as they cross the road. It's just the way the streets of New York work, no one stopped and cared, so neither would Abel.

He attempts to restart his legs and run through the tightness of the muscles in his legs and arms, but he ends up walking after making it a block down the road. The large facility could be seen from his location, looking like it is around a mile and a half from his current position. He quietly considers himself lucky to even see it due to the way the treeline blocked every part of the building except for the standout extremity on the roof, which is the New York Breakers logo; the LED lights on the outside of each letter are turned off due to the time of day.

The only real challenge that he could see in the short future is the rolling hills that led to the entrance, he's on the opposite side of the building that he used to approach from his apartment with Warren, so the terrain is brand new to him, and has more change in elevations than he is used to.

Abel tries to come up with a plan of action upon his entry to the building. He only needs one weapon, one thing to wield against the people who ruined his life. He has finally figured out the solution to all of his problems and much more problems to come for every single person in the league now, and the league in the future.

That solution is sitting underneath a pair of his drawers in a replacement room.

He needs to end the USBA, and he finally starts to acknowledge his safety and decides that it is time to end the dance that he refused to end with the organization, no more playing a puppet. He has to leave regardless of the money that would leave him. Yeah, that's what I'll do. It's what I got to do.

Something still feels off about it, but there's no shortage of anger that he didn't hold towards the basketball team that ruined his life.

What am I thinking? I need to play.

He still needs the money, and he has one opportunity to make some. Now what time does the game start?

"SHIT! SHIT! SHIT! SHIT!" He starts to hyperventilate, drawing tears to his eyes. "NO!"

The basketball game. The game that decided if he lived or not. He quickly checks the time on his cheap analog watch. It starts in five minutes. If he ran to the arena, he would make it by halftime. That's barely enough time to score twenty-five points with five rebounds and assists if he even got subbed in right at the start of the second half. He feels pulled between both locations, the arena, and the practice facility, trying to debate which one to go to. It would be a huge gamble for both sides if he went to the game and did his thing, he wouldn't be able to go back to the practice facility because Baird would surely find him and end what is going on, but if he goes to grab the polaroid then he runs the risk of the mysterious chip in his head short-circuiting his brain. Two choices. Possible death, or possible opportunity to change his future.

He takes another step towards the arena. It isn't worth dying over, but what if he's bluffing? The chip could be anything, right? If he didn't expose the league, then the world would continue to be blind to the decades of exploitation that the best athletes in the world were exposed to when they joined the USBA, millions of dollars poured into them and then squeezed right back out when they slipped up or made purchases on things like homes, going right back to the league. That money is his property, he earned it. Even though he never saw it or touched it. The paper he signed entitled the money to him and so he would get it back. He needs to end everything that the league stands for.

Abel is fairly conditioned from the weeks of practice and high-intensity physical activity inflicted upon the team in their preparation for the games. The only thing holding him back is a small tingling in the back of his heel, like an incision that cuts through some of the muscle tissue. His body hadn't eaten anything in what felt like days, but that didn't stop him from continuing to pump his feet out in front of him. His body is running off of pure adrenaline as fuel, very strong stuff in certain situations.

The time seems to slow by in a fashion that turns everything around him woozy, like a trip off of some drug that forced hallucinations upon the user, but the visions were right in front of him. The trees and business buildings are like a background that doesn't feel important, like props, that's all most stuff was to Abel, irrelevant people and irrelevant experiences. Abel only focuses on the next step in front of him, he has no time to lose.

After the longest six minutes that Abel has ever experienced he flies through the double doors of the building, quickly looking at the time again and making his way towards what he thinks is the area where he was staying.

The night he was taken into captivity, he was completely oblivious to where he was, that isn't something that his brain fully processed, he just went through the motions. All he knows is it was some rundown laundromat.

Even now, his brain goes into autopilot and takes him to his temporary sleeping quarters. With the first twist of the door handle it opens. The small room is tidy in the fact that he never settled in when he transferred rooms, making it easy when he throws himself down onto the mattress like a final drop of rain in the spring plummeting down to the warm grass. His bag is still there, and he rummages through the bag as quickly as the motor function in his hands allows, fiddling with his fingers, brushing the glossy exterior of the Polaroid.

"Good." He says under his breath.

He stops.

Alongside the Polaroid that he had gotten from Chris's locker, there is another picture, this one nearly double the surface area, and clear. This photo is clear as day, it is Meek Fant, a dead Meek Fant. The young man's body is hurled across the carpet in what looks like a study of some sort, this photo is almost like an extension or clearer version of the Polaroid that crawled into his bag somehow. The hair on Abel's arms stands up, pulling upwards like a magnet is attracting them to some metal hull above him, but shivers get sent down his spine instead of a buzzing feeling.

Over his shoulder, he sees the small window that rests lonely in the corner of the room, an odd place for a window to be. The curtains are flowing back and forth like a rowboat on a calm sea, Abel pulls back the curtains to reveal the window to be open halfway. Someone has been here, that had to be the way the new photo had found its way to Abel. But who? Abel speculates.

Abel grabs his backpack and the two photos. Against the will of God, he puts on his basketball shoes, realizing that he would have to be forgiven for the sin that he had committed, but there isn't going to be much time to change into certain clothes when he is going to have to check himself into the game. Baird would be opposed to him playing but he had to get himself in and keep himself in. The coach would immediately want to get him out of the game, sending in the substitutions the moment he checked in. The game of basketball in the States allowed the person getting subbed in to stay in the game until there was a dead ball if someone was going to take them out of the game. That means that Abel would have to keep the ball inbounds the whole game, or the hardest part for some of his teammates, his team would have to avoid fouls the rest of the time it took for him to complete his stat line.

He starts his sprint to the arena.

The New York center is all the buzz, the atmosphere of the huge structure acting as a conductor of electricity, that's how much energy there is. Abel finds an entrance from the back where the buses would unload the athletes to prepare them for battle. This is a war.

Abel winds himself through the security without much problem, most of them would give a brief nod, not even questioning his rush to the game. It's a miracle in itself that he doesn't run into a mob of fans on his way to the arena, the culture around basketball in New York drew in many people who weren't attending the game but would hang around the arena watching the game on an immense screen outside the arena. It's a huge party hanging outside of a mass gathering of dedicated fans.

He filters his way through the locker room, slamming his hands into the lockers to stop his momentum from carrying himself right through the hollow metal doors, pushing himself in a different direction. He became acclimated to the spryness and skill required to open a door while still running. Occasionally he stumbles across a door that is pulled instead of pushed which makes him lose valuable seconds.

He sprints right through the northwest gate of the court, finally experiencing the correct traction under his feet with his shoes that are inevitably going to send him slipping in the future due to the bottom of the shoes being worn down in the frantic escapade.

"And- woah! It looks like Abel Richards has entered the building! What is happening with that!" The announcer announces to the arena of confused and frustrated fans. The majority of the fans catch sight of him on the jumbotron and start pointing back to it, at first Abel thinks that they were pointing at him, but after a few more moments he realizes that they were pointing to the scoreboard. The Breakers are down by seventeen points. Only two minutes left of the third quarter.

Abel curses under his breath, reaching the bench and skipping past all of the high fives that his teammates extended, expecting him to sit down right next to them, instead, he goes to the check-in counter, throwing on his jersey in the same motion as dropping to his knees.

Baird looks furious with him, and for a second Abel believes that he might pop a vein in his forehead. "Abel, what the hell are you doing!" He stumbles over some of his words in disbelief that he is even kneeling in the first place.

Abel looks dead into his eyes and doesn't respond with anything. The commotion in the crowd is faced with a newfound excitement for the team, if they were going to go down, they were going to go down biting and scratching. New York never leaves their seats during a couple of possessions where they are down, it could be the fact that many self-made people fought their way for what they wanted in the city where no one sleeps. They were told they couldn't, and they had no other option but to dismiss their opinions and shut them up, their fans for once empathized.

Khalil grips the sides of his jersey, wiping his face with his undershirt and wiping a smile onto his face. He isn't scared of anyone, but neither is Abel. This is the time he's been waiting for, he's getting paid to tarnish the name of the person who ruined his name, and it's going to be a deadly dance.

Wait. Abel thinks. He is a player in the league too. Khalil is just as much of a pawn in the league's games as Abel is. They were both getting paid to multiply the wealth of the USBA. A couple of seconds of empathy drift away at the sound of the buzzer, indicating his ingress into the game. We aren't alike. Not at all.

"Abel! GET YOUR ASS BACK HERE!"

The front-row seat owners, players, and coaches stare at them in silence. The sound of the arena starts to vibrate in Abel's ears, it's like he is underwater listening to the screams and yelling. Or if he is in the bathroom at a party, the noise becomes saturated and causes a floating sensation to wash over him. As Ray jogs by he raises a fist at him, giving him the nod, he knows.

"We gon' get this Abel. I gotcha. And don't forget-" he raises his hands to his face pretends to click a camera and points to the baseline where the media presence is packed.

Abel returns his acknowledgment and they step back onto the court together, as teammates.

"Abel!" Baird continues to shout out as he lunges at Abel, trying to grab him back towards the bench but Abel quickly snatches his hand off of his jersey and jogs out to center court, not taking his eyes off of Khalil.

"I got Khalil." Abel quips.

TWEET! "Ball in!" The ref calls out.

Khalil advances down the court into Abel's territory. Abel has studied his movements, he's dreamed about an opportunity where he took away everything from him. He observes his hips as he sways with the ball, looking for an opening. Dribble. The ball gets poked out as soon as he moves the ball towards Abel, and he shoots out towards the ball like a bullet, scooping up the ball and sprinting towards the basket. Khalil is faster than Abel and makes it right in front of him, Abel reacts quickly to his steal attempt picking up the ball and spinning while maintaining balance. They both jump up

-SLAM! TWEET!

The rim shakes like an earthquake and the ball collapses on top of Khalil's head as he gets launched backward and onto the ground.

The Abel before would have been in his face. Abel now is a stone-cold killer and holds up a finger to his lips as he steps over the corpse.

The entire arena has lost their marbles, patting their heads and jumping along with each other, shocked at the sequence of events.

While Abel stands on the baseline, he looks at Ray and pulls out the two photos from a small pocket in his undershorts. He holds them up in front of the camera workers, making sure that they look clear as day. The display goes up quickly to the jumbotron and time seems to stop. The brains of the thousands of fans in attendance attempt to wrap their head around what is being shown.

Abel looks up to Baird who is too shocked to move for the first few seconds of commotion before speed-walking his way out of the northwest gate. No one knows what they are watching, the recent sequence of events is never seen before. The entire arena is so out of hand that the refs stop the game for a second, waving toward the people at the check-in counter to pause the game. The players walk back to their benches, just in time to see Chris exit his seat and follow in the footsteps of Baird.

Over the shoulder of a fan, Abel sees the hundreds upon hundreds of posts being sent to social media with the picture, racking up numbers faster than the time it takes for light to travel. The whole world had blown up, and all it took was a photo, an and-one dunk, and a broken and determined boy, man, boy.

The game is over, and the employees start to send the fans back home, disappointed yet still staggered at the events being portrayed in front of them. They had made it to a historical and monumental event in basketball and even global television. An entire organization much less a league at the mercy of a physical photograph being put in front of a camera.

Abel accepts this, finding peace that there is going to be some form of justice among the athletes and their families who were controlled by a twisted puppeteer.

It is only a matter of time before the chip in his head does whatever the chip is supposed to do.

His mother would be alone, but she would have enough left behind to get by for the rest of her life, he starts to think about the amount of green paper that is going to support his mother but he stops himself short. What a mistake.

Abel sighs. I'll see you soon little brother.

He closes his eyes.

Chapter 19

The Owner

After opening his eyes he is somewhat underwhelmed that nothing happened. Instead he gets greeted by the light yet again. The roller coaster of emotions doesn't fail to send him over slopes with his stomach dropping, just now reaching the trough of the wave of tracks. The court resumes its normal state, the fans climbing out of their seats, making sure that they have all of their things before exiting the arena, trying to make their way past the highly concentrated points that lead to places like the parking garages and towards the subway.

Most of the Breakers staff is already gone, and the same goes for the Titans staff, they immediately leave the arena with a sense of urgency. As for the players, they stay around the court area listening to Abel as he describes the sequences of events that he undertook when they didn't see him, the coma, the phone, the chips, the underground rooms.

Everyone had very similar experiences with how their families had disappeared off of the face of the earth, and their phones were all wired too. It is systematic.

Ray pipes into the conversation, "There was one night where Warren was called into an office, entering with nothing and leaving with a pen. He told me that he couldn't say anything, but he had to sign something regarding the money."

"I think we all signed some agreement about the money," Barry says.

"But with Warren, he left with something a bit more than an agreement, he was bound, trapped. The next day he left practice early because he said he had something to talk to Baird about. Warren said that since Baird wasn't there he went to talk to Chris who was in his office instead. He found him going through things like a maniac, holding up a Polaroid camera and pulling out the most recently taken photo out of the top."

"The polaroid."

Ray nods. "There was the same thing in the photo, but that's not it. That Polaroid wasn't clear enough, Chris went on a sort of hiatus throughout the city and found out how to clear up the image, the only reason that Warren knows this is because Chris started to tell him things when he would get back later that night. Warren was getting information filtered through him, and he was talking with his family the entire time."

"And what? Baird found out and got rid of him?"

"Baird never found out, Abel."

They all stop.

"Then who murdered him?" Abel finally ventures.

Ray looks up at the booth sections of the complex, only one of them is lit up. The kitchens and TV are visible from their angle. There is no physical representation of people there, just a shadow of a man drinking out of a short glass cup, watching them.

"I don't really know. I didn't pick up on anything in my time here. I haven't had many problems, the league didn't expect me to succeed and set the contract and Incentives pretty low and attainable for me."

"Ray, they told me that some microchip would shut down my brain if I didn't complete my Incentive. Feel your neck, they're not lying about the chip, it's there."

"I don't know, I guess I haven't realized that they were in my head in the first place. The chips aren't even visible either, we got to get them removed."

"So is this it?"

"What is it?"

"Basketball."

Ray laughs, "And what, what do you think that I will do if I stop playing basketball? I rejoin society with my uneducated ass!" He mocks the question, triggered by the topic.

"What do you think I'm going to do? I don't know! I'm going to make it work! And you have plenty of money to retire and live comfortably for the rest of your life." Abel comes across with just as much distress as the rest of them.

He shakes his head. "No, no I don't. Or I won't. These chips are going to have to come out of us, and if we don't soon then the effect that we all heard about them might kick in. The medical bill will strip away the money I have left."

"But you should have millions, right?" Abel quips.

"I lost most of it. They have control over our bank accounts, what comes in, what comes out. The money that they pay us is temporary, it is only used to keep us in the system and make us think that we are the ones making the decisions. The houses that you buy are the league keeping you close and again, making you think that you have control over your life. Those houses are probably wired too. We don't have any money, none of it is ours." He stops himself for a few seconds. "It did help me for some time though, some things did get paid for."

There is a long pause. It should be hard for anyone to figure out that everything you had worked for was for nothing.

"So you just expect things to blow over and return to normal?"

"You saw the attention that was gained. The league will never be the same. Some people should pick up the ashes and start anew, and this time we'll make that real money we all wanted."

"But what if they don't change?" His voice stays monotone, solemn even.

"Then we would have lost our lives for something that we were told wasn't tangible, we invested time into a dream that ultimately didn't pan out."

"What if I told you I'm out, I can't put up with this any longer."

"I would respect it, but-"

"-but what?"

"Nothing," Ray says, peeking back down at his phone. "You're just lying to yourself Abel, you know you have to stay. You know you have to stay. Just like me and just like all of us, all we care about is money right? Screw everything else but our money. We stay, we at least have another chance at wealth again, and I'll take that chance any day of the week- oh my god."

"What?" Abel tries to look over Ray's shoulder to see what his reaction is.

"It's gone."

"What's gone?"

"Everything. Everything is gone, all of it."

"All of- oh. How?"

"They cleaned it up, they cleaned it all up. We need to leave Abel. We need to leave now."

The two of them pull their bags onto their shoulders and start off the building, trying not to attract any unwanted attention, peeking behind their backs ever so often. "Abel look." Ray starts. "I'm going to stay. You have- no need to leave, you were the one that started the spark, but I need to find a way to get paid, I think I have it figured out. Once I get a check I'm going to cash it out as soon as I touch the envelope, no more keeping it in the online expanse, and waving it in front of the USBA."

"Ray, I'm staying too, you said it best yourself."

Ray gives no acknowledgment to Abel's statement, they both know that Abel would go by his own rules if he stayed, a personal agenda. Revenge. So instead of feeding his delusion to the uncertainty of a check and possibly lifetime trauma, he changes the subject.

"Abel, we need to do something real quick." Ray drops his bag and takes a paperclip out of his pocket, holding it up to Abel. "Here, I need to take your chip out, and you need to take out mine."

"I don't think I can."

"It doesn't matter." He says starting to grab Abel's head, turning it and holding it stern so that he has the best view of the small lump under his skin. Without warning he unwinds the paperclip and stabs at the chip, digging around it before driving it as deep as he can and leveraging the paperclip up to create a slit in the skin. From there he maneuvers his hands and rough fingers to push the chip out of the slit that he made. "There." The chip falls to the ground in a light Ting! Abel bends down and picks it up with one hand, the other hand gripping the waterfall of liquid flowing down his neck while the air dries it cold onto his skin.

"Why do you think I'm still walking?" Abel says as he uses his fingernail to peel the layer of blood that cakes on his neck like the roots of a tree.

"The Incentive wasn't fulfilled, but the game never officially ended. When you exposed them, it saved your life."

Abel tries to think past the wall of pain that grabs at him. He takes the dirty paperclip out of Ray's hands and wipes it with his shirt so that it is sort of clean, it certainly looks cleaner than if the residue of his flesh is still there. "This is the end of the road for both of us Ray, I can't make up my mind to stay here, I don't know if it's worth it."

"What are we going to do then?"

Abel drives the clip into Ray's skin, imitating the same motions that he did when it was his turn, wincing from the painful images that he's taking in. "I don't know, I don't. I haven't experienced the world without looking through the lens of basketball."

"You'll learn. I guess we'll learn. We've made it this far."

"We have." Abel agrees, releasing the paperclip from his grip and letting Ray slip the metal chip out of the burrow that Abel formed.

They make their way through the last stretch of the tunnel, each holding their hands to the side of their head, trying to stop the blood flow with their hands.

Duhh-dunnnnnnnn. The sound of the lights turning off drags out long, in an alien-like sound. For a few seconds, the extended hallway is pitch dark with no form of light guiding their way, but after a minute of trying to find their way, the dim red reserve lights are turned on periodically down the stretch. "The hell?" Ray vocalizes.

"They don't turn off the lights like this. They never have in the time that I've been here. It's only seven o'clock."

Ray turns on his flashlight from his phone, pointing it forward, jumping an inch off the ground at the sight of what looks like an inanimate person down the hallway. He laughs, blowing out a load of carbon dioxide before repeating this process with a higher tempo, startled. "I thought-"

"Ray."

"What?"

"What is that?"

The thing that scared Ray blocks the door to the bus lane behind the arena, remaining in its tracks.

"This is my building."

"What are you talking about Ray." Abel quips, turning towards a space. Ray is gone, the only thing left of him being the receding volume of his footsteps.

"Ray?"

Abel completes a three-sixty, trying to cover as much area as he can, straining his eyes like a lighthouse trying to find a lost boat at sea.

"Abel." The voice calls out, causing him to stop clear in his path. This is the same voice from the locker room. This is the same person who knocked him out and sent him to get chained up. This is the same man in the video orientation that he watched.

"Oh, you can't be serious."

"Oh, I am very serious. You probably know what I'm going to say, it's very redundant and upsetting to have to keep repeating myself." The general shape of the man can be seen as he steps into the partially flashing red light, part of his features revealed momentarily in the parts of the hallway that aren't completely pitch dark. The thing that Abel picks up as he steps closer to him is that his height has to be similar to his own. "I have an offer actually, before I repeat the same old things that I've been saying." The mysterious man continues.

"An offer?" Abel scoffs.

"An offer, Abel Richards."

"What is it then?" Abel listens halfheartedly, not expecting the words coming out of his mouth to be anything of value.

"We want you to become part of the organization. You'll have an early retirement from the league to pursue your passion for leading the teams and running the program.

"Hell no, why on earth would I take that as an option?"

"You haven't let me finish, Richards, what I have to say I guarantee you will be interested in."

"Then what is it?" Abel says, adding staccato to each word, like hopping from one to the next like a game of hopscotch.

"The Breakers are going to give you the chance to accept a one-time offer for one billion dollars."

"Over a lifetime?" He says, laughing.

"No. A year."

This draws drama to the shared space. He was just offered a billion dollars for a year of work for them, currently, he was being paid in less than pennies previously compared to the offer.

"What- what would I even do?"

"You would take my place as the owner of the New York Breakers."

"You aren't being serious."

"You know I'm serious because I'm not going to shove a piece of paper and a pen in front of you like that fool of a coach that you had."

"What about-"

"You have to understand that I work in an industry, I have to handle many things, and follow the rules that were set in place for me. We are all puppets in a greater show, that's just the way it is. It's not just the USBA, if you go into any field of work there is a hierarchy and a system of work."

"If I say no?"

"You walk out of here with nothing to go back to, no money, you have hardly any family, and no purpose."

"I still have a family."

"You are alone now, you have been alone."

"You're wrong, I still have my mother."

The owner chuckles over and over and over again. "You silly boy. Why must you act timid about what you are hiding, I assure you I am well aware. This mother character you have made up yourself."

"Wh-what are you talking about." Tears start to build up in his eyes. "I don't believe you, I have lived with my mom for years since then."

"You are slowly killing yourself, Abel. He wants you to suffer, he wants what you have, he wants you dead."

"WHO'S HE YOU CRAZY OLD MAN!"

"You." The Owner brushes a small piece of lint off of his suit, slowly turning away.

"What?"

"I said what I said. And now you need to reply to my offer, I don't like to be kept waiting, too much anticipation."

"What happens if I say yes?" Abel slowly calms down.

"Then you are the owner of the Breakers, and paid one billion dollars for one year of work."

"But?" He says expecting some caveat, or silver lining.

"But nothing."

"Nothing?"

"Nothing. Look, think about it Abel, there is no logical reason that you would decline the offer that I'm putting down."

"Yes, there is. There are many reasons why I should run my ass out of here and not ever look back, you killed my friend!"

"You don't understand Abel, I've done great favors for you for not throwing you into a rotten jail cell for all your hidden little secrets, it's somewhat of a miracle that we are the only ones that found out about it."

"You're sick. My mother is at our place right now" Abel coughs out.

The Owner chuckles softly again, taking the jab while being a fair sport, but there is still some irony in his cold-hearted laugh.

"So what will it be?" The Owner rushes him.

Abel tries to wrap his head around the whole concept, but all that his pain-induced brain can think of is the money, guaranteed money, and no contracts that could trap him. He could be free. His mother would have to understand him.

"When do I start?"

CHAPTER 20

This House is Not a Home

Abel's mother expected him home at nine. She found a way to get a place in the New York area in her price range. Talking over the phone she nearly sounded optimistic of the future, the first time since the last time that they've talked face to face.

As part of the deal, Abel got paid nineteen million dollars per week, which at first seemed like an infinite amount of money that couldn't be spent but it was later found that he could use it all in a sitting, leaving no crumbs.

He bought his first car at a modest price of around two million dollars. If he's going to roll in anything, he wants to roll in some Hot Wheels. Almost the exact moment after he accepted the deal, he called his mom and told him the news, telling her that he was going to buy him the biggest and best house in New York, he told her that he would find her the highest point in the New York skyline and put her up there.

She declined over the phone, resistant to anything other than a home that is comfortable and not too luxurious. Abel didn't understand why she wouldn't want to celebrate and live a little now that they had the means. She didn't say anything else over the phone that night.

Abel's car pulls to the side of the curb without having to parallel park, sliding right behind his mother's car. He steps out and locks the car before noticing that he left his wallet in the driver's seat, opening the car again and grabbing what he needs before taking his time as he walks up the steps to the brownstone apartment.

The outside of the apartment is decorated with fresh greenery in pots that have to be new. Abel's mom never obtained the luxury of having the time to decorate the exterior of a home, and for the first time in a long while she had an exterior to decorate.

Abel steps onto the welcome mat that doesn't feel worn through, it must be new, Abel thinks. He prepares to knock on the door, raising his hand in a fist, but before he can hit the door a second time the door opens to reveal the person that he misses the most, the one that he hadn't been there for like she was for him.

"Abel." She looks extremely proud as she gazes into his eyes, making Abel frightened that if she looked hard enough into his soul she would see too much.

"Mom," Abel responds trying to keep his voice from shaking and cracking as a tear starts to form in his eye.

Luckily for Abel, he isn't the first one to start crying, his mother starts to draw the waterworks from both of them, moving together in a cold embrace that sends warmth through their bodies. It was too long, way too long.

"Baby boy." They hold each other for what might be an eternity, but neither of them wants to give up the other. "Come in! Come in!" She says enthusiastically, waving him in as she opens the door.

She made the apartment very nice, the layout had the staircase right where you walked in with a small view of the kitchen from the front door, everything is close. It's like a home. To the left of the stairs and the hallway leading to the kitchen is a small living room with the same sofa that he would lay down on as a child with a bag of ice over his legs.

There is something very missing from the place, Abel thinks he can tell exactly what it is, but he doesn't say anything about it, and his mother doesn't either, they would keep it that way. It is time to honor the past but look toward the future and the next steps.

The first few days after the deal he had a hard time coming to terms that he wouldn't play a game of basketball for the rest of his life. He had depended on basketball and used it as a crutch to a breaking point. Life without it left an odd taste on the tip of his tongue, something that he couldn't and would not be able to get rid of, and that's just the way it is. He told himself to suck it up and enjoy the little things in his life while he could, and it wasn't like he was disconnected from the sport, he was making good money by running the program.

Things were different now in his attitude, he couldn't get rid of the shadow that hung over him on most late nights and early mornings, unable to escape the feeling of dread and loneliness. He had a very hard time explaining what was happening to him, and it only got worse after he became the owner of the Breakers.

As he walks through the foyer and into the kitchen, he stops every few steps to observe his surroundings, accompanying himself with the new environment.

"I like what you've done with the place, Mom," Abel says, brushing his hands over the countertop.

"Oh, thank you! It took some time, but, well it's done!"

"Hey?" Abel inquires, looking at the three plates set at the table.

"Yeah?" His mother says while washing some dirty dishes from what is used to prepare the meal that sat comfortably in the oven.

"Why did you set out three plates on the table, I thought you were only expecting me?" Abel looks at his Mom, who seems unreceptive to the comment, avoiding eye contact in a manner that requests a follow-up question.

"It's- well-" She tries her best to let the words escape out of her mouth but they don't.

"Well, what Mom?" Abel doesn't know whether to be concerned about an unsuspecting guest or to be more laid off in the approach to receiving the information.

"-Your father is going to be joining us."

As if not enough nuclear bombs could explode in front of Abel, surely enough he looks up into the sky and sees one descending. "I'm sorry, what?"

"I didn't think it was an emergency." She hushes down.

"An emergency! Mom, he's been gone for years! I told you that if that man showed up to speak one word-" His temper releases phlegm from his mouth, he is truly frightened, and his mom is frightened for him. "-one syllable! The same thing goes for Mikey's dad. Those men are monsters."

"I invited him okay?" His mother matches the intensity and some, sending Abel reeling back, not expecting her to bring back the same level of sternness that she once used to when he got mixed into things at school or just outside in the neighborhood.

"You what? Invited him? He left you, left us."

"I invited him." She wipes her eyes, trying to conceal her face from the outside world, no shell to protect her from the weight being inflicted upon her.

"Mom- I-"

"-No. I didn't know what to do, with your brother gone and you gone I didn't know what to do. I didn't know what was happening to you and I got lonely. Your father called me recently and started talking to me again."

"This isn't okay. I understand that you were trying to fill the gap, but I'm here now, okay?" He squeezes her forearms with his hands, bringing everything down to surface level, it couldn't be that bad, it is an overreaction from a very stressed man who didn't know his place, that is it.

"Abel, I can't uninvite him."

"I know. I'll take care of it, don't worry, do you think he's already on his way."

She shrugs, and then chooses to nod, "I would assume so, oh and Abel? There's something else you should know."

"What Mom?" Abel replies, rubbing his forehead until it turns red, the massaging of his temples curing whatever is going on in his body.

Knock! Knock!

Abel's mother looks back up at him, who is already advancing towards the door, he points to it, then looks at his mother in approval. She clasps her hands together, her smile fading from her cheeks slowly as Abel does the same.

"Hello, Abel." A voice pipsqueaks, brandishing the widest grin in the whole wide world.

Abel's eyes widen to the size of watermelons, shaking his head and returning his neck angle to face his mother.

"What is this-"

"Hello, Abel." A deeper voice takes center stage, and from behind the little girl with pigtails comes a voice that had changed since the last time he heard it, having only faint memories of the rough around the edges sound that he projected when he spoke.

"Hello-" He stops to clear his throat, still trying to turn the stagnant gears functioning in his mind. "-Mark."

The girl from behind him is around the age of someone just passing the toddler stage, but that doesn't stop Abel's reflexes from shutting the door dead in their face.

"They can't be welcome here, Mom." He says matter of factly.

"Abel!" She scolds. "Open that damn door, we all need to talk."

Abel's choice to reopen the door and extend it out is in no way shape or form because of his mother, if anything he should be protecting her from that villain, but there is something that eggs the muscles and tendons in his arms to reach towards the handle and bring back the demons of the past. It seems like nothing mattered in the grand scheme of things to Abel, and his conscience took it a little too seriously. Any cycle of forgiveness would be a slippery slope, and he did not intend to respond to any subject that had to do with that word.

"Abel look-" Mark says, maneuvering his hand right in between the crack of the door.

Instead of giving any recognition to the middle-aged man he stares dead at him in silence, not exactly giving him the silent treatment, but making him feel bad for what he did, and for some reason it does not affect him, he still maintains a monotone voice and isn't on his knees repenting for his past actions.

His mother has nothing else to say for the time being, ushering the group inside of their home, and welcoming them straight to the kitchen table to be comfortably seated in the fancy wooden chairs that were new additions to the space.

Abel decides to sit down on the couch with a very slight view of the group. His mom is laughing with the group, she is expressive, her heart is beating, and there are signs of life. Signs of life ever so distant after her heart rate had become a straight line with the loss of her son. Maybe that wasn't the only thing she lost that night, Abel was away during that time, gaps had to be filled, ties had to be cut, and at the end of the day she had to move on.

Quite a time earlier:

"Mom?"

"Yes, sweetie?" She says, brushing back his wild hair after too many months without getting a haircut, she is told that he is still finding his style, and his baby brother enjoyed running his hands through it too, it isn't that bad as to cut it off.

"What would you do if I wasn't here? Because I know exactly what you should do."

"Why are you talking like that?"

"Well... I don't know. I just thought that- maybe I should ask." Their youth of Abel implies the occasional stumble of the insanely confusing ever-changing linguistic system that is the English language, but that didn't stop him from having his best go at it.

"I don't even know what you mean." His mother says

"What if I am gone today?"

"Honey, that's not something we have to worry about."

"But what if it was?" Abel responds, looking back up at his mother, at a point in his life where he still had to do that to see her. "Would you move on?"

"-I. Abel?"

"Would you move on?"

"I- no! No, I wouldn't!"

"I would want you to." Abel returns his hands to his lap, folding them softly and reaching them out to meet with his mother.

Abel's mom squeezes them back with a force to move mountains, the kind of force you expect from someone like her, the resilience she has, and her capacity for love. She is left speechless at the sheer confidence he had in asking such a question that warranted further diving into his intentions where he came up with the question and why it even crossed his mind.

"Abel we have someone we want you to meet." He hears his mother calling from the dining room, increasing in volume as she finishes speaking. Behind her is Mark and the child, walking towards him in a slow manner that adds to the drama even more. He isn't ready for confrontation, and he certainly isn't the type for it, if anything he wants to avoid it, but instead, the problem is coming for him, and as per usual, he has to play the defense.

The little girl with pigtails pokes out from behind Mark's arms, immersing herself in what is like a new world for her, she is a butterfly exploring the world outside of the cocoon. She still holds onto the fingers of Mark as she makes her full appearance to Abel, enough to see her little boots and raincoat despite there being no sign of clouds in the sky, even for a cold winter day.

"Alright, munchkin, this is Abel. Say hi!" Mark says, making his voice suitable for the child's ears, something that he didn't think he did with himself when he was young, but he did remember the soft side that he had with his mother. It is all a facade for him though, they were both pieces in his game, and they didn't know the rules and the roles that they had to fulfill.

Abel can sense what is about to happen, it makes him feel like he is getting slingshotted out of the atmosphere, launched straight to the moon, and then sent towards the burning sun. He isn't ready to hear what is about to be said because he believes that it isn't something that he would ever say to him, or about him.

"This is my child, Abel. Her name is Sarah." Mark leisurely explains, trying his best to minimize the damage. Abel's mother is completely unsurprised, instead wearing a face of pity while waiting for his reaction, clasping her hands and praying.

Sarah waves. Abel nods. He knew what was going to happen, but it didn't prepare him for the reaction he had, which led to him fighting back waves in his eyes, hiding from the painful reality and hatred that he had stored up inside of him, locked in the strongest metal safe that the world has ever seen.

Mark continues, "This is our child." He looks at Abel's mother, strafing a step or two to get closer to her.

Abel tries to let out words but snaps his mouth shut.

His mother closes her eyes, shutting herself off from the war she started. "Abel, he never left us! He has always been here! It's just been- it's been so hard-"

"No. No. You're lying. You're playing a prank, this can't be real. He left us, he left you!"

"No Abel, he never left us." She tries to be soft and in the process feels a bit pushed over, and she lets it happen, she is disappointed in herself, ashamed of what she resorted to.

"Yes, he did! I saw him leave!"

"Abel you're sick! You are SICK!"

Something goes off in Mark's head because, in almost a blink of an eye, he appears different to Abel, a completely different outfit. His mom, the girl. They are gone. Nowhere to be seen. Just two men sitting down.

"Mom? What are you?" Abel trails off mid-sentence, trying to figure out the disappearance of his mother and the strange child.

"What are you talking about, kid?" Mark looks up, gaining slight irritation with the comment.

"My mom, she was just here, and so was your kid, they were both right here." He points to their last point of origin.

"Your mom is gone Abel, I don't know why you keep bringing her up. Some bastard, pfft." Now it's his chance to return to kneeling over, rocking back and forth.

"So why are you here Mark?" Abel questions, turning his body calmly and keeping a lower tone.

The next few words come across as hardly intelligible, as severe roughness and pain come from every word. "I want to know why you did it, I want to know why you killed my wife."

What happens next Abel has no possible control over, his body seems to speak for him, taking full command over the shared space of his brain, "Because she was the reason you left."

Mark unravels his pack of cigarettes and takes a smoke.

Marlboros.

CHAPTER 21

The End...

I have to do this. I have to do this. I have to do this.

The repetition of his thoughts rings in his head and sticks with him like a common holiday jingle that just wouldn't leave him to his solidarity. He was told that this night would be the hardest, which isn't saying much for him, he wasn't considered a night owl by any means. His entire life he became very accustomed to the endless loop of time that spiraled and twisted at some sick villain in his head's will. He was at the mercy of no one else except for himself.

The darkness isn't a help either, which doesn't scare Abel because of the dark necessarily, he is scared of what his mind would do to him when those lights turned off in the night and he could hear the roaring rustling of the sheets as his body tossed and turned all hours of the night. It's a miracle that he could get up and function each day and the one time that he had gone to the doctor they had recommended that he should start taking things easier.

Spoiler alert, he would not make things easier. He put his car into drive and floored it against what anyone said. There was no point in listening to someone who didn't understand him, and he refused to abide by the meaningless packet of papers that they turned in to him alongside a few clear orange bottles that his mother made him pick up.

With everything that built up, nothing is stopping Abel from clawing at his eyes, everything feeling like it's twitching uncontrollably. He couldn't stop thinking about the night and what came with it. It's like a daunting task that remains in front of him on his way to glory or the top of a mountain, blocking his way and he has nothing else to do except to go through the thick of it.

The television emits a cold blue light that can be seen from another room, with the small whispers of voices echoing and bouncing around in the small box.

"And what exciting news at that, it'll sure be a very tight race between the two, Randy. I mean, we've seen such amazing things from each player consistently throughout their commitment to TSU and Washington, would you say one has an advantage over another, is there some gap that separates the two?"

"Now don't look at me funny Michael, but I just have to say that there is a slight gap in athleticism between the two, not to mention just sheer drive and defensive capabilities of none other than Khalil Henderson. Let's look back, he dominated in all four years in collegiate-level basketball, averaging a total of four rebounds over his first two seasons as a Tiger. We take a peek at his next season: eight rebounds. The next season: eleven rebounds. There is a constant trend of improvement throughout Khalil's game that I have major respect for, I expect him to go far."

"If you're going to speak about improving you have to mention this last season where Abel led the league in points, and nearly every other offensive capability. Khalil sold out arenas, and Abel sold out cities. The boy is only twenty. " Michael quips, straightening his suit before returning his stance towards the camera.

"Who won the finals the year before Michael?" Randy's hand gestures make a grand display of his argument.

"Tha-" His excitement is short-lived as his incoming response is shot straight out of the stratosphere.

"-No!" He chuckles and scoffs at his coworkers' simple stupidity for having such an opinion, his words coming out faster than his mouth allows him, causing him to choke over some of his words. "Khalil Henderson is the real deal, he averaged thirty-five points per game in the tournament throughout all four of his seasons. Instead of winning just one he built a dynasty for the three years before, where he won three straight national titles." He straightens out his papers, his eyes panning over to the camera for dramatic effect. "I'm sorry but there is no discussion to be had-"

CLICK.

The TV turns off, and the room returns to its poorly lit regular self.

"I can't believe-" Abel sighs, talking to himself. "You know what, it doesn't even matter."

He meanders around the hotel room sluggishly, like his legs are two stiff wood boards, trying to fit himself into the small crevice between the countertop and the barstool. Smooth granite. A nice type of material. A perfect material to leave plenty of empty and full plastic and glassware of food, sent by family, friends, and neighbors. These gifts were all filtered through his momma of course, who made sure to label them because she knows how picky he is about certain foods, especially foods not made by his momma. One of them is labeled: spaghetti and meatballs without the meatballs. This makes Abel laugh and just because of it, he pops off the lid and throws it into the microwave on top of the dresser. Yes, the dresser, and hotel room designers are very special people…

The digital clock beside the microwave reads 9:50.

9:50.

9:50.

BEEP!

BEEP!

Abel tries to rub off the sleepy feeling from his eyes, afraid that he would be a zombie by the end of the day if he didn't down eight cups of coffee. The feeling would have to go away due to the lack of a supply of coffee that he had access to while temporarily staying at the hotel.

The compelling nature that is the science of decision-making causes Abel to take a few steps towards the door, ignoring the food that he had put in the microwave. He would never have believed that he would deny an opportunity to "nourish" his body with the best feeling in the world. Sure, it did cause a couple of close friends to get on him and insult him saying that he was "fat", but the only reason that hands weren't thrown is that he was the skinniest in the friend group by a mile and a half.

The cold steel of the elevator feels vaguely familiar as his hand rests behind his back as support while trying to stand straight up and away from too close in proximity to the other passengers of the hellbent vehicle dragging them back down to ground level. It might as well be considered the depths, humans were starting to spend more of their time above the clouds, trying to escape their reality that most people were made to stay with the others with both feet nestled safely on the ground. The innovators and changers were the ones who sought ways to make sure that their feet never felt the grace of grass and the natural path through life. The path that Abel planned on taking is the search for the uncomfortable pursuit of perfection, he would drive himself to the point of exhaustion and he would reach heights that have never before been explored.

Ground level is designated by the buttons with a star, these Vegas hotels take a more interesting approach to the floor system by making ground level the "ground level", and making the first floor the floor that you would reach by walking up one set of stairs. It's off-putting and it reminded Abel of a horrible Spanish class that he took in early high school, when talking about floors in a building, the first floor is the second, and so on. That was the kind of stuff that Abel never understood, learning a new language stuck with him and it is only by god's grace in one of the teacher's hearts to pass him and round the grade up to passing grade just because he gave some effort in the class and isn't as annoying as the rest of her students.

However, the elevators work just fine, delivering a fresh batch of people to the lobby floor. Most of the people in the lobby are traveling through the area or looking for cheap and quick thrills in the city, some people with brains use the low hotel room prices to gamble more and spend less on other things, the others fruitfully spend their cash on pretty much everything with a price tag, which to be honest would be, well, everything, including their expensive and increasingly addicting hobby that flourished in Vegas.

Abel takes another look at the pills, examining them closely before becoming even more frustrated, cursing and closing them up tight in their container before throwing them away.

"I knew they wouldn't work."

The wave of deja vu comes back stronger than ever as he looks at the oncoming paparazzi, he had been there before, it was on the very tip of his tongue. If only he hadn't neglected what the doctor said about writing them down as soon as they finished, they could mean something.

"How has your confidence shifted since the recent interview with Khalil Henderson?"

And as if a switch had flipped inside of him, bits and pieces came back slowly, fragmented by the tough time he had deciphering the whole thing when he woke up in a cold sweat. It isn't very often when the entire night had permitted him a long enough time to reach the morning without the normal twisting and turning, waking up in a cold sweat meant he made it that far.

He shivers at the thought, returning his trembling hands to his pockets in his sweatshirt, trying to keep his stomach from kicking and the butterflies from pecking out his insides. Nearly every part of him he can feel is on fire, every pressure point flooding with gallons of sweat despite the deodorant that he put on in layers that morning.

He exits the doors of the hotel, lowering his tone so that no one in the world can possibly know what he is saying or thinking, "Must have been a bad dream."

ABOUT THE AUTHOR

Oliver Talmadge

Oliver Talmadge is a sixteen-year-old writer from Renton, Washington, where he lives with his five siblings and two parents. His passion for storytelling began in elementary school, where he discovered his love for narrative-driven projects and the creative freedom they offered. While Oliver initially focused on short stories and anthologies as achievable milestones, his writing journey soon took him beyond those early works.

When he's not writing, Oliver enjoys playing basketball, spending time with friends and family, and serving as a student leader for Renton Young Life, a global Christian organization dedicated to supporting local youth. As a member of the Lindbergh High School basketball team, many experiences from his time on the court, both real and dramatized, have found their way into his writing.

The spark to write his first novel came unexpectedly during a parent-teacher conference, where his English teacher introduced him to an after-school club that provided students with a place and resources to write a novel during November. Initially hesitant, Oliver changed his mind after his mother mentioned his interest in writing, and he decided to take on the challenge. With the support of his father and family, he completed the fifty-thousand-word manuscript by the end of the month—a story that Kitsap Publishing later decided to publish.

Oliver dreams of becoming a full-time author, continually honing his craft and sharing his stories with the world, while also working within his community through Young Life. His journey is just beginning, but his passion and dedication are already shining through.

Oliver Talmadge

anyway, there are these guys hanging about and they saw me come out of the drug house and I—"

"Stay in your car, okay?" Alex got into his car. The idea of Joe being watched by street thugs made his stomach churn.

"Okay," Joe said.

"Where are you?"

"Smith Street. Near the corner of Pahiatua Street. Can you find it?"

"Of course. Don't worry. I'll be there in ten minutes. Maybe fifteen."

"Alex? I'm sorry."

Alex rang off and explained the situation to the others, leaving out the bit about the drugs. "Do you guys want to go back to the bar? I can pick you up on my way back through."

Chris looked at him through narrowed eyes. "Think I'll come with you."

"Of course, we'll come," said Miguel. "Is your friend all right?"

"Well, I'm not drinking alone," William said. "Can't you get an Uber for this guy?"

"No," Alex said.

As they were pulling out of the car park, Chris asked quietly, "Deal gone bad?"

"It's car trouble, like I said. But you're right about why he's out there."

"Sure you want to get involved? Mig and I could go."

"I'm going," Alex said.

"Don't hit anyone."

"I won't. Things are better these days."

"*Hit* anyone?" William said from the backseat. "Good grief. How macho. I think I'm getting excited."

"I haven't hit anyone since kindergarten," Alex said.

"Can't we drop you somewhere, William?" Chris asked, turning in his seat.

"I wouldn't miss this for the world," William said.

Smith Street was grim under the orange street lights, utilitarian state housing with broken down cars and letterboxes that looked as if someone had taken to them with a baseball bat. A smashed TV and an old fridge with a gaping door sat on the grass verge, but there were no people to be seen.

Alex realised he was gripping the steering wheel as if it was trying to escape. The lemon, lime, and bitters he'd been drinking felt like acid in his stomach. Terrible scenarios kept popping into his head: Joe with a knife in his side, Joe beaten to a pulp, Joe missing entirely. He slowed to a crawl, scanning for Joe's white car with the one red door. He was still searching for the car when he saw running figures up ahead, first one, then another, peeling away from a dark huddle against a tall wooden fence.

"Stop," Chris said, but Alex had already stopped in the middle of the street. He leapt out and tore across the road. Two more figures dashed away, leaving one with his back against the fence; Joe. Alex ran to him, grabbed Joe's upper arms. The adrenaline made him rougher than he meant to be. Joe winced.

"Alex, I'm okay."

"What the hell are you doing out of the car? I told you to stay inside."

"They were rocking it. Said they'd flip it if I didn't get out. I was scared. I thought it would be better to just give them the…Alex. *Alex*! You're hurting me. Let go, okay?"

Alex made himself remember the terrified jaywalker he'd bailed up and yelled at. He didn't want Joe looking at him like that. It wasn't Joe he was angry with, it was the little wankers who'd just scarpered. Alex took his hands away from Joe's shoulders one at a time. It took every ounce of will he had, but he did it. Chris and Miguel were at his side. William was standing by the car, arms crossed as if he was already bored.

Alex turned away from Joe, breathing deep, clenching his fists. He focused on the empty fridge. The wind was strong enough to make the gaping door swing, and swing, but never quite close. Chris asked Joe questions, voice professionally calm, a little clipped. Joe answered shakily; no, he didn't know who they were, no he didn't want to call the police, no he didn't think he needed to go to hospital.

"What about your head?" Chris said.

Joe put a hand to his forehead. He looked younger than usual, even less sure of himself. "It's nothing. Really."

"They hit you?" Alex asked.

"No, but they shoved me, and I banged my head on the fence."

Chris said in his cop voice. "Sure you didn't pass out? Not even for a moment? Your vision didn't go dark?"

"No."

"No headache?"

"Maybe a bit."

Chris peered at Joe's forehead. Chris was dealing with it, making a decision. Alex longed for Kahawai Bay with a ferocity that almost swept him away. To be there, with the surf thundering on the shore, the wind rustling in the flax bushes, and the house at his back. Safe.

But it would be bloody nice to have company tonight. Chris and Miguel would go to their own bed. If sex with William was the price to pay for having a warm body in bed with him, then so be it. *Christ, just to feel someone's arms around me.* If he couldn't have Joe, it didn't really matter who the arms belonged to.

"Alex. *Alex.*" Chris stood in front of him. "Okay with you?"

Alex was uncomfortably aware that he had zoned out at a time when he should have been paying attention. "Uh, yes. Fine. Home, then?"

"Yeah." Chris gave him a long assessing look. "How about I drive?"

"I can."

"You're a bit distracted, mate," Chris said. "I had one glass of wine with dinner. And two beers. Over about four hours. I'm fine. I'll drive."

It was too much trouble to argue. And anyway, maybe Chris was right. If Alex drove and caused an accident because he wasn't concentrating properly…it was easier to acquiesce.

They got in the car. Chris and Miguel in the front. Alex and William in the back with Joe between them. William looked unimpressed. Joe kept glancing at Alex, face white in the dark car.

Alex closed his eyes, picturing the house at Kahawai Bay; the cracked concrete step at the front that was so good to sit on, the front door freshly painted the same turquoise-grey as the winter sea. The living room, with Joe's seagulls hanging on the wall above the kitchen table. Alex's photograph of the wild south coast hanging on the wall opposite. The door to the sunroom. The step down into the sunroom. The old wood, which smelled like a memory of summer. The Chesterfield, which, when he lay on it, moulded to his body like an embrace.

When the motion of the car told him that they were on the Makara Road, he opened his eyes and watched the dark hills and fields rush by. His heart had stopped pounding. He could feel Joe's thigh and shoulder pushed up against his, the warmth like sunlight. But Joe was only touching him because, in the narrow back seat, he had no choice. This whole thing must be horrible for Joe. To be forced to cosy up to someone he didn't fancy must be the final straw. Alex tried to lean away from him.

Joe's place appeared, old Blue like a ghost horse in the front paddock, dozing beside the hedge. Chris drove straight past.

"Chris, Joe's place was back there," Alex said.

"Joe's coming with us," Chris said. "Remember?"

"Oh, are you?" Alex turned to Joe in surprise. He must have missed that part of the conversation. It felt right, though. He didn't want Joe to be home alone after what had happened.

"That's a head injury," Chris said. "We've not taken him to a doctor. We're keeping an eye on him tonight. I did ask you. You said it was okay."

"Sorry." Joe didn't look up.

"No, it's fine," Alex said.

Chris parked the car outside Alex's place. Alex had left the lights on and the house glowed like a beacon in the dark, showing them the way up the garden path. They got out and took backpacks and bags out of the boot.

Alex was walking around the car to get his keys from Chris, when Miguel took his elbow.

"Alex," Miguel said quietly, and nodded his head sideways.

Joe had got out of the car, but wasn't following the others to the house. He was leaning against the car door, face in his hands.

"Headache?" Chris said.

"No." Joe's voice was muffled. He didn't take his hands away from his face.

Alex heard a stifled sob. He realised, belatedly, that not only had Joe been mugged, he'd then had to be a passenger in a car driven fast along the motorway by someone he didn't know. It was impossible not to go back and put an arm around him.

When Joe didn't shrink away, it was impossible not to put the other arm around him as well.

"We will go in," Miguel said. "Come on, carino, you have the keys. We'll make a cup of tea and explore the mansion without you, Alex. William, you can chase away the spiders."

No matter the circumstances, standing in Kahawai Bay with Joe in his arms and the sea wind icy-fresh in his face was a moment to savour. They'd made it. They were home safe. Alex murmured reassurances into Joe's hair, which smelled of cheap shampoo, and stroked Joe's back, making sure to stay in the friend zone between the shoulders. Even that little part of Joe was good to touch, even through his clothes. Alex found himself wishing Joe would stop crying so he could kiss him. But that wasn't going to happen. Alex wasn't proud of the way he'd behaved so far tonight, first grabbing Joe, hurting him, and then more or less ignoring him. Alex might be a bit fucked up, but he'd never hit on a friend who'd had a night from hell.

"Sorry," Joe said, finally, stepping back. He pulled what looked like a painting rag from his pocket and blew his nose, wiping his eyes with the sleeve of his coat.

"It's okay," Alex said, wishing he could go in for a second hug.

"It would have been all right if my stupid car had started."

"Were you so desperate for drugs?"

"No. I was just having a shit night. I thought I'd have a smoke and do some work and it would be less awful."

"Was your shoulder hurting?"

"No, it wasn't that." Joe took a deep breath. Let it out. "I've ruined your evening, haven't I? Sorry."

"Not at all. We were on our way home."

"I won't get in the way. I really am fine. I could go now if you like. I could walk home."

"Are you kidding? I don't want you to go. Chris would kill me if I let you. Why would you—oh, William? No! Don't worry about that. He just tagged along."

"But you were going to, weren't you?"

"I told him he'd be sleeping on the couch," Alex said. It was technically true. But Joe was watching him, the light from the house making bright points in his eyes. Anyway, what did it matter? Why pretend anything to Joe? "I suppose I might not have enforced that. I don't like him, but, you know; he was there."

Joe frowned, looking as annoyed as Alex had ever seen him, but all Joe said was, "Well, anyway, if I'm not going home, we should go in. I'd better face the music."

"There's nothing to face. No one's pissed at you. Chris acts like a cop because he can't help himself, but he isn't going to make trouble or tell you off. He's fine. He's a nice cop."

"William's pissed off."

"I'll drive him back to town if you like."

"You don't have to do that. Come on, let's go in before I lose my nerve. Waiting makes it worse."

"Okay, but no one's mad. I promise. It'll be fine."

Inside, they'd got the wood burner lit, and Miguel had made tea. They sat around the kitchen table drinking it. Chris gave Joe a bag of frozen peas to put on his forehead. William's mouth had taken on a discontented pinch, and he sat back from the table, affecting boredom when he wasn't glaring at Joe.

Alex felt halfway guilty; he had sort of let William think something might happen. Something might have happened if Joe hadn't rung. Joe sat hunched and unhappy over his tea, a lump the size of a quail's egg on his pale forehead, bruising beginning to darken around it. William had been given a chance to bail out, and had not taken it. Suddenly, Alex couldn't care less about William.

"I've got a story about a drug deal that went a bit unexpected," Miguel said.

"Oh, God," Chris said under his breath.

"Shut up, carino, or I'll make you tell it."

Chris groaned and shook his head in surrender.

"Right," Miguel said. "This story didn't happen to me, but it happened to someone who is not very far from here. And this person went to buy drugs at the house of someone he didn't know. This was a long time ago, you understand, when he was very young, and had no intention of joining the police. And luckily, he never got caught and so can now look very handsome for me in his uniform."

"All right, all right," Chris said, smiling.

"And this person got a proposition from the drug dealer, and because the dealer was quite hot this person said yes. And so, they did what they wanted and afterwards the dealer said, 'well, I will not charge you for the drugs because you are such a cute boy.' And this person says, 'thank you' because he is an English gentleman, you understand. And he is so charming and sweet that at the front door the dealer says, 'I'll give you a free bonus because you are so cute' and this person says 'oh, thank you, that is jolly decent of you'."

"Is that meant to be me?" Chris said. "You sound like Dick Van Dyke."

"Shut up. And so, this person is waiting by the front door for his bonus. And we are all wondering what it will be. And then, the dealer does two things: he kisses this person with something very small in his mouth, and at the same time he unzips this person's fly and reaches in and rubs Tiger Balm on his balls. And then, he pushes him outside and locks the door, and this person is walking through the dark streets with his balls blazing on fire, and then—"

Miguel paused, glancing around the table. Joe's mouth had fallen open. The frozen peas sat forgotten on the table. Even William was staring. Chris was looking at the ceiling, half smiling, half wincing.

"—then the acid trip starts to kick in."

"Yes, and I still made it home," Chris finished. "And they were the best pills I ever had."

Miguel smiled. "So, Joe, I think your night is actually not so bad, because you have not had to catch the Tube home with the bright lights and a thousand people staring, and with Tiger Balm on your balls and a trip coming up."

Joe gazed at Miguel for another second with his mouth open, then smiled, ducking his head. "No, it wasn't that bad."

Everyone laughed, even William. Even Joe.

"Well, since you've told them that, *carino*," Chris said. "I think I'll tell them about the time you had too much cocaine with royalty and took all your clothes off in Trafalgar Square."

"But it's not true!"

"It is."

"He was not royalty, but only an earl's son and a bishop."

"A *bishop*?" Joe said.

"It's true," Miguel said. "I didn't know at the time, of course, because he wasn't wearing his bishop's hat in the club. He was just a nice man who was sharing drugs with me and watching the boys dancing. But then I saw him on television a few nights later. There was such an important church service, it was televised. And he was up the front with the Archbishop of Canterbury. But I will never tell who he was because I am a gentleman too."

Outside, the wind was getting up again. Joe had taken his small sketchbook out of his pocket and was drawing quick little scribbles inspired by the stories they were trading—a bishop gyrating around a pole, a be-wigged lawyer chasing a poodle across a courtroom, a sketch of Miguel and Chris both standing with different groups of people, both looking over their shoulders, gazing into each other's eyes.

Joe gave that one to Miguel, who said, "Look Chris! Isn't this a talented picture? It's just like you, carino, except back then you were thinner. And he had more hair, Joe. We will keep it as a souvenir, and one day you will come to London and see it on our wall, maybe?"

"Maybe," Joe said, blushing.

Getting ready for sleep was awkward, because they had to make a bed up for William on the living room couch and the stony silence was bad enough. And then, Joe seemed half paralysed with embarrassment at the idea of sharing with Alex.

"I could sleep in the sunroom," Joe mumbled, staring at the ground.

"Are you kidding? It's freezing in there at night. It'd be like sleeping in a greenhouse. You wouldn't rather share my bed with William, would you?"

Joe shook his head, mute.

"Didn't think so. Come on, I'm not some jerk, you know. We're going to sleep. Except for when I wake you at six in the morning to check you're still all right."

"I am all right. I could go home," Joe said.

"Well, I wish you wouldn't, but I'll take you if that's what you really want."

There was a long pause. "I'd better stay."

"Yeah, because otherwise Chris will give you a talking to, which is really something to avoid."

"Yes."

"And I'd have a go at you, too. Come on, am I really that scary?"

"No."

"Well, then."

Joe sat on the edge of the bed and removed his old Dr. Martens, then lay down, all his clothes still on, on his side, facing the wall. Alex thought about this for a moment, then lay down fully dressed himself. He spread a blanket over them both. The heater was on, and they weren't likely to need more than that. He left the bedside light on out of some sense of propriety, and set an alarm for six a.m. because Chris thought it was a good idea to wake Joe early, to make sure he hadn't developed a headache and could still be roused.

The rain had come again, but between gusts of wind Alex could hear Chris and Miguel talking quietly in the room next door, the occasional chuckle. Living alone, he hadn't realised how thin the walls were. *Christ, I hope they don't have sex.* The idea of lying there with Joe, listening to people have sex, was too much to contemplate. Alex shifted, trying to relax, and ended up on his side, looking at the glossy chaos that was back of Joe's head. Bad idea. He twisted his neck and stared at the freshly painted ceiling instead. *I did a good job with that ceiling. I'm not going to sleep a wink tonight.*

"Alex?"

"You all right?"

"I…I wish I'd said yes. I wish I'd gone out with you tonight."

"Oh." Alex frowned at the ceiling. "So, why didn't you?"

"It's silly. Don't be angry, okay?"

It's because I'm too fucked up, isn't it? Or too old, too boring, too much of a has been. I don't drink, don't take drugs. Don't go dancing. I've never heard of Dylan Horrocks. You've never heard of Yousuf Karsh.

"Well, going to tell me?" Alex prompted.

"It's two reasons really. It's…you can be kind of intimidating, you know?"

Oh, great. Fucking awesome. I freak you out with my freaky ways. Grabbing you when you need a hug, storming off or ignoring you when you need looking after. Well, fair enough, I suppose. Sean treated you like shit. You don't need another fuck up in your life.

"…because you've been to all these amazing places and met all these glamorous people. And I thought your friends would be the same and I wouldn't know what to say to them. But the main reason was the theatre, because I can't go there. I'm too scared they'll do some awful audience participation thing and I'll have go on stage and everyone thinks it's so fun and it terrifies me. So, I just said no."

"Well…fuck. But couldn't you have told me the truth?"

"Yes. Sorry. Sean used to laugh at me when I was honest so I got out of the habit. But it wasn't fair to you. I should have known better. Because you never make fun of me."

"I don't really intimidate you, do I?"

"Not any more. But I thought your friends would be all...I don't know...scary. Talking about the theatre, and thinking comics are geeky and lame."

"Want a recap of the evening's conversation? I can tell you now it wasn't highbrow stuff about theatre. What you heard earlier was a fair sample."

Joe turned over to face him. "Do you think those stories are true? The Tiger Balm and the trip?"

"That one's true. Chris told me himself once."

"It'd make a great comic. Do you think he'd let me use it?"

It was hurting in some deep exquisite way to have Joe looking at him, face so close on the pillow. Alex's heart was pounding. Because if Joe wished he'd said yes, then what did that mean? That he would have enjoyed a night out? Or something more?

"Ask him in the morning," Alex said.

"God, I'm glad I've told you all that." Joe yawned and closed his eyes. "I felt terrible. I didn't sleep much the last few nights. It's warm in here, isn't it? Like lying in a bath."

"You Kiwis need to learn about home comforts."

"We're tough. What's a bit of frost on the blankets in the morning?"

"Watch it, I'll make you sleep in the sunroom."

Joe smiled, eyes still closed. The lump on his forehead had gone down, but the bruising was coming up. "You wouldn't. You're intimidating, but you're nice." His voice was sleepy.

"Is that possible?"

Alex thought Joe had fallen asleep, but then Joe said slowly; "Do you know that line? 'Good is better than evil, because it's nicer'?"

"I never heard it. From a comic, is it?"

"Mm." Joe had his hand open on the pillow. He was lying in almost exactly the same position as when Alex had first seen him. Relaxed, unguarded, beautiful, his breathing slowing, deepening. Only now, he wasn't just a handsome stranger. He was Joe, with all his strength and talent, and all his foibles and weaknesses too.

"Goodnight, sweetheart," Alex said. And winced.

It had just popped out. But Joe didn't flinch, or turn away, or even open his eyes. He was probably asleep.

And in that moment of exhaustion and relief, the truth seemed to well up. It needed to be said, even if Joe wasn't listening. Alex added, "I wish you'd come out tonight too. Things are always better when you're around."

Joe didn't reply, but he made a sound in his throat and curled closer, so the top of his head was nearly touching Alex's chest, his knees up against Alex's thighs. It wasn't what Alex had expected the night to bring. If this had been William, they'd both be naked by now, possibly fucking, or sucking each other off.

This was much better.

Chapter Seven

The following morning, Alex's alarm went at six. He'd just dozed off. Joe opened his eyes sleepily, said he was fine, obediently counted backwards from ten, and fell asleep again. Much later, they both woke up. The house was silent. Alex found a note from Chris on the kitchen table: '*Gone for walk. Brunch at Makara Beach café*'. Fine. Nice not to have William around, glaring at Joe.

Joe kept staring at him. Not in the usual way, but big-eyed, slightly dazed. Maybe he'd hit his head harder than he was letting on. Alex made coffee. He'd hardly slept until after the alarm went off, and then slept too deeply.

"I should go," Joe said.

"Stay."

"I don't want to see William again. It's too weird."

That meant something, but Alex felt too tired to decode it. "I'll take him into town as soon as they come back."

Alex yawned, sipped coffee, leaning against the kitchen bench, Joe next to him. Typical that now he was up and had coffee in his hand, Alex could hardly stay awake. Joe was watching him again, sideways, through his hair. He had dark smudges under his eyes, which made him look smoking hot.

"So, I'm too nice and also intimidating?" Alex said. "I know you were half asleep, but how is that possible?"

Joe grinned and ducked his head. "It's your superpower."

"Great. You're going to put me in a comic as one of your awful superheroes, aren't you?"

"Actually, if I put you in a comic, you'd be the love interest," Joe said to the floor.

Alex froze, cup halfway to his mouth. The silence stretched out for at least an hour. But suddenly he was more awake than he'd been in years. "Oh, yeah?" he managed. "Whose? Can I be yours?"

Joe turned, taking Alex's hand, lifting it to his lips. At the same time, Joe pushed his face against Alex's shoulder. Alex stood frozen, eyes wide, not sure what was happening. Was Joe making a move on him, or about to tell him, with the aid of some platonic hand-holding, that they would always be friends? Or was Joe's headache suddenly back and he was grabbing hold of something to stop himself falling?

Alex fumbled his coffee cup down on the bench behind him and put his now free hand on Joe's shoulder. Joe pressed against him, trembling, breath coming fast. Alex tried not to breathe for fear he'd disturb the equilibrium of whatever it was that was happening. His right arm was crushed between them. He could feel Joe's breath on his hand.

When he felt something wet and warm on the back of one of his fingers, at first, he couldn't identify it. Could it be a tear? Then it came again—deliberate, warm—and arousal crashed through him like a breaker. Joe was kissing his finger. No, he was *licking* it. Little, light, cat-licks. Then a kiss, feather-soft. Alex's whole body was quivering. And he was hard. Joe would surely be able to feel it.

Then Joe slid his tongue in between two of Alex's fingers. The entire world slipped out of focus. There was nothing but the sensation of the tip of Joe's tongue between his fingers. He'd had blowjobs that were less erotic. Greatly daring, for he felt one wrong step might break the spell, he bent a finger so the knuckle stood proud of the rest. Joe took it between his teeth and bit gently, breath catching, pushing their hips together at the same time. Alex pushed back and was rewarded with a nip of teeth around his knuckle and a sound like a sob. That was definitely an invitation. But Joe's head was still bent. Why would Joe kiss Alex's hand when he could kiss his mouth? But then nothing Joe did was ever quite what Alex expected.

Alex put a finger under Joe's chin to lift his head and kiss him properly—when footsteps sounded outside and the front door opened.

Joe sprang away. William. Of course, bloody William, with Chris and Miguel behind. Alex shifted position, aware that if anyone cared to look, the bulge in his pants was a dead giveaway. He was about to make some inane comment to change the subject, but he glanced at Joe, and Joe's expression made his mind go blank. Because Joe didn't seem a bit embarrassed, like someone caught making out; he looked stricken, guilty, like he'd sinned. Oh shit. What was going on?

"Well!" said William, glancing from Alex to Joe and back again. "God, can't you keep it in your pants for five minutes?"

"Shut up, William," Chris said.

"No, I won't." William whirled and poked a finger in Chris's chest. "You invited me on a double date. And then this bell-end," he jerked his thumb at Alex, "decides to pick up some little twink cock-tease—"

"Double date?" Chris said. "Where did you get that?"

William turned to Joe. Joe shrank back, averting his white, appalled face. He put his hands up in an awkward defensive position.

"You think you're shit hot, don't you?" William said, conversationally. "Coming in here with your scribbles and your swooning artist act?"

"Hey!" Alex said, sharply. "William, cut that out."

William ignored him, took a step closer to Joe. "I can see right through you. You don't even want to be here, do you? But you won't leave and let the grown-ups play, because you're a tease who—"

"Enough!" Alex shouldered in between Joe and William. "Don't speak to Joe like that."

"You're being a twat, William," Chris said, in a weary voice. "Don't be that guy."

Joe sidled out of the house, cheeks beet-red. Suddenly, William was an irrelevance.

"Shit. *Joe!*" Alex shoved his feet into his old sneakers, tucked the laces inside. "Chris, get William out of here, will you? Keys are on the table."

Joe wasn't on the step, nor on the grassy area that led to the dunes. He'd probably started for home using the back way, cutting through the scrub, up the valley. Alex jogged down to the road, then headed up, away from the sea, through a tall stand of manuka trees. And there was Joe, about twenty metres ahead of him, about to cross into open farmland.

"Joe! Wait!"

Joe turned, crossing his arms, shoulders hunched defensively, head down, staring at the thousands of tiny brown leaves that formed a fragrant carpet under the manuka. Joe had fled the house without putting his boots on. His socks were wet. *Please God, don't let him step on something sharp and take them off and—*

"Alex, I never meant—what he said. I never meant to—to—"

"Of course not! What does he know about it? Joe, sweetheart, can't you see he only said that to be a jerk?"

"Yes." Joe still wouldn't look at him.

"So, will you come back? In a minute, when he's gone? Chris is taking him to town."

"I need to tell you something." Joe unfolded his arms, but then tangled his hands together, fingernails biting into skin.

"Okay." Alex did his best to keep his voice level and encouraging. *Here it comes. And whatever it is, it's going to be bad.*

Joe spoke to his socks. "I have scars."

For a moment, Alex just stared at the top of his head. At that lovely glossy hair he always longed to touch and smooth away from Joe's face.

"Okay," Alex said, aiming for the same tone of voice as before. It came out more stunned-sounding than he would have liked.

"On my shoulder. And hip. And leg, and well, lots of places. You know, the car accident. I had compound fractures. I lost a lot of skin. They did a graft, but I got infections and uh…"

Alex remembered a dozen small incidents: Joe never rolling his sleeves up, no matter how warm the room; Joe carrying things awkwardly clutched against his chest; the way he hunched when he walked; his clumsy gait. Even last night, Joe keeping all his clothes on in bed. Alex had known all this time Joe had been in a car crash, but he'd had never thought Joe's injuries had gone beyond a broken shoulder. And that raised scar on his bottom lip that sometimes kept Alex awake at night.

Joe managed a fearful glance at him. He was biting his lip, the scar hidden under his teeth. "I look kind of…horrible. I didn't know how to tell you."

"Well, you've told me now." Alex wanted to kiss away the misery on Joe's face, to kiss him until there was nothing there but pleasure. "Can I give you a hug?"

Joe made a gesture that could have been a shrug. "You don't have to."

"But if I want to?"

Alex put his arms around him, but Joe was rigid with tension. After a moment, Joe pulled away.

"We don't have to mess around anymore. If you don't want," Joe said.

"*What?* You think I would stop wanting you because of this?"

Joe wiped his eyes roughly with the sleeve of his ragged old jumper and tried to glare. But his eyes were scared. "But it's like the hook in my foot, isn't it? It's like…weird body stuff. Scars. They're gross. They'll remind you."

Understanding jolted through Alex like an electric shock. "No. *No.* It's completely different."

"You haven't seen them."

"I don't care. It makes no difference. Scars are fine. Come here. Please?"

"But, my foot."

"Joe, you want to know what triggers me? It's two things. Three, actually, but one seems to be pretty easy to avoid. Look, your foot…the thing is…"

"You don't have to tell me."

"But I want to. I'm ready. If you don't mind hearing about it?"

"Of course, I don't mind."

"Well, the foot thing is because…Khamane—that was his name—our interpreter. The first thing I knew about the explosion was this terrible blast and then there was his foot in front of me on the ground. It—"

Alex's skin was crawling, sweat pricking out in his armpits. He took deep breaths. The manuka-scented air was pungent, medicinal. The sea whispered in the background. *Everything's okay. I'm in Kahawai Bay. With Joe. Telling him.*

"His foot was blown off. And it landed in front of me. Sole up. And now, if I see the bare sole of a foot at a certain angle…"

Alex closed his eyes, shaking his head, as if to dislodge the image that was tattooed there. He would never dislodge it, but perhaps, like a tattoo, it might one day begin to blur. He took more deep breaths. Consciously relaxing. Joe was standing, waiting. Not interrupting. Bless him.

"So that's one. And there's a certain kind of glaring light together with a certain kind of palm foliage." It was getting easier. The worst one was told. "Don't ask me to go to Hawai'i okay? Or into a greenhouse with palms in it. And then the other one is walking on loose earth. The beach is fine. Grass is fine. Even packed-down soil is fine. But a freshly dug garden or a ploughed field, I can't do it. We were on a ploughed field when it happened. Crazy, eh? The field had been cleared by a bomb disposal team. The farmer had ploughed it. The chances were a million to one of anything being there. Anyway. So, I've told you. But scars are fine. I couldn't care less about them. So, will you come here now? Because I could really use a hug."

This time Joe came, hiding his face in Alex's neck, clinging to him. Alex was trembling so hard it felt like having a fever. Or maybe it was Joe trembling. It was difficult to say.

"Alex, I'm sorry for not telling you sooner. I wanted to, I swear, but at first, I didn't think you could possibly be interested in *me*…I mean, I thought you were just being kind. And then, later, I was scared because I thought when you knew, all this," he gestured helplessly, "would stop. Dr. John said I should tell you. I knew I should."

"It's okay." Alex closed his eyes. Joe was so good to hold. Alex felt he could stand there all day, just holding him. "Ah, Joe, and I thought you weren't interested. Who's Dr. John?"

"The psychologist at the pain clinic."

"Pain clinic? You have pain?"

"You know I do."

"Yeah, I guess I do. I'm sorry too, Joe. I've been blind, haven't I?"

"No, you haven't. I don't like people making a fuss anyway. It's not so bad these days. I got new meds, just before you came. I think it's getting better, over time."

"And you've been worrying about how to tell me about these scars?"

"Yes, for weeks."

Alex heard voices in the distance, one raised higher than the others in complaint.

"So, can I check something?" Alex said, to cover the noise. A car door slammed, then another. "It doesn't bother you that I'm older?"

"Do you think I'm too young?"

"Never. But sometimes I think you might rather have someone who's a bit more fun."

"Fun? Like parties and getting drunk?" The disdain in Joe's voice was obvious.

"Well…"

"I just want to make comics and…and…" Joe's voice sank to a whisper. "…be with you."

Alex held Joe's chin so he couldn't look away. "Sure?"

Joe blushed, breath catching. "Yes."

The car engine started and they both jumped.

"Okay, but you want to wait, right? To take things slowly?" Alex asked.

"No!" Joe sounded almost angry. "I just had to tell you first."

"Oh, so, in fact, all this time you've been wanting to rip my clothes off?"

And there it was, that shy, delighted smile that made life worth living.

Joe put his face back into Alex's neck. "Yes," he whispered.

Alex smiled. "Come back to the house and tell me some more about this 'not waiting' thing."

The house was empty, and the moment they were inside Alex caught Joe around the waist and kissed him. Tenderly at first, then open-mouthed, not holding anything back. He'd wanted it for so long it was hard to believe he was allowed to. But Joe was pressing up against him, mouth soft and eager. Joe was making breathy noises, one hand in Alex's hair, pulling him close. Alex took Joe's bottom lip gently between his teeth. He could feel the raised scar with the tip of his tongue. His knees were going weak, balls aching, hands trembling. Time to move things on. He drew away.

Joe gazed at him, lips kiss-swollen, breathing hard, eyes shining like he was about to make a declaration of love. "Alex."

"Mm?"

"My socks are wet."

"I…what?"

"But should I leave them on? Because, you know, bare feet."

Alex grinned, accepting the change of pace, even revelling in it, because there was something so Joe-like about it; from passionate kisses to wet socks in a heartbeat. It was the kind of shift Joe put in his comics. But it was caring too. Joe was looking after him.

"Trust me, when we're having sex I won't be looking at your feet," Alex said.

Alex kissed him again. It still felt transgressive, like kissing a friend. But then, Joe *was* a friend. It was just that soon he'd be something more as well. "Come on, I want you in there."

"The sunroom?"

"Yeah. On that old Chesterfield. I've been wanting it since the moment I saw you there."

"But, there aren't any curtains."

With anyone else, Alex would have said 'let's do it anyway'. But this was Joe. Adorable, shy Joe who'd had to ask a psychologist how to tell Alex about his scars.

"Okay. Not in there," Alex said. "Though I think you should know I've been jerking off to the idea of fucking you on that Chesterfield."

Joe laughed against his shoulder, part disbelief, part delight.

"So, if we're not doing that, why don't you tell me what you've been wanting to do?" Alex said.

"Well, I…uh…want you to decide," Joe said.

"Don't want to tell me?"

"No, that's what I want. You to decide what happens. You to tell me what to do. I mean, if you want."

Joe blushed, staring at his feet, his hands resting lightly on Alex's hips. It *felt* as if he'd shoved his hand down the front of Alex's pants and squeezed.

Alex swallowed. "You want me to be bossy? I can do that. It works for me."

"But you can't be mean, okay?" Joe added, voice wavering. "You can't hurt me. I don't like that."

So, Sean was mean to you, probably. And hurt you. "No, okay. Got it."

Alex gave him one more kiss, chaste, on the cheek. What Alex really wanted was to strip Joe naked and fuck him into the floorboards. He suspected if that was as simple as it sounded, they'd be doing it right now. He would have liked to say, "strip for me", but that would be too much, too soon. Joe had hang-ups about these scars.

Joe was watching him, eyes wide. Tense. So, how to make it easier? Best to start off slow.

"I think we'll start with you on your knees," Alex said.

Joe knelt, gazing up at him. Alex stroked Joe's face, ran his fingertips along Joe's lips. Joe looked, already, more at ease. He could probably guess what was coming next. He was going to be right. Next time, Alex might surprise him. This time would be about a different comfort zone.

"Hands behind your back," Alex said. "Close your eyes."

Joe obeyed. Knelt there, waiting, breathing growing ragged.

"Lick your lips. And open your mouth."

It was a beautiful sight, Joe kneeling there, receptive, accepting Alex's caresses on his face. Alex could see the front of his old black pants tenting.

"God, Joe, I could not want you more."

Alex undid his own belt and fly. He cupped one hand around back of Joe's head. Joe startled at the first touch and then leant into it. With his other hand, Alex took out his dick and said, "Lick your lips again. Then open your eyes."

When Joe opened his eyes, they grew gratifyingly round.

Alex said, "Suck me. Really slow."

He suppressed a groan as Joe did as he was told. Couldn't suppress the next one as Joe drew back, then took Alex down again in one long, smooth movement.

"*Christ!*" Alex said, voice strangled. "Slower. I want to see if I can feel that scar on your lip."

He couldn't, but Joe sucking his dick with painstaking concentration couldn't have been better anyway. Joe was trembling with the effort of moving so slowly. Alex guided him with the hand on the back of his head, tugging gently at his hair when he moved too fast. But soon the temptation to grab Joe's head and thrust into his lovely mouth became too much. Joe wouldn't have minded. In fact, Alex could feel him willing it to happen. But that wasn't what Alex wanted this to be about. Not with Joe. Not when Joe still had all his clothes on.

All the same, it was difficult to pull away.

"Stop," Alex bit out.

Joe stopped. Reluctantly.

"Stand up," Alex said.

Joe stood up slowly. Now, they were getting to it. Joe knew it. They both knew.

Alex said, "Come on, sweetheart, that old sweater first. Think it'll behave itself if we leave it lying on the floor?"

Joe tried to smile, but it didn't reach his eyes. All the same, he took off his sweater. He did it clumsily, not raising his left arm. It couldn't have been more different from a sexy striptease act in a club, and it made Alex's heart race.

Underneath, Joe wore a long-sleeved, blue shirt, faded from too much washing. He looked over his shoulder. The closed door was behind him, but to his left was the long row of windows letting in the winter sun and the view of valley and hills. "Should we go to the bedroom?" Joe asked.

But somehow that felt wrong. Because Alex could sense what Joe *hadn't* said. *"So, I can hide. Because I'm ashamed."*

"Listen, Joe, you spent the morning making decisions, didn't you? What's best to say to me? Should you stay? Should you go? Should you kiss me? What if you tell me about the scars and I freak out?"

Joe was staring.

Alex said, "But now you don't have to make any more decisions for a while. Because I'm making them. I won't let anything bad happen to you."

"Okay."

"Good. Now, no more talking. Get that shirt off."

But Joe still stood there, arms at his sides. "Are you sure?" he said.

"Are you doing as I tell you?"

Joe's mouth fell open, pupils shooting wide. But then his brows knit, face falling into the same misery Alex had seen outside under the manuka trees.

"Uh…I just meant. You know, the scars. They're not very…uh…with Sean I would always leave my shirt on, because he…I…I mean, I'm glad the scars won't be a trigger for you, but…um…maybe I should leave my shirt on anyway?"

So, *this* was where Joe's fear and shame was coming from. Alex remembered Sean, calling Joe a "pity fuck". At the time, he'd thought it a slur from a fashionable young man to a less stylish one. Now, the cruelty of it took his breath away. He thought of the words Joe had used about himself: horrible, gross. Alex was willing to bet Joe had heard them first from Sean.

"Joe." Alex stepped close, heart nearly breaking. He said into Joe's ear, "Sweetheart, you're not with that dickhead. You're with *me*. And I could not want you more. Scars or no. Now take it off."

Joe unbuttoned his shirt. The old cotton looked soft as silk. He let it fall to the ground. He had a puckered red scar all the way up the underside of his left forearm. Under the shirt, he was wearing an ancient T-shirt with a flaking picture of a unicorn jumping over a rainbow.

Alex smiled. "So, you *are* gay."

"Well, I suppose I'm bi…" He broke off, puzzled. "*What?*"

Alex nodded at the T-shirt. When Joe realised what he was wearing, he smiled. It was a tremulous smile, but it was real. There was something hopeful about it. Joe was finally realising that everything was going to be okay.

Joe said, "This—"

"Uh-uh. Explain it to me later, if you like. Get it off. Actually, pants first. Leave that rainbow unicorn a moment."

The sight of Joe undoing his belt and unzipping his fly, with his face as pink as a dawn sky, and his hands trembling, was so overwhelming that Alex caught hold of the back of one of the kitchen chairs for support.

"Jesus, Joe. Do you know what you're doing to me? I'm not going to last very long at the end of this."

Joe was holding his pants up. He gave Alex a nervous look and slid them down, pushing his wet socks off as he did it. He wore greying white briefs, and his dick wasn't hard any more. A purple scar ran down the front of his left thigh, all the way from briefs to knee. The outside of his thigh was pink, the skin pitted and raw-looking. About a hand's width beneath his briefs there was a horizontal scar and an expanse of coarser skin that wasn't quite the right colour; that must be the graft. Alex couldn't help wincing internally, not out of disgust, but from a visceral sympathy. It was difficult not to imagine the accident, to think of Joe lying broken and bleeding on some horror roadside.

"Alex?" There was a plea in his voice.

"OK, maybe I'll help for a bit." He took Joe in his arms.

Joe clung to him. "Are you sure you don't mind?" he whispered.

"Sweetie, I couldn't care less." He took Joe's hand. "Does this feel like I mind?"

Joe made a circle with fingers and thumb and slipped it up and down Alex's dick, feeling its hard length. "No."

"Good. Now, stand still. I want the pleasure of taking your dick out myself."

Alex dropped to his knees and pulled Joe's briefs down. Joe's dick was beginning to plump up against his thicket of dark pubic hair. He was uncut, foreskin still loose. He was much hairier than in Alex's imagination and the difference between expectation and reality sent a pulse of excitement through his groin. Alex put his hands on Joe's narrow hips, feeling him flinch when he touched the side with the graft.

"Don't like being touched there?"

"Uh…I don't know."

You don't know? That seemed odd, but anyway. Alex tugged Joe closer and took his dick in his mouth. Joe gasped, grabbing at Alex's hair. Alex set a slow pace that soon had Joe groaning and thrusting forward. Joe had a nice dick; it was thick and strong, and as Alex lavished it with attention, it blushed as fiercely as Joe's cheeks did. But after a while, Alex tasted sweet pre-come, stopped sucking and glanced up. Joe gazed down, eyes black with arousal. Still wearing the unicorn T-shirt.

Joe's shoulder was the worst; it hurt the most, and with Sean Joe had kept his shirt on. So, Alex was going to make damn sure Joe took it off, and didn't get any more time to worry about how he looked. Alex stood and helped Joe take the T-shirt over his head. Joe's left arm didn't go as his high as the right one, so Alex took care not to force it. A big scar snaked up Joe's abdomen, more scars criss-crossed his ribs. His left pectoral muscle appeared to have had a bite taken out of it; his left nipple was a nub of scar tissue. His shoulder was stippled pink and red.

Alex kissed his mouth and said into his ear, "C'mon. Bedroom."

He could see the relief in Joe's eyes. Joe might like being told what to do, but taking all his clothes off had been enough of a challenge for today. From here on, Alex would only ask for things Joe would find easy to do.

Alex stripped his own clothes off as they went. His sweater dropped next to Joe's, his T-shirt outside the bedroom door. He toed his old sneakers off, yanked down his jeans and underwear. Joe stood by the bed while Alex closed the curtains. The chances of anyone peering in were practically nil, but Joe would be happier. Joe was holding his left hand up to his heart, unconsciously trying to hide the worst of the scars, and that ruined nipple. From the back Alex could see a great curved scar, curled around Joe's shoulder blade like a sickle moon.

"Come and kiss me," Alex said.

Joe liked that. He liked being told to lie back on the bed and spread his legs. He liked a wet finger up the ass and more head. Alex found his prostate. Joe gasped, writhing, eyes closed, clutching the bedsheets. He seemed to have forgotten about his scars. For now, anyway.

"Want me to fuck you? I have condoms," Alex said.

Joe levered himself up on one elbow. The right, of course. Alex had a split-second vision of Joe standing on the beach, as he stood so often, arms crossed over his chest. Alex had always thought it a shy, defensive posture. Now, he could see Joe had simply been cradling his left arm in his right. Because it hurt.

"No. I mean, sorry. Do you mind?" Joe said.

"Of course not."

"It's too intense. For the first time."

"Joe, you don't need a reason. 'No' is fine."

He told Joe to lie back again, got on top and fucked his mouth instead, nice and slow. Then he turned around and sucked Joe off at the same time, until Joe was squirming and bucking underneath him, cries muffled by Alex's dick. Joe exploded into his mouth like shook-up champagne, and the taste of him tipped Alex into his own climax. Pure pleasure, making him shudder and shout and clench. Pleasure spiking so sweet, because he was with Joe, who'd seen him at his worst, and wanted him anyway.

He thrust one last time, and Joe gagged and spluttered, pushing at Alex's hips. Alex pulled away.

"You okay?" Alex said, flopping down next to him.

"Uh, yeah." Joe's eyes were closed, his hair plastered to his forehead with sweat. "Sorry. You're bigger than I'm used to."

"Ah, you're sweet."

"It's true." Joe opened his eyes. He blinked. "Wow, that was amazing."

Alex smiled. He thought it had been a bit scattershot, a bit awful for Joe, having to show his scars for the first time. Next time would be much better. And one day, Joe would forget about the scars completely, the way he forgot to be shy with people he trusted.

"Just wait until I know you inside out," Alex said. "I'll make you come so hard, they'll hear you yelling in the South Island."

Joe grinned, though it was obvious he didn't quite know where to look. "I can't wait."

"You want me to keep away from that graft, eh?" Alex said.

"No, it's just that no one's ever touched me there before. Except doctors. It feels strange, because I can't feel your fingers, but I can feel the pressure of your hand deep down. But…I don't mind if you don't."

No one touched it before? It was on the tip of Alex's tongue to say, 'what about Sean?'. But he didn't want Joe thinking about that dickwad. If Sean hadn't wanted to see Joe's scars, it was all too easy to imagine him refusing to touch them as well.

Alex put his arm around Joe, and kissed the closest part of him, which happened to be his nose. Joe ran his fingers up Alex's chest, brushing a nipple. Some guys Alex had slept with had only been worth it once; the novelty had been the most erotic thing about them. With Joe, it would get better and better. One day, he'd get Joe fucking on that Chesterfield in the afternoon sun, and it would be slick and sweaty and sublime. He slid his hand down to Joe's ass.

Joe pressed his face against Alex's shoulder. "Remember when you came to art group? I went home afterwards and thought about you all night."

"Oh yeah? And I thought I put you to sleep."

"No, the opposite. Actually, I didn't just think about you." Joe squirmed, blushing, but smiling. "God, I wished I'd had the guts to go and talk to you. It made me realise I didn't want Sean very much by comparison."

"That night sounds fantastic. I'm going to have to ask for a re-enactment," Alex said.

"We already did some of it. But I never thought, in a million years, I would get to be with you for real."

"That's because you're too much of a kumara. It's obvious you're perfect for me."

"I'm not perfect." Joe's voice wobbled.

"No, you're not," Alex agreed, feeling Joe go completely still against him. "You're better than that. You're like one of those china bowls the Japanese mend with gold. Have you seen them? They were attractive enough once, but quite ordinary. They're much more beautiful for having been broken and mended. That's how I'd photograph you, if you'd ever let me. Naked, with gold streaks painted on you, looking straight at the camera. It makes the hairs on the back of my neck stand up thinking about a shot like that."

Joe lifted himself up on his right elbow. "You'd photograph me naked?"

Alex smoothed the hair away from Joe's eyes. "I've wanted to photograph you since the moment I saw you. Because you're gorgeous. Nothing's changed."

"Naked?"

"We could try with clothes on first if you prefer."

A car door slammed right outside. Then another; Chris and Miguel.

Joe's eyes widened. "I left my clothes on the living room floor."

"I left some of mine. I think they can handle it."

"But the unicorn T-shirt! It was a present from my mum."

Alex started to laugh and couldn't stop. Joe joined in. And around them the old house creaked, as if it too was sharing the joke, and the voices of friends were at the door.

Epilogue: two months later

Out Loud

Joe woke to a kiss on the back of his neck and the sound of surf. He was at Alex's place in Kahawai Bay, in Alex's warm wide bed. Joe rolled onto his back. Alex was leaning over him, a dark outline against grey dawn light.

Happiness swelled in Joe's chest. *Now. Tell him now. Just say it. Whisper in his ear.*

Joe reached up to pull him closer and got a handful of woollen coat. Of course, Alex was working. Early start. He'd mentioned it last night.

Alex sat on the edge of the bed and kissed him, soft, close-mouthed. "Sorry, didn't mean to wake you."

"Alex—" *I love you.*

"Hey! No. Don't start with that tone of voice. I know where that leads and I have to go."

"Okay." Joe grinned, in spite of himself. Now wasn't the time for declarations. He switched to a formal, stilted voice, "Goodbye, Alex. I hope you have a good day."

"Mm, slightly robotic. Much better. See you later? Back here?"

"Yeah, five o'clock. I've got work today."

Joe stretched, cautiously, not letting go of Alex's coat. Nothing hurt much, not even his shoulder. There was only that stiffness he was starting to trust in and to think of as normal. The warmer spring weather—and being at Alex's well-heated house so often—was making a bigger difference than he'd expected. *I'll say it the moment I get back from work. I'll walk through the door and tell him: I love you.*

"Aren't you meeting someone after work? To talk comics?" Alex asked.

"Oh. Oliver. I forgot."

"Okay." Alex took Joe's chin, turned his head and kissed the side of his neck, teeth nipping the skin. The sensation shot all the way down to Joe's cock, which twitched. His breath caught.

"Don't forget I'll be waiting for you," Alex said.

Joe could hear the smile in his voice. And the promise.

"I won't," Joe said. *Because I'll be thinking about you all day.* "I'll be back around six thirty, okay?"

"Great. Bye, sweetheart."

Alex's fingertips lingered in the newly trimmed hair behind Joe's ear, eliciting another pleasurable shiver. Then Alex stood up. Joe listened to the creaks as he crossed the living room floor, the quiet sounds as he gathered together about a hundred pieces of camera equipment, the front door opening to let in the roar of the sea, and closing. Alex's car engine starting, and receding along the gravel road.

Sweetheart.

Joes toes curled with delight. It was two months since Alex had first called him that. Two months since Joe had told Alex his secret. Joe had expected everything to be over, but instead, the opposite had happened. Alex had led him into this room, already naked, clothes in a pile on the living room floor. Two months since they'd become lovers.

Joe still couldn't quite believe it was true.

The first time he'd seen Alex at art group had felt a bit like the car crash. Without the nightmare element, but with the same sense of unreality, the same 'oh, God, is this really happening?' Because men as gorgeous as Alex didn't usually turn up in Edith's living room, smouldering at Joe while he tried not to die of blushing.

And now, Joe was waking up in Alex's bed.

Alex called him 'sweetheart'.

Alex read his comics and laughed in all the right places.

Alex didn't seem to care that Joe was like a cobbled together Frankenstein's monster from the neck down. Alex didn't seem to notice the scars, except to be careful of them. He said things like 'you're gorgeous' and apparently meant it. And the sex was fantastic. Joe had *known* Alex would be dynamite in bed, and he was.

With Blessing, sex had been good, but not very exciting because at first Joe had been too young to know what he wanted and then, once he'd worked it out, too shy to tell her. Sex with Sean had been hot in a way, but it had felt like a public affair because Sean told his friends everything. Joe knew some people would have laughed along, but he never could. And when he blushed and protested, Sean teased him about that too, and the constant minor embarrassments began to feel like a series of slaps to the face. Joe could never relax in bed with Sean, because whatever he did might become a snide joke the following evening.

Alex understood that some things were for him and him alone. He never made fun of Joe afterwards. He let private things *be* private. By now, Alex had only to *look* at Joe in a certain way and Joe's inner critic was silenced by lust in a way that was almost alarming. Of course, it wasn't just sex. Alex was everything Joe had dreamed he'd be: clever, kind, cultured, funny. He was also everything Joe wasn't: well-travelled, self-confident, sexually experienced, good at public speaking. Hell, Alex could even *talk to strangers*.

Yes, Joe was in love all right. But what about Alex? Was the relationship as good for him? He seemed happy. Mostly. He didn't act like Joe was just one more guy. Alex hadn't said 'I love you', but then neither had Joe. Although, Joe had *almost* said it.

A couple of weeks ago, Joe had arrived at Alex's place one evening to find him sitting on the old sofa in the sun room, hands over his face.

"Hey," Joe had said softly, pausing in the open doorway. Seagulls were calling, high and harsh. The setting sun was streaming in, making everything glow.

"Hey," Alex said. It came out part sigh. Fed up. Not inviting.

It was on the tip of Joe's tongue to ask, "Are you okay?" but it was clear Alex wasn't. Either Joe had done something heinous without realising or something had triggered Alex's post-traumatic stress disorder. Probably the latter. Joe settled for, "Did something happen?"

Alex took his hands away from his face, but didn't look up. "No. Just more boring shit."

"Oh. Okay."

Joe could guess what that meant. Alex had had therapy, but from time to time he still had flashbacks. Or bad days. Joe sat next to him on the sofa and sifted through a number of things he could say, but they all felt wrong. The sea wind buffeted the old house. Outside, the long grasses hissed and the surf was a muted thunder.

Eventually, Alex said, "I had that job today—photos for the theatre company." His tone was reluctant, as though he might stop telling the story at any moment. "At the last minute they wanted to go to the Botanic Garden. They're doing *A Midsummer Night's Dream* so they wanted some woodland shots. Fine, right? But when we got there…" Alex dragged his hand down his face. "It's November, so the spring flowers are over and there were these empty, dug-over garden beds everywhere. Just like the ploughed field we were on when it happened. It's not like I had to walk on them, but they were all around and it…it just fucking blind-sided me. I was sweating and shaking…and…and everything's so great and then that happens. I had to delay everyone while I got my head together and then I did a bad job. I can't bring myself to look at the shots. And just…fuck…this will *never* be over. You know? And I am so fucking tired of it."

"I know. It sucks. I'm sorry." Joe put an arm around his shoulders.

Alex let out a deep breath. Then another one. But the tension in his shoulders didn't lessen. "Enough from me. How was your day?"

"It was okay," Joe said slowly.

There was something Alex wasn't saying, but he was trying to change the subject. Perhaps he wanted to be distracted.

Joe said, "I drew beetles for those conservation pamphlets. I did a nice huhu bug. And a tiger beetle."

"Uh huh." Alex was sitting hunched forward, forearms resting on his knees. He glanced at Joe, expression unreadable. "Look, I'm not going to be any kind of company this evening."

"That doesn't matter."

"Why don't you head home?" Alex stood up, leaving Joe alone on the sofa.

"Do you want me to?" Joe asked.

Alex sighed, a sound without hope. "I don't know, Joe. Do what you like."

Alex didn't look around. He walked away, through the living room. Joe heard the bedroom door open and close, and then silence.

Joe sat in the red-gold light, perched on the edge of the sofa. The sun room was usually one of those magical places where it was impossible to imagine anything bad happening. And now this. He'd been dying to see Alex all day. He'd been hoping Alex might be dying to see him.

Did Alex want him to go? But Alex had said 'do what you like'. Joe wanted to stay—in case Alex changed his mind and wanted him.

Joe took out his sketch book and tried to draw the view through the sun room windows: the wind-tossed flax, the sea, and the jumbled rocks of the northern headland.

But the sketches were lifeless and Joe wasted page after page. Alex would be lying on the bed feeling awful. Or maybe sitting on the floor, forehead on his knees. Joe had seen him sitting like that once before. But that time Alex had stood up when Joe arrived and offered him tea and seemed happy to see him.

Joe turned to a fresh page and began to draw a comic. He drew a picture of himself— all skinny wrists and bony knees—sitting on the old sofa, brows furrowed, eyes anxious. In the next panel he drew himself again, same expression, same position—only now a Joe-shaped outline was leaving his body like a ghost. The outline was transparent, but it had a heart inside it from which lines radiated bright and bold. The outline drifted past the kitchen and through the living room. It slid under Alex's bedroom door.

In the final panel, it curled its empty arms around Alex where he sat slumped against the wall in his bedroom.

You can't feel them. Maybe you don't want them. But they're there.

Joe studied the comic, strengthened a few lines, added shading. Was it dumb? Sometimes simple ideas were strong, sometimes they were cheesy, but Joe meant every line of this one. He'd left a comic for Alex once before and that had worked out okay. Alex had liked it. It had cheered him up.

Joe tore the comic out of the sketchbook, crossed the creaky boards of the living room, knelt, and slipped the paper under the bedroom door. Then he stayed where he was, kneeling on the floor, unsure what to do next. Maybe *now* he should go home. The comic said what he wanted to say. Alex could have some space and come and find him whenever he was ready.

But the bedroom door opened. Alex stood looking down at him, the comic in one hand. He looked tired, and not happy, but he didn't look angry. Hope flared in Joe's chest.

"Joe." Alex ran his free hand through his hair, as if he didn't quite know what to do. Then Alex was sitting down next to him, holding him close. It was like in the final panel of Joe's comic, except their positions were reversed, as if Alex were comforting him.

"Oh, Joe," Alex said, into Joe's hair.

"I'll go if you want some space. I won't be offended."

"I don't want you to go. I *never* want you to go. I feel guilty for laying my shit on you and bringing you down."

"You don't bring me down," Joe said.

"No, I'm a laugh riot. Your day got way better when you came over here."

Joe lent into him, resting his head on Alex's shoulder. "It's better *now*."

Alex half-laughed, a rueful huff of breath in Joe's ear. "What did I do to deserve you?"

"You laugh at my jokes? You like comics?"

"I like *your* comics." Alex pulled him a little closer. "Joe, you could probably have anyone you like. You'll realise that soon, I think. I'll understand, you know, if one day you decide you've had enough of me. I don't want to hold you back. You get that, right? Christ, you're twenty-six! You might want to travel. You might want a family—children, all that. I want you to be happy, not worrying about me and having to deal with my bullshit."

"I don't want children. Blessing and I used to argue about that all the time."

"Well, you might want something else. I want you to know I'll understand if you decide to move on."

"When I was with Blessing I felt guilty—at the end anyway—because we wanted such different things. And when I was with Sean I felt like everything about me was wrong or not good enough. But when I'm with you, I just feel happy. You never bring me down. I know you're having a bad day. I'm not happy about *that*, but it's just a bad day, isn't it? It's not who you are. I want to be with *you*."

Alex shifted his left arm, giving Joe a more comfortable angle to lean at. How did Alex do that? How did he know how to make their bodies fit together in a way that always felt so right?

Alex said, "I used to think I was the luckiest man alive, and then I doubted that for a long time. But now I know it's true. You're the sweetest boy in the world and somehow you've ended up with me. How did I get so lucky?"

"It's not luck. It's because you manage to overlook all the terrible things about me. I don't know how you do it, but I'm not complaining."

"What terrible things?" Alex pulled back so they could see each other's faces.

Joe relaxed a little more. Alex was looking him in the eye.

"I'm not listing them," Joe said. "There might be some you haven't noticed."

"I guess there is your tendency to bring me flowers—which is *very* gay and absolutely repulsive."

"You see, I knew you hated that."

"And your other idea of a romantic gift is a dead fish."

"At least I make sure they're dead before I give them to you," Joe said, with exaggerated dignity.

Alex actually smiled. "I used to think the fish was less sweet than the flowers, until I realised you always fillet the fish for me. You don't gut fish for anyone else. Other people get given them whole and have to do their own dirty work."

"That's because you don't know how, you city slicker. Everyone else around here could gut a fish with their eyes closed, but you have no idea. And Mrs. Rakete gives me the flowers from her garden because I mow her lawn. I told her I like to draw flowers, which I do sometimes. And then I bring them to you. They look nice on your kitchen table."

"If you can't see how that story makes you even more adorable there's no hope for you," Alex said.

Joe grinned. Alex was smiling at him. It wasn't a big smile, but it was there in his eyes. He looked exhausted, but they were together. Alex wanted him; the day was golden again.

Comics were *always* a good idea.

Joe stretched again and sat up in bed. Out of the corner of his eye he could see the comic he'd drawn that day. Alex had tacked it to the wall above his bedside table.

I should have told him that day. I've been thinking it for weeks. Why can't I be the kind of person who just says things?

It's just…

What if he doesn't say it back?

Joe had a shower, using Alex's expensive shower gel. It had a fresh, citrusy scent that would make Joe smell a little like him all day. He shaved, towel-dried his hair and combed it with his fingers. It felt strange to not have hair falling in his eyes all the time. The way the air touched the back of his neck was still a surprise.

Bella's girlfriend, Emmi, had cut it last weekend, after lunch at Alex's place. Joe usually hated having his hair cut because the person doing it so often wanted to talk. Small-talk too, which Joe was terrible at: things like the weather and rugby and politics and celebrities he'd never heard of. It was different with Emmi. She took him outside onto the concrete step at the front of Alex's house and began to cut his hair in the spring sunshine. The dark feathery clippings drifted off to catch in the flax bushes. She didn't talk. She hummed a little under her breath. It was clear Joe wasn't expected to say anything. Alex and Bella followed them outside to watch, Bella carrying the mirror from the bathroom.

When Emmi stepped away, Joe hardly recognised himself. He glanced at Alex, who had stopped smiling and was staring at him.

"Is it okay?" Joe asked.

"Gorgeous."

"You should keep it like this," Emmi said to Joe. "I'll do you a deal, okay? You draw Bella for me, but as a cat. Got it? Then I cut your hair forever."

Bella spluttered something and went scarlet.

"Okay." Joe grinned. Alex liked it, so that was fine. He liked it himself. He felt lighter, as if Emmi had cut away more than just hair.

Joe finished combing his damp hair with his fingers. He was getting dressed in Alex's bedroom when he noticed a streak of something white down the front of his old blue shirt. It was probably pasta sauce, but it looked like dried come. He scraped it with a fingernail and made it worse. He could get a clean shirt at home, but Alex often lent him clothes and Joe loved borrowing them. Wearing a shirt of Alex's was proof, a tangible reminder that Alex was real. Also, Alex's clothes were *nice*. Everything was high quality, natural fibres: cotton, linen, cashmere, silk. Things that felt good against Joe's skin.

Joe chose a long-sleeved shirt in a creamy unbleached cotton/silk blend. It was so soft, and he remembered Alex wearing it around the house. The shirt settled around Joe like a caress. It was a bit loose, but all Alex's clothes were big on Joe. Nothing chafed.

He drove the short distance home through the bright morning to check on Blue. The old white horse was growing fat on spring grass and had bidibids all through his mane. Joe picked the seeds out, pushing Blue's nose away from time-to-time so Blue wouldn't slobber all over Alex's nice shirt.

Joe had an idea for a comic coming. He tossed bidibids into the hedge and thought about panels and lines. The black lines between panels were spaces in time. They were bits cut out of the action, but sometimes what happened there was as important as the main story. Because those moments counted too. Those were the times when someone sat with you in silence or said something mundane about dirty dishes. They were moments when nothing happened, but somehow, when examined all together, they made a pattern that was revelatory. Why did the way Alex park his car or button his shirt make Joe love him more? Joe wasn't sure, but he could imagine the comic – the panels getting smaller and smaller, the bigger picture that lay underneath becoming clear.

Joe drove to work and spent the day selling canvas and graphite blocks, pastels and drafting paper. It was a good day. Not too busy. Being on his feet all day made his shoulder ache, but today he got to sit down between customers.

At four o'clock, he closed the shop and walked to the café where he was meeting Oliver. It was a new place: polished wooden floors, comfortable-looking booths, the walls decorated with old-fashioned pictures of duchesses waving fans— only someone had given the duchesses tattoos and nose-rings. Joe got a flat white and sat down. At the same time, someone sat opposite. Joe looked up, expecting Oliver, and found Sean lounging there, all blue eyes and smiles. Joe froze.

"Hi," Sean said. "Cute haircut."

"Thanks," Joe said automatically. "Uh…Sean, I'm meeting someone, so…"

"Who? Not that old guy? Bryan Adams?"

"He's not…it's none of your business," Joe said, trying to sound off-hand. His shoulder twinged. He took a deep breath, tried to relax.

"Jesus, settle down. I'm only being friendly."

"Great. You've been friendly. Can you go now?"

"No, I can't." Sean smiled. "I work here. I get off soon. Got your car? You could give me a ride home if you were feeling nice."

"Why would I do that? I'm meeting Oliver."

"Oh, God, the comics nerd? Although, that doesn't narrow it down much, does it? Wait a minute—he's the 'mum caught me wanking' one, isn't he? Jesus, Joe. Come home with me instead."

"Sean!" A woman called from behind the counter.

"You have to go," Joe said.

"Yeah." Sean looked over his shoulder, yelled, "Just a sec!" then added, to Joe, "Text him and cancel. You know you want to."

"No way."

Sean leant across the table. "You pissed me off last time, but I forgive you because that haircut makes you look like you stepped out of Brideshead Revisited. You look different all round actually."

"Do I?" Joe asked, in spite of himself.

"Yeah. You look hot. What are you doing? Yoga, or Prozac, or something?"

"No."

It's Alex, of course. It's because I'm happy. But he wasn't going to talk to Sean about Alex.

"I was always hassling you to get a haircut and wear decent clothes. You never listened to me, did you?" Sean said.

There was genuine hurt in Sean's blue eyes. Joe shrugged, not knowing what to say. It was true that Sean had always been on at him to smarten himself up, to take some pride in himself. It was also true that Joe had clung to his crappy old snowflake jumper partly to annoy Sean.

It hadn't started out that way. Joe had worn the jumper because it was the warmest thing he owned and it helped against the aches that plagued him in cold weather. But Sean had made such a fuss about it that Joe had begun to wear it more out of contrariness. Perhaps it had been petty, but that was Sean; he brought out the worst in Joe.

Sean said, "I don't see how it was so hard to buy clothes that aren't *hideous*, and get a haircut from time to time. You seem to have managed it now."

"A friend cut it." Joe ran his fingers through his hair.

Once Emmi had finished cutting it, and she and Bella had gone, Alex had grabbed Joe's hand and led him straight to the bedroom. Alex had kissed Joe's exposed neck and ears, and stroked the short hair on the back of his head. Then Alex had stripped him naked, and kissed him some more. Finally, when Joe was whimpering with need, Alex had fucked him, from behind, teeth on the bare nape of Joe's neck.

It had been so good they'd done it twice. The second time had been slower, more languorous, and just before he came, Alex had whispered Joe's name.

I should have told him then. I love you. It would have been so easy to say.

"Joe! Jophiel! Wake up!" Sean waved a hand in his face. "Come on, Joe, come home with me. I'm feeling *very* bossy. You'll love it."

"I don't want to. I wouldn't come with you anyway, because I'm meeting a friend, but if that's not enough for you: I'm seeing someone. I'm in a relationship."

"I knew it! It's that old guy, isn't it? It's the daddy thing." Sean sat back. "Oh well, I'll call you in a month, eh? Those things never last. He'll get bored, Jophiel. I bet you don't know anything about his old-person crap. I bet he likes jazz. Oh, God, how fucking tragic."

"*Sean!*" The woman behind the counter called again."

"Bye, Sean. Don't call me. I'll be blocking you anyway."

"Well, fine. Last time I try to be nice to you. I hope you like geriatrics wards. Hope you like incontinence pads, and zimmer frames, and…and fucking *prunes*."

And with that, Sean was gone to get a hissed bollocking from the woman at the counter. Joe left his coffee untouched and went outside to wait for Oliver. They'd go somewhere else instead.

Joe drove out of town, shoulders tense, a headache coming on. Oliver had been in a bad mood—worried about his job, having trouble with his girlfriend, down on his comics. Not that Joe minded talking about stuff like that—that was what friends were for. No, Oliver wasn't the problem.

Alex wouldn't get bored of him, would he? They always seemed to find plenty to talk about. But it was true that Joe didn't know much about photography—although he was learning—and he'd never heard of most of the music Alex played. Nor visited any of the countries Alex had been to. And when Alex went running, he always had to go alone, because Joe couldn't run. Not anymore. Would Alex have preferred someone he could go running with? Someone lithe and fit and laughing? Someone who never worried about anything?

Joe pulled over and turned the ignition off with a shaking hand. This was bullshit. And he *wasn't* going to take it home to Alex. He was only worrying about it because Sean had put the idea in his head. If he let it, it would circle around until it paralyzed him and he'd be silent and awkward and never be able to tell Alex: 'I love you'.

In case Alex didn't say it back.

But he would. Joe knew it.

Probably.

Joe took slow, deep breaths, hands on the wheel, forehead resting on his knuckles.

What did Sean know? He knew nothing. He knew *nothing* about Alex and how he and Joe were together.

In Kahawai Bay, Alex would be waiting. Not in a finger-drumming 'you're late' kind of way, but in a pleasant 'I'm expecting you' way. Alex was easy-going about time. He never fussed if people were a bit late. He'd be working through the photographs he'd taken that day, weeding out any unsuccessful shots, editing the rest, and putting them in order if the client had requested it.

But the moment Joe came through the door, Alex would get up, smiling. He would hold Joe close—as if to have Joe in his arms was the most important thing in the world. And they would kiss, and the kiss might deepen and they might go to the bedroom. Or the kiss might turn affectionate and one of them would discover he had something to say. They might talk, or cook, or walk down to the beach. And whatever they did would feel right and natural and easy, and Joe wouldn't feel like a freak who never knew what to say and who liked the wrong things. He would feel like himself, only better.

Joe started the car, checked his mirrors and blind spot twice. To be alone with Alex. That was all he wanted. He pulled out into a gap in the traffic and was soon turning onto the Makara Road. He negotiated the sharp, familiar turns, past steep fields of gorse and sheep. He passed his own place with Blue grazing out the front, and turned left, heading south along the gravel road that led to Kahawai Bay. The hills rose high, blotting out the sun and cell-phone coverage. And then there was the sea, with white surf and menacing dark patches. And there was Alex's place, perched on the far hillside, nestled amongst the flax and the remains of Mrs. Addison's salt-bitten roses.

There was an old red Toyota Corolla parked next to Alex's shiny new model Mini Cooper. Joe pulled up next to it and got out of his car. The air was hot. The sea wind had dropped and a chorus of cicadas came from the stand of manuka trees up the valley. He glared at the Toyota. He didn't recognise it, but it was parked too close to Alex's house to look as if it belonged to beach visitors. Alex appeared, waiting for him on the concrete step at the front of the house. At least he seemed to be alone.

"Hi," Joe said, walking up the garden path. "Whose car is that?"

"Hey."

Alex gave him a quick kiss. He wore jeans and a pale blue shirt with the sleeves rolled up to his biceps. He looked so *good,* so handsome, arms tanned and strong-looking. Joe's brain momentarily shut down. Later, those arms would be wrapped around him, or braced above him.

"Nice shirt," Alex added, touching Joe's shoulder.

"Thanks. The car?"

"We've got visitors. They're for you, really. They wanted to surprise you, but they've gone down to the beach because the kids have been cooped up in the car all day and couldn't wait any longer. I said I'd wait for you."

Joe frowned. A surprise visit, with kids, in an old car. He glanced down at it. A car with a crystal hanging from the rearview mirror. A car with wooden beads on the dashboard and a pale orange muslin scarf that was just the kind of thing—

"Oh, shit, my mum's here, isn't she?" Joe said, breaking out in a cold sweat.

Joe loved his mother, but she was an acquired taste. Sean had met her once by mistake and treated her with a condescending scorn that had made Joe cringe inside. Mum had responded by getting extra cosmic and telling Sean that he had a spirit watching over him whether he knew it or not. Alex was polite to everyone, but he did prefer rational thinking and had no time for crystals and ley lines. Joe's incipient headache, which had almost gone away, pulsed through his left temple.

"Uh huh," Alex said. "And Blessing. Very pretty, isn't she, your ex? And—" Alex ticked off his fingers, "—Summer, Thor and Kahurangi, who are kids. And Sarah and Jake, who are dogs."

"Why are they at your place?" Joe asked.

"Okay, so I guess you haven't mentioned me to them?"

"No, I…no."

Was Alex hurt? Should Joe have told Mum about him by now? The thing was that being with Alex was so big, so important, so all-encompassing, that telling other people hadn't seemed right yet. Joe had wanted to be sure it was real before he started doing that.

Alex said, "Okay. So, they went to your place first, but you weren't there, so they drove to Makara Beach to buy ice-cream, and someone in the café told them if you weren't home you might be here, so here they are."

Joe could almost see them; a car-load of kids and dogs emptying out, Mum laughing too loud and hugging people she didn't know, Blessing doing cartwheels and handsprings, all intruding on Alex's privacy and quiet.

"Oh, God, Alex, I'm sorry."

"Are you?" Alex was looking at him closely. "Well, I didn't tell them anything. As far as they know, we're just friends."

"I don't mean that! I haven't *not* told Mum about you. I just haven't told her. You could have said anything."

"Could I?"

"Of course. Mum's fine about whatever I do. Girlfriends. Boyfriends. Whatever."

"Whatever?" Alex cocked his head. "Is that what I am?"

"No! You're…"

All the words Joe knew were inadequate. What *should* he call Alex? Boyfriend? Lover? The Most Amazing Thing to Ever Happen to Me? What did Alex want to be?

"Your boyfriend?" Alex asked. He was smiling, but his eyes were serious. "Although, I'm hardly a boy."

"I can't say 'man friend'. I'd have to die."

"Partner?" Alex said.

Joe blinked. He hadn't thought of it. Maybe because it was a word he wouldn't have dared to use, because it sounded so permanent, so committed. To him, at least. Maybe, to Alex, it meant something else. Joe hadn't thought about the future too much, in case he jinxed something, or tempted fate. But 'partner' wasn't a word people used for a fleeting thing, was it?

"Partner," he repeated.

"Okay. Sounds good. Hey, are you all right? This is a nice thing, eh? You get to see your mum. You get on with her, don't you? And Blessing, who seems lovely. You two are friends now, right?"

"Yes, but don't you mind a pack of strangers turning up at your door?"

"They're hardly strangers." Alex grinned. "I've met your mum before."

"*What*? Where?"

"Well, our spirits have met before. On another plane. She recognised me straight away."

"Oh, God."

"Joe, I like her. She gave me a big hug, and told me she could tell I'd suffered, but that my future was clear. She can tell from my aura."

"Alex, look—"

"I told her she was quite right and that I have post-traumatic stress disorder. They'd been here for about two minutes when I told them that."

"Oh, God. Alex, look, Mum asks people all kinds of things. Just tell her it's private."

"Joe, listen. Do you know one of the worst things about having PTSD? It's that it's invisible. And yet it's hard to tell people because it's not the sort of thing that comes up in casual conversation. It's not the sort of thing you can say to most people after two minutes acquaintance. But I could tell your mother and Blessing, couldn't I? Because they work on a different level to most people. And they're not scared, or embarrassed. They don't think it's weird or intense. They think it's normal that I would tell them that. Do you know how amazing that is? So, stop worrying. I *like* them – even if your mother is younger than me, which I have to admit is slightly freaking me out. Anyway, I've invited them to stay the night."

"No, she's not younger than you. She's—" Joe did the maths and said reluctantly, "Er…forty-five."

"Uh huh? Same as me, eh? Well, that's all right then. I can stop worrying about that, can't I?"

Joe found himself smiling. But it *was* funny, because it was so unimportant. Alex's eyes had sparks dancing in them. He didn't care either. Not really.

Alex said, "I've also found out they're not vegetarian, but they won't eat anything battery-farmed and they don't believe in processed foods, although when it comes to ice-cream for children they make an exception. Also, they'd like to get up early tomorrow because they have a wedding to go to over in the Wairarapa. It's at midday and we're invited to the party afterwards. There's no dress code, except everyone should wear flowers, and Blessing is a dab hand at garlands. Want to go?"

"Do you?"

"I want to see you in a garland, that's for sure. Maybe we could get flowers from Mrs. Rakete?"

"Maybe. Who are the kids? Summer is Blessing's, but the others? Will *more* people be coming? Will anyone's parents be arriving?"

"Not that they mentioned. Thor and Kahurangi are just friends, I guess, who came along for the trip. Kahurangi told me in confidence that if we come to the wedding she can show me her party trick. But she won't say what it is."

"It might be fire-poi" Joe said, absently.

He was still wondering what the word 'partner' meant to Alex. Maybe he should just ask. His stomach lurched and his heart started pounding. Was now the time to say it?

"Fire-poi? I doubt it. She's only about seven," Alex said.

"Alex, if I tell them you're my partner—that's important. It means something, doesn't it? It does to me because I..." Joe's breath had all run out. He reached for Alex's hand and stood looking at it for a moment. Alex was holding onto him, a strong, gentle grasp. Joe managed to look up, into Alex's eyes. "I...love you. So much."

"Come in here a moment?" Alex pulled him inside and kissed him, slow and thorough. He took Joe's face in his hands. "Joe, I've been wanting to tell you for weeks that I love you. I didn't want to come on too strong when we've just got together. But it's true. I've loved you since the day you sat on that concrete step out there and told me about Fox's glacier mint wrappers, and put that comic under my front door."

Fireworks were bursting in Joe's belly. He was burning with joy. He stood there, alight, Alex's hands on either side of his face.

"I've wanted to tell you for weeks as well," Joe said.

Alex smiled and brought their foreheads together. "You know, I am delighted to meet your family, but I wish they weren't here so I could take you to bed right now."

Joe squirmed, involuntarily. "Me too."

Alex let him go. "Well, I will get my hands on you later. I promise."

"But we can't...you know...do it, if my mother is in the next room. It's not like when Chris and Miguel were staying. And even that was a bit weird."

"Ha, listening to you trying to be quiet was *almost* more of a turn-on than listening to you normally. But, anyway, I have a plan. So, come on, let's go down to the beach and find everyone, but I want you to know we're not missing out on *anything* tonight."

They went down to the beach. Alex might have walked, but Joe floated there on a golden cloud. Joe introduced Alex properly. Mum hugged them both, and said, to Alex, "I knew there was something special about you." Blessing hugged them both too.

Alex made dinner. Alex and Mum turned out to have been to some of the same places in Morocco and India and Thailand. They talked about cities Joe had never heard of and looked at some of Alex's photos from those places. They discussed the benefits of ecstasy as a treatment for PTSD and dance parties as a form of transcendental meditation. The kids and dogs invented a game dodging around all the flax bushes in the garden and Joe sat with Blessing on the concrete step, half watching the kids, half listening to Alex and Mum talk.

Joe couldn't help remembering the first time he'd seen Alex at Edith's place—how unobtainable he'd seemed, the hot-shot photographer from London. How talented and stylish and sophisticated. How absolutely out of Joe's league. And now—Joe glanced over his shoulder.

Alex was standing by the kitchen bench, a knife in his hand, cut lemons in front of him. He was listening to something Mum was saying, smiling. He noticed Joe looking at him and his expression changed for a moment into something far more intimate.

I love you.

I love you, too.

Joe looked away, cheeks growing hot.

"Joe?" Blessing said. The sea breeze had sprung up again and her long blonde hair blew towards him. It was so fine that a few strands kept floating straight up, as if she was about to start ascending. Her eyes were pale, pale blue, clear as the evening sky.

"You're really in love, aren't you?" she said, quietly.

"Is it that obvious?"

"Yeah, it's glowing out of you. I'm not big into auras like your Mum, but you've got one at the moment."

"Well, okay."

"Don't worry, it's just as obvious with him. When we got here, I asked about that picture of the seagulls on the wall because I could tell you'd done it. I thought you two had something going on because he lights up when he talks about you."

"Really?"

"Yeah, he thinks you're wonderful. Which you are. You won't have to pretend, with him."

"Pretend what?" Joe said, feeling exposed. He hoped she wasn't talking about sex, although it was true he didn't have to pretend in bed with Alex.

"Anything. You could tell him anything. You could trust him with your life."

"Oh, yes. Of course."

Later, when Mum was talking about going to Joe's house to sleep, leaving Blessing and the kids at Alex's, Alex said he wouldn't hear of it. He said it was an old Canadian custom to give up one's own bed to one's guests. He added that he'd already changed the sheets, and would be devastated if Joe's Mum didn't take him up on his offer.

"Joe and I will go to his place. He should check on Blue, anyway," Alex said.

"Can I come?" Summer asked. "I can help. I know lots about horses. I could sleep on Joe's sofa. I've done it before."

"You're staying here," Blessing said.

"But I want to see Blue!"

"In the morning, eh Joe?" Blessing said.

"In the morning, Joe and I will come back and make breakfast," Alex said. "Maybe Joe could bring Blue along with us?"

Alex and Joe said good-night and began walking to Joe's place using the back way, past the manuka, through farmland. The night was scented with dried grasses and crickets sang at their feet. It was about nine-thirty. There was still an amber streak of light to the west, and, in the east, a half-moon bright as a pipi shell. It was too dark to see much, but Joe knew the way.

"This is your cunning plan?" Joe said. "That we go to my place? Blessing guessed why we were leaving. Mum, too."

"I never said it'd be cunning. Anyway, so what? I hope you realise your mother's slept with more guys than I have."

"Alex, don't."

"Ha. She's one of the least embarrassed people I've ever met, and you're so sweet you blush if I mention sex when we're alone. Are you sure you're related?"

"Families have embarrassment quotas. I do hers for her."

"Young people today," Alex said loftily. "So prudish."

Joe snorted. Alex might as well have said 'okay, bye, we're off to have sex now'. But then, Alex didn't care who knew. Mum and Blessing didn't care. Sex was just something people did. Why did it still make him blush?

"I saw Sean today," Joe said, surprising himself. When he was with Alex, remarks just popped out. Sometimes, even things Joe had decided not to talk about. Like this.

"Oh? Bad luck. And how is the Prince Frog? Is he taking up painting?"

"No." Joe had to smile, the idea was so ridiculous. "He didn't come to the shop. Turns out he works in the café where I went to meet Oliver."

"That *is* bad luck."

"He wanted me to go home with him. Can you believe it? He was such a *jerk* to me, and then he thought I would go with him like nothing happened."

"He's an idiot."

"Yeah. He liked your shirt, though. My green snowflake jumper used to drive him crazy."

"Ha! I bet it did! That's its benevolent side. It drives away unsuitable lovers. Maybe I owe it something. What do you think? Would it like a bottle of fabric softener?"

Joe grinned. "I think that would offend it."

"You're right. I expect it drinks rum. Or maybe blood. There is something a bit terrifying about it."

"Do you want me to get rid of it?"

"No way! If I said yes, it'd *know*. It'd come back to haunt me. In any case, I want you to keep it so you can write more comics about it."

"I think it likes you. Have you noticed the strange tracks around your house when I'm not there at night? It pines for you."

"Okay, now you're scaring me." Alex took his hand. "Come on, I've got plans for you tonight. And they don't involve your sweater."

They came out onto the Makara Road, crossed it, and walked the few hundred metres up the road to Joe's house. Joe opened the door, went into the bedroom and turned the bedside light on. The house had been shut up all day and was stuffy. Joe's grandma had been dead for three years, but at times like this he could still smell her lily of the valley talcum powder. He opened the window.

Alex had closed the front door behind him, but stopped in the bedroom doorway. "Actually, this is your place, isn't it?"

Joe frowned. "What?"

"I'm just thinking: Your house, your rules."

Joe frowned a bit harder. They both knew how sex usually went. Joe liked Alex to be in charge. It meant Joe could stop thinking. He could relax, because Alex called the shots and Alex would look after him. Alex always made it great.

Alex leaned a shoulder against the doorframe. "Yeah, I think you should be in charge tonight."

There was a gleam in Alex's eyes that made Joe tremble with anticipation. Alex had done this a couple of times before, confusing him, so he couldn't guess what was coming next. With anyone else it would have been awful. Because it was Alex, the uncertainty morphed into arousal.

"So, you'd better tell me what to do," Alex said.

Joe opened his mouth and closed it again. Alex had a half-smile lurking in his eyes. Joe glanced away, trying to collect himself. If he was going to have to tell Alex what to do, he was going to have to say things like—*oh*.

He looked back at Alex, eyes widening.

Alex smiled. "Yeah, you want it, you're going to have to ask for it. Out loud."

Joe blushed. He couldn't. He'd forgotten how to speak anyway.

"Want me to start you off?" Alex said. "I think you want to take out that lovely dick, and show me how hard it's getting at the thought of all the dirty things you're going to have to say to me."

Joe swallowed. Why was it easier to suck Alex's cock than to say he wanted to suck it? It would sound so *rude*. But he *was* getting hard. And of course, Alex knew that.

"Come on, sweetheart. Do you know how much it'll turn me on to hear you say it? And then you'll come for me. But only if you tell me what you want. So, dick out, and the rest is up to you."

Joe put his trembling hands to his fly. His breath was speeding up. He was already aching with the need that had been building since Alex had woken him that morning. He wanted Alex to fuck him, but quite how he was going to get them to that point was a hot blur of taboos. His face was already burning, and he hadn't even opened his mouth.

Of course, he could tell Alex he didn't want to do this. Alex wouldn't mind. He'd say something like 'okay, dumb idea. Now get over here'.

But maybe it would be exciting. Joe could start with some easy stuff. If he didn't like it, he could always change his mind. He undid his fly, pushed his underwear down enough to free his cock.

Alex exhaled, shakily.

Joe said, to the carpet, "I…I want you to come closer."

Alex obeyed, stopping about an arm's length away. Joe could only see his feet. Joe glanced up. Alex had the intent expression that meant he was turned on.

"Um…I want you to take your clothes off," Joe said.

Alex did it slowly, fingers lingering on buttons. Joe managed another glance at him.

"Faster," Joe said.

Alex smiled, and pulled the rest of his clothes off. He was trim from all the running he did, but not as skinny as Joe. There was nothing boyish about Alex. He had a man's set strength, a man's broad shoulders, hairy chest and strong thighs. And, of course, a fine, jutting erection, slightly fleshy, foreskin starting to pull back. Joe was used to the size of it by now. He couldn't wait to get his mouth around it.

Joe sank to his knees, and Alex stepped back, out of reach. Joe looked up. Not fair. Alex raised one eyebrow.

"Come closer," Joe said.

Alex didn't move. "Why? What do you want to do?" He put his hand on his cock and jacked himself a few times, lazily.

Fine. Two could play at that game.

"I want you to undress me," Joe said. His left knee was hurting from kneeling on the hard floor. "On the bed." He got up and knelt on the bed instead. Much better.

Alex knelt in front of him, smiling. "You little tease. This is *not* what you want, and you know it."

Joe couldn't help smiling back, shame-facedly. Alex took the hem of Joe's shirt, and took it off, careful not to force his left arm too high. Alex pulled Joe's trousers and underwear down around his knees. Joe kicked them off. He couldn't help noticing that Alex took care to only touch the clothes, not him. Alex was going to make him ask for that.

When Alex was done with the clothes, he knelt there, almost touching Joe, but not quite. Joe twisted his head with frustration. He could smell Alex, could feel the warmth coming from him, their cocks were nearly touching. But not quite.

"What next?" Alex said.

"I want you closer. I want you to kiss me."

"Uh huh. Where?"

"My…neck, and mouth. Just kiss me, Alex." The second sentence came out a bit impatient-sounding.

Alex put one kiss on Joe's neck, making him moan. A lingering kiss on his mouth, quite hard, tongue swirling over Joe's. Then it was over.

"Don't stop," Joe gasped. "Kiss me again. Put your hands on my arse."

Joe writhed against him, grinding their cocks together, letting his head fall back so Alex could have full access to his mouth.

"Alex, get the lube. I…I want…"

"Mm? What do you want?"

"You to get it."

Alex grinned, but reached for the bedside drawer and got out the tube.

"Put some on your fingers," Joe said.

Alex did as he'd said, then held his fingers up. "Well? What could you possibly want with these very slippery fingers?"

"Um…" *I want them stroking my hole. I want them stretching me and teasing me. I want them inside me.* "Uh…Alex, can we just do it now?"

"Do what?"

Joe groaned in frustration and let his head fall forwards onto Alex's shoulder.

"Do what, sweetheart? Where do you want my fingers? Huh? Do you know how much I want to hear you say it?"

"I want them…up my arse." Joe's face was burning again.

"Mm," Alex said, and slipped his fingers under Joe's balls, first to stroke his hole, and then to push two fingers inside, quite fast. Joe gasped, grabbing at Alex's shoulders, cock twitching. Alex slipped his fingers out, circling the rim, and then pushed them in again. Then he stopped.

Joe kissed him. Alex didn't move.

Joe groaned, half in frustration, half in pleasure. His thighs were trembling. It was as if Alex controlled Joe's entire being with those two fingers.

They knelt there, chest to chest, Joe with his knees apart to give Alex access. Joe could feel the sweat beading on his skin in the close air of the bedroom. Being made to say what he wanted was excruciating, but it was also making him as hard as he'd ever been. Because Alex was in charge, really. If Joe wanted more, he *had* to say it. And he *had* to have more. It didn't feel like a choice. It was a necessity.

"Move your fingers. Do what you did before. Push them in. Oh, God, yes. There…harder." A moment later, Joe gasped, "Fuck me."

"With my fingers?"

"Alex, just fuck me." It was a demand, not a request.

"Be more specific." Alex's breathing was hitching.

Joe pulled away, glared at him. "Fine. Stay still. You touch me and it's all over."

He went down onto his hands and knees and took Alex's cock into his mouth, one long, smooth movement, making Alex say "Oh, Christ!". Joe sucked him until Alex pushed at his shoulders to fend him off.

"Joe, stop. Seriously."

Joe looked up. "Why?"

"*Why*? What'll happen if you don't?"

"So?"

"You don't want that," Alex said.

"Don't I? What do I want?"

"You tell me."

"You're *infuriating*," Joe said.

"Say what you want then."

"All right. *Fine*. I want you to…to…" Joe blushed, but he was too turned on by now to care. "…rim me. And then fuck me. Hard. And no stopping. Fuck me until I come. Happy now?"

Alex grinned. Wolfish, not like his usual smile. "Oh, I'm happy. This evening is going *great*."

He pushed Joe down onto his back and flipped him over. "God, you have no idea," he said, into Joe's ear. "You have no *idea* how much I want you right now."

Joe was shaking with anticipation. It would feel *so* good. If he had to wait a moment longer, he would scream. Alex was kissing his way down Joe's back, hands moving lower, stroking his arse. Joe could feel Alex's breath, hot against his skin.

Then Alex's tongue was on him, soft and wet. Joe's eyes fluttered and closed. He could hear himself making breathy moans. He grit his teeth, but his breath kept catching. He wriggled, lifting his hips to let Alex get at him better. He clutched the bedclothes in his fists, cock aching. It was a torment of pleasure, because while it felt as if the whole world had melted away, it wouldn't be quite enough to get him off. Although, tonight, it nearly was.

"Alex," he gasped. "Let's fuck. Quick. Because—"

Alex didn't let him finish. He grabbed Joe's hip and pulled. It meant 'turn over'. Joe obeyed. Alex liked this position best. He liked to watch Joe falling apart, liked to see him come. Alex kissed him, mouth greedy, fingers probing and stretching again, but this time he didn't stop. This time, his fingers were moving faster, almost jerkily, and

Joe realised, with a pulse of pure lust, that Alex was coming apart too, that usually he was more in control, but this time, Alex was getting swept away along with him.

Joe turned his head away from Alex's kiss.

"Fuck me," he demanded. "Quick."

Alex took Joe by the hips and pulled him onto his lap. Joe wrapped his thighs around Alex's waist, crying out when he felt the tip of Alex's cock easing into him. He would come any moment. He needed it *now*.

"Quick," Joe sobbed.

Alex pushed in. "Oh, Joe," he groaned. "Oh, Christ!"

Alex rocked his hips, settling himself, sending shivers of ecstatic tension throughout Joe's body. He writhed, helping Alex find a rhythm that got swiftly faster and harder. Joe's hips were jerking, breath gasping. He grabbed his cock with a sweaty hand and convulsed, painting his scarred chest with ropes of come. Alex bent over him with a wordless shout, eyes closed tight, jolting into him. Joe was spiralling around in that place where there was nothing but sensation. It was a black-red place, like the colour you see behind closed eyes. It was the void before life, the place you go when you die. It was the space in between panels, where nothing happens and everything does. It was pure, and he was there with Alex.

They stilled, both gasping for breath. Alex opened his eyes and shook his head like a dog to get the sweat and hair out of them. Joe gazed up at him. In these moments, Alex was truly his. The sophisticated, award-winning photographer was gone; Alex was a man and nothing more, and yet at the same time, he was more himself than ever. Joe was looking into Alex's soul and Alex was looking into his. The taboos that made Joe blush were nothing. The memories that haunted Alex were forgotten. They were naked before each other. Two people in love. That was all that mattered. It was all that would ever matter.

Alex lowered himself to kiss Joe's mouth, making a little surprised sound that Joe had never heard from him before.

"What?" Joe said.

"What do you mean 'what'? *That*. It was mind-blowing."

He withdrew, and groped on the floor for something to mop up with, coming up with the cream shirt Joe had worn that day. Joe made a noise of protest.

"What? It'll wash. Here." Alex finished with it and tossed it to him, then flopped down next to him on the bed. Joe wiped the come off his chest, and from between his legs. He was dripping with sweat. Alex was shining with it.

"Want a shower?" Joe said.

"No. Can't stand up."

Joe looked at him.

"You've fucked my brains out," Alex explained. "I'm putting you in charge more often."

Joe smiled, an unfamiliar feeling of victory coursing through him. He lay back too, closing his eyes. If Alex couldn't be bothered to have a shower, neither could he.

A breeze was coming in through the open window, carrying with it the scent of grass and pine and a base note of cooling tar from the road. Joe lay, limp and naked, letting the breeze play over him, over the scars and the raw-looking, shiny red areas where he'd lost too much skin for it to ever look normal again, and over the numb patch on his hip that was the graft. He'd learned not to hide from Alex, because Alex didn't want him to, but usually Joe covered up after sex – with a t-shirt or the covers – as soon as he could without it being too obvious.

Tonight, it didn't seem important. His bones were molten honey. The breeze washed over him, warm and gentle, intimate and gloriously impartial. Alex touched him like that. Alex had hands like a summer breeze. He had hands like a summer night. Joe's thoughts were scattering into sleep.

Fingertips touched his cheek, bringing him back from the brink.

Alex said, "Joe?"

Joe opened his eyes. Alex was leaning over him. There was a strange look in his eyes, so tender he might almost be going to cry.

"What is it?" Joe mumbled, dragging himself back into wakefulness. "You okay?"

"You're falling asleep on top of the covers," Alex said. "Get under. You'll get cold in the night."

Joe groaned, but Alex was right. Joe did as he was told. Alex brought the covers up over them, smiling down at him.

"You love me," Alex said, gentle triumph in his voice.

"You love *me*," Joe said. He didn't blush. He was too sleepy, too relaxed. He could say anything to Alex and it would be all right.

"Yes, I do. Good night, sweetheart."

Joe wanted to gaze at him forever, but his eyes were closing again. Sometimes it was like this after sex—all the tensions of life had been exorcised by Alex's touch. Alex switched off the bedside light. Joe turned over, getting comfortable. Alex was behind him, solid and safe, breath even, one hand on Joe's hip. Joe couldn't feel Alex's fingers, because they were on the grafted skin, which was numb to the touch. But he could feel the weight of Alex's hand. He could feel it deep down, inside, where it really mattered.

Joe fell asleep to a kiss on the back of his neck.

About the author

Lee Welch wrote her first book—a pastiche of *The Lion, the Witch and the Wardrobe*—aged seven. She lives in Wellington, New Zealand, with her family. By day she works as an editor and business communications adviser, mainly persuading people not to say 'utilize' when they mean 'use'. Her favourite authors include Ursula Le Guin and KJ Charles.

98

Website: https://leewelchwriter.com/

More by Lee Welch

Salt Magic, Skin Magic (historical fantasy m/m romance)
Seducing the Sorcerer (fantasy m/m romance)